Soft Target

By

CONRAD JONES

The DI Braddick Series
Brick
Shadows
Guilty
Deliver us from Evil

The Detective Alec Ramsay Series
The Child Taker
Criminally Insane
Slow Burn
Frozen Betrayal
Desolate Sands
Concrete Evidence
Thr3e

The Soft Target Series
Soft Target
Soft Target II 'Tank'
Soft Target III 'Jerusalem'
The Rage Within
Blister

The Anglesey Murders
Unholy Island
A Visit from the Devil
Nearly Dead
A Child for the Devil
Dark Angel
What Happened to Rachel?

CHAPTER 1

The Downtown Disney Bombings

The overhead traffic lights changed from red to green and flashing chevrons pointed toward parking lot number two. Yasser Ahmed pulled the black people carrier off Buena Vista Drive, into the car park, his passengers were silent and the tension in the vehicle was palpable. Yasser looked up into the rear-view mirror trying to read the thoughts of the other occupants and the image reflected in the mirror was like a weird dream.

Mickey Mouse sat directly behind Yasser in the back seat and next to him was his partner, Minnie Mouse. Donald Duck and Goofy sat a row behind them, at the rear of the vehicle. All the cartoon characters stared silently back at him, the fixed cartoon grins on the costume masks disguising the evil intent that hid behind them.

Yasser pulled the black vehicle into an empty parking bay and turned off the engine. Without saying a word, the man dressed as Mickey Mouse placed his hand on the door handle and hesitated a moment before opening it. One by one, the cartoon characters stepped out into the hot evening air and headed toward the lights of the Downtown Disney marketplace. They had made this journey many times before, dressed as tourists wearing shorts and sunglasses. This time it was not a dress rehearsal, this time it was the real deal.

As the characters neared the packed tourist area, they parted company and headed in different directions. They didn't look back, each one of them dealing with their own fear and trepidation. 'God goes with you my friends,' Yasser said aloud in the empty darkness of the vehicle.

Yasser Ahmed was born in Iraq, and he was the spiritual leader of the extremist group 'Ismael's Axe'. In 2005, over a three-month period, Yasser and his affiliates were responsible for more than a thousand attacks on coalition and Iraqi forces in Mosul alone, many of them were suicide attacks typically using cars and other motor vehicles. The plague of sectarian violence, which was spiralling out of control in his country, had placed his own life in danger and so he had decided to leave and bring his Jihad to the land of the aggressors.

The Disney marketplace was an entertainment and shopping metropolis packed with tourists. It was the home of nearly one hundred shops and restaurants, not to mention the famous Cirque du Soleil. Schools all over the country were already well into their summer recess and families from the world over wandered around, enjoying the magic of Disney. The evening's firework display was still a couple of hours away, and long lines of hungry tourists waited patiently, forming snake queues around the Downtown Disney restaurants.

Pamela Rodriguez smiled as she looked around the table; her three children laughed, talked, and ate chicken nuggets simultaneously, as only kids can. Her husband, Raul was talking to his parents. They clinked their beer bottles together every time they agreed on something. It had taken Pamela eighteen months to plan this trip to celebrate their in-laws fiftieth wedding anniversary. So far it had been a perfect holiday. Her father-in-law, Pappy, was a second-generation Puerto-Rican American, he had left his homeland as a young man to come and live the American dream. America had been good to him. The idea of sitting in the Rainy Jungle café, in Downtown Disney, eating New York steaks with his grandchildren had once seemed a world away; what was once an impossible American dream had become a wonderful reality. Pamela loved her in-laws like they were her own mum and dad. They were simple people and they worshipped their grandchildren, most of all they enjoyed spoiling them at every opportunity they could. Sometimes they would spoil the kids too much, but that's what grandparents are for.

Her husband caught her eye as she looked around the table; he smiled at her, Pamela's heart flipped, even now after all this time when he smiled at her that way, she would have the same reaction. Raul had just six months left to serve in the American Air Force until his retirement. He had served in both the Afghanistan and Iraq wars. Pamela wasn't sure if it was a good thing or not for him to leave the service behind, it had been his life. He loved the service and his buddies were like his brothers. She couldn't see what else he would be if he took retirement. Pamela knew that despite all the promises people make when they leave the Air Force for Civvie Street, they would lose touch, everyone does.

Raul smiled and turned away from Pamela's gaze. His kids, who were gesturing excitedly toward the restaurant's entrance, took his attention. 'Look, Daddy! Mickey's coming for dinner!' The families that were already eating and the people waiting in line for a table, pointed as the man dressed in the mouse suit walked by them. The volume in the dining room rose to fever pitch as he headed toward the centre of the room waving to the kids as he walked by table after table.

The Rainy Jungle's manager smiled a Disney smile as if all was well. He pretended that the famous mouse came to dinner here every night, he looked from one waiter to another, hoping that someone could give him an explanation as to what was going on. The Disney characters appeared on scheduled days and charged a huge fee. Today was not a scheduled day for the mouse to appear. Disney did nothing for free and this extra visit was not in the budget. *The bastards are just trying to put the rent up*, he thought, but he couldn't let his customers see how annoyed he was. He couldn't disappoint his excited customers by asking the mouse to leave. This was Disney after all; this is what they want to see.

Pamela couldn't believe her luck as Mickey headed straight toward her table. *Wow*, she thought, *this is what makes the time and expense all worthwhile*. Pamela's eldest child, Christopher turned in his chair as the mouse approached the table. 'Hi, Mickey,' he shouted, he had a smile from ear to ear, exposing the half-chewed chicken nuggets in his mouth. The mouse stood still for what seemed an age; the cartoon grin never fading however, the waving had stopped. *The man in the mouse suit has stage fright or something. What's he doing?* she thought. 'I think he has forgotten what to do, maybe he's new,' she said quietly across the table. Raul took out a digital camera to make the most of the photo opportunity, being so close to the mouse. 'It's still perfect for the kids. We are so lucky that he came in while we are eating,' Pamela said to her in-laws.

Just as she was wondering what was wrong with Mickey Mouse, the bomb that was strapped around his waist, beneath his costume exploded; it took her family and her thoughts away forever.

CHAPTER 2

San Francisco

Hassan finished praying in his San Francisco motel room, and then dressed in his clean white smock-type shirt with a beige, sleeveless long jacket over the top. He pulled on his matching white cotton trousers and slipped his feet into rope sandals; the white skullcap was last to be put on. Hassan was Pakistani, born and educated in Karachi, which was a luxury not afforded by many people in his country. His family had been displaced from their home in India during the partition of Colonial India, when the British forces forcibly created the Islamic state of Pakistan. Over twelve million Hindus, Christians and Sikhs had to leave their homes and belongings behind them during the partition and a further two million Muslims were slaughtered as ethnic tensions exploded between the displaced religious factions. The chaos left behind by the British led to many young Muslim men growing up to hate Britain and its Western allies. Hassan had met Yasser at a religious training camp in Somalia some years before. The camps were originally set up by Osama bin Laden and his followers in 1996, to train Islamic extremists to use weapons and manufacture explosives. The trainers at the camps were veterans of the war in Afghanistan, where the struggle against the invading Soviet Union had drawn Muslim brothers from all corners of the world to fight alongside the Mujahideen.

Hassan dressed and watched the news of the chaos that Yasser and his terrorist cell had caused in Florida the night before. The death toll was in the hundreds and still rising. 'Now it is my turn, my brothers,' he said to the man reading the news on the screen. The man at the CNN desk ignored him and continued to read the news. Hassan had no doubt that what he was about to do was right and just, however he felt scared and very alone. During their planning they'd decided that once the terrorist cells had been given their targets, there was to be no further contact between them. Hassan had no idea of the others' whereabouts and he did not know what their missions would entail either. He knew that some of the others were to work in groups and he wished that he had been assigned an accomplice on his mission, but Yasser had told him that this glory was to be his alone.

He glanced in the mirror; the clothes and his long dark beard left no one in doubt that he was from the nation of Islam. He left the hotel room and headed down to reception where he enquired at the reception desk if any messages had been left for him. The receptionist handed him an envelope, and he read the two words that were printed on the page inside. 'DiMaggio, Monroe'. Hassan understood the meaning of it straight away. His instructions from

Yasser three weeks earlier had specified that he was to travel to San Francisco and check into a motel. He then had to change his accommodation every six days until he was contacted. Hassan was also told that he needed to take open-top tour buses from the Fisherman's Wharf at least twice a week and to travel with a different operator for each trip. Most of the tours used the same routes and were an excellent way of getting to know the city quickly.

The tours had taken him past a beautiful granite church in a part of the city called Little Italy. Apart from its architectural beauty, it was famous because Joe DiMaggio and Marilyn Monroe had their marriage blessed there. The tours pointed it out because the postal address was '666', the sign of the devil, and Hassan thought that was very apt for the house of the Christian devils to worship in. Hassan knew that the truck would be parked near to the church, the two words that had been written on the note gave him all the information he needed to find the vehicle. Everything else that he needed would be inside.

That morning in his prayers he had asked for the strength and courage to complete his task; his prayers had settled his nerves and steeled his resolve. The next time he spoke to his god it would be face to face.

The original plan was to take a cab to the area where the vehicle had been parked, but he decided time was on his side and that he would walk one last time through the streets that he had become familiar with. He wanted to feel the bay breeze on his face one last time before he met his maker.

Hassan stepped out onto Polk Street. The wind chilled him as he pulled his waistcoat tighter around himself and started up the hill toward San Francisco Bay. The bay area was the hub of San Francisco's tourist industry and he had walked up the hill toward the bay every day since arriving in the city. This part of San Francisco was the area that the locals called, 'The Tenderloin', and it had been the centre of the drugs and vice trade since the 1900s. The nickname had come to fruition, as the only people in the city that could afford such expensive cuts of meat as 'Tenderloin', were the corrupt policemen that worked this part of town. The police force pay was lousy, but the perks and bribes made it a job well worth doing from a financial point of view.

As he walked along the sidewalk toward the bay, neon signs flashed from windows on every block, and a myriad of colours promised sex for money from dusk till dawn. Each massage parlour that he saw hardened his resolve to rid the world of as many of these non-believers as he could, and he wanted to join his dead brothers in their Jihad. 'Spare change, sir?' A vagrant stepped from the alley on his left. This scruffy man was one of the thousands that chose the city of San Francisco for their home. It had amazed Hassan just how many tramps there were in this city and how the people and police tolerated their presence. Even the well-trimmed lawns in front of City Hall were home to a dozen slumbering rag-bag people at any given time. The last time he had gone by on one of his city tours he had decided to count how many vagrants were sleeping on the lawns of City Hall, he had counted twenty-two there, right under the noses of the mayor and his colleagues. Madness; they would be stoned to death in his world unless they repented and changed their idle ways. Hassan felt no pity for these lost people, only the dull glow of hatred for a society that accepted the vagrants and sex shops so freely. He hated the homosexuality and the drug abuse that the city's inhabitants and tourists found attractive. The infidels found these vices part of its charm. He was about to tarnish the city's charm forever and he knew that a place in heaven with his brothers would be his reward.

He reached the crest of Polk Street and looked down the steep hill to the bay. The hill took him down past the huge Ghirardelli chocolate factory on his right, and the old maritime museum stood in front of him at the bottom of Russian Hill. The museum building was under a major repair programme as the facade was showing signs of its age. Its position next to the sea made it vulnerable to erosion from the weather. Construction workers covered the scaffold's walkways like little yellow ants in their hi-viz jackets and hard hats, and they seemed to swarm left and right all over the building's facade. Hassan's thoughts were on the task ahead, when suddenly a loud whistle from above drew his attention. 'Hey, Osama, where the fuck have you been, Dude?' A group of construction workers laughed loudly, patting the speaker on the back in congratulation of his joke. 'The police have been looking all over for your ass, boy!' another comedian in a yellow hat joined in from higher up the scaffold.

'What the fuck have you done to Mickey Mouse, man? That shit just isn't funny, Dude!' The first hard hat added. News of the Islamic terrorist attack in Florida was plastered all over the news, and it had obviously provoked the racist abuse that Hassan was receiving. A supervisor from the construction company heard the commotion and decided that enough was enough. 'You aren't funny, McAlister! Get back to work.' The men ambled away from the rails slowly going about their business. The laughter and jeering continued as Hassan walked by the museum. He put his head down and walked faster, his face flushed red with anger, his fists felt sweaty as he clenched them tightly. Hassan put as much space between himself and the catcalls as he could; he also mentally added an extra job to his plan. 'You will not laugh any more today, you will not laugh for a long time,' he hissed under his breath as the voices faded into the distance.

CHAPTER 3

Grand Canyon

Muktar backed slowly away from the canyon's edge; small stones rolled over it and fell toward the canyon floor thousands of feet below. He stood when he felt that it was safe to do so and stepped back up onto the canyon trail. He walked backwards a little to check if the sniper rifle that he had placed beneath an overhanging rock could be seen from the path, then he walked down the path in the opposite direction and looked again. Eventually he was happy that it couldn't be seen. Even if an eagle-eyed tourist spotted the green baize material that he had wrapped it in, it would look just like moss. If anyone was stupid enough to lean over the rim that far, it would still not be obvious what was hidden there.

This was the third and final rifle that he needed to hide that morning. The sun was rising higher into the sky. The light was changing the colour of the rocks from grey to red, shifting the dark shadows, and revealing the true marvel of the canyon. Muktar looked back toward the Bright Angel Lodge through the short-sight glass that he had. The footpaths around the lodge were still quiet as the tourists had not arrived yet or were still sleeping.

He had booked into his room at the Bright Angel Lodge a week before. The rooms were basic to say the least, there were no televisions and the shower facilities were shared. The carpets that covered the long corridors were bright red and embroidered with American Indian symbols and patterns. Early that morning he had tiptoed down the long corridor and out of the rear of the building to his car. He had collected the three sniper rifles that were folded into a sports holdall and hidden them along the rim trails.

Muktar, who was an Egyptian national, had given the idea of using snipers in sensitive tourist areas to Yasser months before. Yasser Ahmed and Muktar had met many years ago at a religious terrorist training camp in Syria. Muktar had told Yasser stories of how the Islamic fundamentalists in his country had become disenchanted with President Mubarak. Resentment was growing among young Egyptians because of his capitalist policies and in 1992 Egypt had started to suffer a series of terror attacks largely aimed at tourists. Tourism represents the most lucrative part of the country's economy and the attacks on Western tourists proved to be very damaging. Western governments had always associated these attacks with al-Qaeda; however, it was never clear who was responsible for them. It appeared to Muktar and his associates that in general, these were attacks by Islamic fundamentalists, against the westernisation of Egypt. Muktar told Yasser how in recent years his country had become transformed into a modern capitalist economy. Huge tourist resorts full of luxury hotels, swimming pools, and golf courses were built by Mubarak's government. Large sections of the Egyptian indigenous population felt ignored and lived in poverty. 'Is it any wonder my people feel aggrieved when we are starving, whilst being constantly surrounded by foreign wealth?' Muktar often asked.

In September 1992 the Egyptian group Gama'a al-Islamiya warned the government that tourists must not enter the province of Qena, which was renowned for its ancient archaeological history. In October snipers opened fire on a cruise ship full of German tourists that was sailing on the River Nile. In the same month, a tourist bus was attacked resulting in the death of a British tourist. In total that year, the gunmen had murdered nine foreign nationals. Egypt became a dangerous place to visit and the attacks threatened to do lasting damage to the well-established tourist industry. Terrorism did not need to be sophisticated to work; just one determined man with a weapon was enough to cause mayhem.

In 1995 the group that was dedicated to the overthrow of Mubarak's undemocratic government continued their campaign against Western capitalism within their own country. They had warned all foreign tourists to leave the country immediately and two days later, seventeen Greek tourists were gunned down outside a hotel in Cairo. Yasser had learned much from their discussions about the Egyptian insurgents and the devastating effect that attacks on tourists could have.

Muktar looked through the glasses again and panned down to the rock face below the Bright Angel Lodge, following the path of the orange looking zigzag trail. The narrow tourist trail snaked down the canyon wall to the Indian gardens a mile and a half below. His task was simple enough; from sunrise tourists would start to descend the Bright Angel Trail toward the Colorado River. Walkers usually only got as far as the Indian gardens before fatigue, and the heat, forced them to retrace their steps back up the steep trail. As they descend, the heat increases, as does the realisation that they have to walk back up. There are no cabs or buses from the canyon floor, no chair lifts or cable cars to relieve weary travellers. If you walk down the Bright Angel Trail, then you have to walk back up. Many seasoned hikers had headed off with the intention of reaching the Colorado River, only to collapse, many fatally from dehydration and fatigue.

These people were not his target today though; he was to wait for the mule trains to start their decent down the narrow path. Muktar was to take three shots at the mules or their riders before moving to the next rifle. He knew that the noise would be sufficient to make the mules panic and cause havoc on the busy, narrow trails. Then he would leave the weapon where it was and move onto the next hidden rifle and begin again. The confusion of the moving shooter and bullets coming from different positions around the canyon should make his capture or death more difficult. There would be many deaths if his aim was true and his luck held.

His task was finally prepared, and he headed back toward the lodge. There was time for prayers and one last meal before the mules started their journey down.

CHAPTER 4

Las Vegas

Mido looked out over the balcony at the busy strip. The streets were lined with giant hotels of all shapes and sizes, a medieval castle, a pyramid, and even the Eiffel Tower were below him. He paced up and down the balcony nervously, looking from the busy streets below, to the blank screen on the mobile phone that he held in his hand. It was as if the answer to his dilemma would appear on the screen if he stared hard enough at it. His hand felt hot and clammy as he held the mobile phone tightly. The desert heat had already started to rise making him sweat. The temperature was already in the high nineties and it wasn't 9 a.m. yet. He walked inside to the hotel room and took a cold bottle of water from the fridge. He took a long gulp from the bottle trying to quench the thirst that his hangover had gifted him; Mido had spent the previous night drinking heavily at the bar in the huge hotel casino; it was supposed to be his last night alive, after all.

At around midnight he had been approached by a call girl called Laura, or Lara, he wasn't sure which and didn't really care. He had taken her to his hotel room and enjoyed what can only be called a brief encounter, before asking her to leave. His Muslim brothers wouldn't have approved if they'd known, but from what he had seen on the news this morning, they were already dead. Whisky always made his headache in the morning, and today was the mother of all headaches. Today was supposed to be his last before he joined his brothers in heaven; they'd completed their tasks already, and now it was his turn. The television news told of nothing but the chaos that Yasser Ahmed and his affiliates had caused in Florida the night before. The problem was that Mido's part of the plan was messed up. He was alone and did not know what to do next.

Mido had said goodbye to Hassan in San Francisco three days before and had then made the long drive to Las Vegas, across the desert, alone. He had met Hassan in a religious terror training camp in the Sudan some years before. Mido was from Iraq, but he had been forced to leave his country shortly after the American and British forces invaded in 2003. The invading armies were using 9/11 as their justification for a war on terror against the 'axis of evil'. The invading coalition forces had begun a generalised offensive against elements of the Arab world including Mido's homeland. The reasoning behind the hostile invasion confused Mido and his compatriots as the United Nations had not sanctioned the war. He could almost see the justification for the invasion of Afghanistan, as many countries believed the Taliban

13

were giving shelter to Osama bin Laden and the US firmly believed that bin Laden had sanctioned and financially supported the 9/11 attacks.

Mido's country was secular with strong links to the West. America and Britain had armed Iraq when its borders were threatened by a Soviet backed Iranian invasion. Iraq and its people were polar opposites in terms of Arab culture to bin Laden. The general opinion of Mido and his compatriots was that this invasion was a ploy to control Iraq's oil fields. Resentment and anger spread across the country as it descended into a religious civil war. Centuries old feuds resurfaced between Shia and Sunni factions. The illegal invasion had the effect of ratcheting up the tension between the two cultures tremendously. Many of the neighbouring Arab nations started to regard America and the West with hostility. Mido believed that the invasion itself was an unprovoked attack on an independent country and was a form of state terrorism itself. He had stayed in Iraq during the conflict but the removal of Saddam Hussein and the destruction of his army and police forces led to total anarchy. The invaders couldn't quell the many conflicts that ensued once the regime had fallen, and with the collapse of the infrastructure, Iraqi tribes began to fight among themselves to establish their dominance in their ruined country.

Mido had watched his country fall into disarray as rogue elements from the Iraqi military started fighting among each other, and the hospitals and water supplies crumbled into chaos. Insurgents all over the country stockpiled dangerous weapons and ammunition. Mido had joined in a guerrilla war that included improvised explosions, suicide bombing, and the sabotage of oil wells. Water and electricity supplies were destroyed by grenade attacks as the opposing ethnic and political factions of Iraqi society continued to do battle with each other.

Mido felt frightened for his life and left the country. It was when he had left fearing for his life that he met Yasser Ahmed and the others. The training camps were full of angry young Muslim men from a myriad of Islamic countries; it was there that he decided to take the fight for his country's freedom to the aggressor's door.

Yasser Ahmed told Mido and Hassan that once they'd been given their task, there was to be no further contact between them. Mido told Yasser that he would dispose of his mobile phone on his journey across the desert, so that it couldn't be traced, but instead, he had kept it in the event that something went wrong. It had gone very wrong. He was desperate for an answer, a plan B. He had a rental car in the parking lot beneath the huge hotel. In the boot of the vehicle were three tactical M40-A5 rifles, the same type Muktar had taken for his mission in the Grand Canyon. Mido had trained for many days in the camps in Sudan with similar weapons, and he had learned to use them with deadly accuracy.

14

Yasser made the plans for the Grand Canyon and Las Vegas attacks to be almost identical. The idea was that one man with three sniper rifles hidden in different positions could cause chaos on a large scale. When he arrived in Las Vegas, Mido was to check into three different hotels, he was to book rooms that had balconies overlooking the strip. Then he was to set up a sniper nest in each room. Once his attack was prepared, he was supposed to choose targets on the streets below indiscriminately. Mido was to fire at tourists; however, police officers would be even better. Each attack was to last for three minutes and then he was to set fire to the room, leave the weapon, and travel to the next hotel where the next rifle was already hidden and waiting for him.

Once his mission was complete, the authorities would only find one body or kill one shooter. The police would then be left with many questions to answer. How many shooters were there? If there was more than one, had the others got away? Was there one shooter or three? The fires would cause confusion and hamper any investigations that were made, and the police would never know the truth about the number of terrorists that were involved in the plot. They could only assume. The public would believe that there were still terrorists out there hiding somewhere and people would imagine that extremists were lying in wait everywhere. Every hotel room on the strip could be concealing a sniper waiting for the next best shot to come along and they may even be lining them up in the sights of a rifle right now. Panic and fear are the one true goal of any terrorist attack, if Mido could complete his grisly task then the streets of Las Vegas would become like a ghost town. Tourists would avoid the city until anxiety settled down, by which time millions would have been lost in revenue.

The events of the previous night in Florida had made tourist destinations nervous and there was tightened security everywhere. Mido had checked into the rooms easily enough, but all the hotels were checking bags and customers with metal detectors as they entered. He couldn't find any way of getting his weapons into the buildings and he couldn't get access to the balconies armed with his rifles. Mido decided that he needed another drink while he thought things through. For the first time since the illegal invasion of his country, he started to have doubts. He left the room and headed toward the lift.

Mido stood in the hallway and waited for the lift to arrive, he was grateful that when it did, it was empty. He stepped inside, held the door open for a second, then pressed the ground floor button and leaned back against the mirrored wall breathing deeply to calm his shattered nerves. Mido had to keep his mind focused; he reached into his pocket and looked at the mobile phone again and then he typed in a text message; *Problem at hotel. Can't get bags in. Advice?* He pressed send to Yasser's mobile phone number.

The lift descended at warp speed and then it stopped suddenly, and the doors opened. A man wearing a dark suit and dark sunglasses stepped inside. He rode the elevator, never looking away from Mido all the way to the ground floor. Mido could feel the man's stare upon him, and it made him even more nervous than before. He was sweating profusely now, and his breathing was becoming laboured. A few seconds later, the doors opened, and he stepped into the hotel lobby, where the air conditioning cooled him down and he immediately felt more in control. Mido checked that the signal on his phone was still good. The lobby of the giant hotel was nestled beneath a million tons of glass and steel and although his mobile phone had a full signal, the screen was blank. *They must all be dead*, he thought, *or captured*, though the news had said nothing of any arrests. He was clutching at straws, trying to think of a course of action but his mind was just a blank. The alcohol from the previous evening had made his head fuzzy and confused.

He looked around the huge hotel reception area, and in desperation approached the reception desk. 'Have there been any messages received for Ramirez?' He asked the peroxide blonde behind the desk. He had used a fake passport when he had checked in, identifying him as a tourist from Honduras. The blonde woman went to check the pigeonholes on the wall behind her. 'What room are you staying in, Mr Ramirez?' She asked him with a sigh. Her shift was nearly over, and she couldn't wait to go home. The man who called himself Mr Ramirez was sweating, and he smelled of body odour and alcohol. 'I am staying in room 1408,' he answered her while still looking down at his mobile phone.

'I am afraid that there is nothing here for you. Would you like to leave your mobile phone number here and I will page you if anything arrives?' she said, walking away into the rear office. Mido had already turned to walk away and he did not answer her question, he had also not seen the receptionist taking his passport through to the back office. She had worked in Vegas for too long not be able to spot a fake passport. She picked up the internal phone and dialled security.

Mido turned and headed down the long walkway that led to the high-class hotel shops. Gucci and Prada stood next to Armani and Chanel. Nothing in the glitzy windows had a price tag on it and if you needed to ask the price, then you couldn't afford it. The corridor led further into the bowels of the giant hotel and then into a huge casino. He saw the main bar area some distance away, it looked like an oasis in the centre of the football field sized gambling area. Mido walked past a hundred slot machines and then sat on a stool at the bar; he ordered a whisky, straight with ice. He lit a Marlborough and fed a fifty-dollar note into the poker machine that was in front of him on the bar. His head was filled with doubts about what he should do next.

16

'That's two dollars and fifty cents for the whisky please, sir,' the barman said. His fixed Vegas smile never fading.

'I'm playing the poker machine. Drinks are free when you're playing the machines right?' Mido answered through clenched teeth, the air conditioning was now doing little to cool him down or calm his mood.

'You weren't playing the machine when I gave you the drink, sir.' The smile did not fade at all.

'Well I'm playing the fucking machine now and I'll take another whisky and another, until I'm done playing the machine, or are we going to have a problem?' Mido said. He was starting to lose the little composure that he had left.

'No problem at all, sir, but we really don't need the bad language though, sir. We just want you all to have a good time, without the bad language thanks,' the barman replied, still grinning like a Cheshire cat. Mido was close to snapping. What was he doing here drinking and arguing with a person who looked like he had a smile glued permanently to his face? He should be in place, in the first room now. He couldn't get the rifles into the hotel. He tried to think what to do next, there was no plan B and there were no rendezvous points because this was a suicide mission. What should he do?

Doubts started to eat into his mind, all the planning and preparation over the months before seemed pointless now. The training in the religious camps had cemented his resolve to sacrifice his life for his god. He wanted to be killed in the Jihad fighting for the freedom of his country, but now it all seemed so far away. The inspirational words of the Imams were a distant echo. The preaching from the Mullahs had seemed to be so absolute, but today he felt different. He could just sit here and get drunk, maybe even get another hooker, who would know? His friends were all dead. Tomorrow he could get into the rental car and head for the coast. He had a bundle of money and fake credit cards. He could leave now. He could live. Maybe this was fate.

Whatever he decided to do, he wasn't going to do it right now. He was too confused to make any decisions. Mido decided that he would take his time and think the problem through properly. He needed to retrieve a small bag from the boot of the rental car, as it contained his money and he had just put his last fifty dollars into the poker machine on the bar. He pressed the deal button on the poker machine; it was his last dollar bet. Four aces popped up on the screen and the animations went crazy. The bartender looked over and waved a hand in Mido's direction. 'Four Aces, sir. It must be your lucky day!' The bartender's grin faded slightly. Mido had just won the equivalent of a week's wages.

'Yes, it must be my lucky day after all,' Mido replied. The casino machine manageress came over to Mido to verify the win. She smiled and made a big fuss of handing him his winnings. He took the nine hundred dollars from the woman and thanked her. He put the money in his pocket and headed for the parking garage.

The garage was situated beneath the hotel and Mido walked down a flight of concrete stairs. His mind was made up. He opened a heavy fire door and stepped into the dimly lit garage, he walked toward the far end, the roof was low, and the smell of exhaust fumes filled the air. He opened the boot of the blue Ford Mustang with an electronic key. The lid clicked open. He reached in, lifted a small bag out of the boot and placed it on the floor next to his feet. The three sniper rifles that were in the boot were stripped down and contained in three sports holdalls. Mido looked at them and felt very confused and guilty. He had not completed his mission. His Muslim brothers were dead, and he had failed them. 'I can't get the rifles into the hotel,' he said. The plan had failed, but he did not believe that it was his fault. He decided that he would dump the rifles in the Mojave Desert the following day. Maybe he could sell them; he would decide when his mind was clearer.

'Step away from the vehicle. Lie down and place your hands behind your head!' A voice boomed in the parking garage. The low concrete ceilings made it echo. A man in a dark suit, white shirt, and dark tie was pointing a gun at Mido's head. It was a big gun and Mido froze. His mind was more confused now than ever. Had Allah read his mind and heard the doubts that were rattling around in his head? Mido thought that his lord had deserted him because he had failed his task. This was his punishment. 'You need to lay down right now, motherfucker, or we will shoot you!' The voice came from a second man and Mido looked in his direction. The second man looked identical to the first, except his gun was bigger.

Mido stayed very still and looked from one agent to the next. He was terrified; he looked into the boot and saw the three bags that contained folded sniper rifles. He wished that he had stayed at home in his beloved Iraq. 'Okay, I'm surrendering. Please don't shoot me.' Mido said as he moved to lie down. His hands were shaking with fear and he could feel beads of sweat running down his face into his eyes. He tried to blink as the sweat stung his eyeballs. He moved slowly, trying to bend down but the small bag that he had removed earlier was in his way. Mido reached forward to move it.

The two men in suits were NSA agents. They fired simultaneously, and Mido's head exploded as the high velocity rounds smashed through his skull. All his confusion disintegrated into a red mist.

CHAPTER 5

Disney Aftermath

Yasser sat on his motel bed watching the television and smoking a cigarette. CNN had a news loop that kept repeating itself. Each time it was replayed by the network, they were adding more information. As new information was gathered, it was added a piece at a time as the story unfolded. Initial reports thought that it was one bomb that had exploded in the Florida resort. The reports that followed insisted that it was three, and then possibly more. No one seemed to be sure at this stage exactly what had happened. The only certainty was that the bombs had caused death and destruction in the heart of an American tourist institution.

We've blown up Mickey Mouse. That's like shooting Kennedy or knocking down the World Trade Centre. Generations of people will remember this day, Yasser thought as he watched the news loop around again.

'Who is responsible for this outrage?' asked a reporter who was at the scene. The local police Chief was trying to give a brief outline statement of what they knew so far, but they did not know very much. Eyewitnesses had given frightened and confused testimony that a series of at least three explosions had killed and injured hundreds of innocent tourists. 'It is too early to speculate at this time,' he replied; then he repeated the same answer to the next three questions.

The truth was that it was impossible to know how many people were holidaying in the area at any one time. The weather had been hot and sunny that day. Tourists headed for the water parks at Blizzard Beach and Typhoon Lagoon in the afternoon to take advantage of the sunshine. Epcot, MGM Studios, and Animal Kingdom were all mostly daytime destinations. Downtown Disney had a combination of shopping and entertainment facilities which made it a perfect destination for families in the evenings, and it had been full.

How many of the tourists in the Orlando area were at the Downtown district at the time of the bombings? There was no way of knowing. The police and rescue services were at full stretch because of the scale of casualties and the uncertainty of further attacks. Identifying the dead and dying after such an attack would be a slow and painful task. The police would have to wait and painstakingly sift through hotel lists; they would need the full cooperation of the hotels in the area to try to assess how many people had not returned to their accommodation that night. Nobody could guess how many of the people that were on holiday in the area had simply packed up and left immediately, many tourists would be heading home fearing for their families' safety from further attacks.

Yasser had heard the first bomb blast from the car park. He knew from the planning sessions that they'd carried out that the Mickey bomb had been timed to explode first at the Rainy Jungle café. The second, third, and fourth explosions were timed thirty seconds apart. It was a much-used terrorist tactic to cause mayhem, as people ran from the first explosion, straight into the path of the secondary blast. When Yasser had driven away from the scene down Buena Vista Drive, he couldn't be sure that he had heard all four planned explosions. He had definitely heard three and he felt pleased with himself because another giant blow had been struck at the infidel Americans.

The shock of what had happened here and the impact of what was to follow tomorrow, would stun the Western world and cripple tourism for years to come. He looked out of the hotel window toward Interstate 4 and saw the tail lights of a thousand cars snaking off into the distance. The traffic would be gridlocked all night as people fled from the carnage. The traffic would be bad, but he couldn't wait until tomorrow to leave. He checked his documents; he needed to fly tonight before the security services tightened the noose looking for the people responsible.

Yasser stood before the bathroom mirror and shaved his dark boyish skin. He was twenty-six years old but looked younger. He was young to be in charge of such operations as these, but his talent to organise, recruit, motivate, and execute such attacks had been recognised years before. When he had first gone to the Sudan to be trained in religious camps, individuals were earmarked as those who would do and die, and those who could organise such people. Yasser was identified as the latter. When it came to motivating others, he was the best. His belief was that the West's invasion of his homeland in Iraq and the oppression being felt by his Muslim brothers in Afghanistan was unacceptable. His ability to convince others to join in this global Jihad was incredible.

He looked at his small frame in the mirror. He was slim and lean, his skin was dark, and his eyes were olive green, they looked through you, not at you, they seemed to be lifeless like those of a shark and although attractive to some, a cold malice behind them chilled you if you looked too long.

Yasser put some eye shadow around his green eyes and applied mascara to his long eyelashes, he put lip-gloss on and pouted in the mirror at his reflection, and then he took the bobble from the long ponytail that he wore on the back of his head and brushed his thick black hair. Yasser dressed in a casual pastel coloured tracksuit and pink trainers and to add to the effect he put on a pair of women's Dolce and Gabbana glasses. The lenses were broad and round, and they covered most of his face. Yasser's long hair and slim frame made him look all the more feminine. He blew a kiss to his reflection in the mirror and as he shook his hair again, Yasser became Yasmine.

CHAPTER 6

San Francisco

Hassan reached the truck that had been left next to the park, in a suburb of the city called Little Italy. A beautiful Catholic church could be seen across the park through the trees; he spat in the direction of the church as he got closer to the truck. He looked down the hill toward the bay; the Coit Tower, which looked like the end of a giant fire hose, was perched on the rocks that overlooked the harbour.

Whoever had left the truck for Hassan had placed four plastic traffic cones around the vehicle, so that it did not look out of place; it simply looked like it was making an innocent delivery. Hassan looked beneath the only traffic cone that had a flashing yellow light on top of it, beneath it was the key. He moved the cone from in front of the truck, opened the lock, and climbed in. It was a small gas storage tanker, the words 'America Gas' were painted down the side of the Mack driving rig which had five thousand litres of propane gas stored in the bulbous tank behind his cab. Anyone looking in his direction may have thought it odd, that this man who was dressed in Islamic clothing, with a 'ZZ Top beard, was delivering propane in Little Italy, but no one saw anything as he started the engine.

Hassan reached beneath the passenger seat and took out a red cool box, which had been hidden there; he noticed it still had the price tag from Publix supermarket stuck on it. He lifted the lid and placed the contents of the box onto the seat next to him. He put a claw hammer and a roll of silver duct tape next to each other on the passenger seat. He then removed two grenades and a reel of fishing twine, which he placed on his lap. Lastly, he removed a 38 calibre Smith and Wesson, which he slid under the driver's seat. He decided to set up the truck in preparation for the attack while it was quiet, as he did not want to be disturbed and he needed to make enough time to enable him to pay a visit to the old maritime museum on the way. The men that had ridiculed him would pay for their insults with their lives.

Hassan recognised the two types of grenade he'd been given, from his training in Somalia. One was a regular explosive fragmentation grenade, the other a phosphorous device. He needed no further instructions; the plan was deadly simple.

21

He turned to face the rear window of the Mack truck and smashed the glass with the hammer. He used the claw to pull the glass remnants into the cab and the broken window left the exposed bulkhead of the gas tank only feet away from him. He taped the two grenades to the tanker's metal bulkhead. He then tied some twine to both activation pins and attached it to his steering wheel. When the time was right, he would pull the twine, which would release the activation pins. Hassan knew that one grenade should be sufficient to rupture the tank and ignite the gas; if it did not, then the phosphor grenade would do the trick.

Hassan firmly believed he was a Mujahideen warrior fighting the Jihad. If he were to fail today, then he would bring shame on Islam. With the grenades in place, he put the truck in gear and drove toward the museum.

Hassan pulled the America Gas truck to a stop, mounting the curb. He was fifty yards from the huge scaffold structure that covered the front of the maritime museum. The truck was facing the Ghirardelli Chocolate Factory at the bottom of Polk Street. The workmen who had shouted insults to him earlier that morning all wore yellow hats and hi-viz jackets. Hassan watched as they swarmed over the scaffold. At every level, stonemasons, carpenters, and painters were all busy repairing the old building to its former glory.

Hassan engaged drive and steered the truck toward the legs and supports of the steel scaffold that resembled a metal spider's web. Hassan slammed his foot down on the accelerator pedal as the truck made contact with the scaffold poles; the vehicle lurched forward tearing the scaffold away from the building as it roared down the road. Steel bars clanged to the floor along with wooden gangplanks, men lay injured all over the road, while some still clung to the building above, hanging on for dear life itself. Hassan looked in the rear-view mirror at the scene. There were bodies scattered all over the road. Men lay prone on the tarmac, some were not moving, while others were crawling and screaming because their bones were broken. Hassan spotted the man that he had heard called McAllister by his supervisor earlier that morning. He was about thirty yards away lying on his side in the road, his heavy moustache and ponytail identified him from the other injured men. The truck's wheels screeched as Hassan put it into reverse, revving the engine as it closed the distance between himself and his tormentor.

McAllister lay on the tarmac, confused as he watched the tanker race toward him. He thought he had been involved in a terrible accident when a gas truck had brought down the scaffold, but as he looked incredulously on, the truck's reversing lights came on, and the vehicle lurched toward him. It was almost as if the driver was aiming for him deliberately. He raised his head from the tarmac, desperately trying to get his broken body out of the vehicles path but to no avail, the last thing he heard was the loud crack as his hard hat collapsed beneath the crushing weight of the truck, his skull split, spilling its contents across the road.

22

The truck lurched forward again. Hassan weaved slowly through the injured men that lay prone and helpless in the road. He aimed the truck at the men that were still moving as he drove down the bay road toward Pier 39.

Hassan had driven about a mile by the time he approached Fisherman's Wharf and Pier 39; they were on his left-hand side as he passed them. Tourists milled around the shops and stalls that sold fresh crab of every size and description. The café bars and restaurants were full of tourists on both sides of the road as he drove the gas truck toward Pier 39. He heard the sound of sirens coming toward him and he slowed as the emergency services passed him by. They were heading toward the carnage that he had left behind him at the old museum. He turned toward the bay and looked out at Golden Gate Bridge. There was mist and low cloud covering the top of the huge red structure. He looked toward the Rock, Alcatraz. He saw the passenger ferries carrying tourists from the famous redundant federal penitentiary. It had once been the home of such famous gangsters as Al 'Scarface' Capone and 'Machinegun Kelly'. The huge white ferries took tourists from the empty prison back to Pier 39. Hassan could hear the incessant barking of hundreds of elephant seals, drifting from the bay on the wind.

Hassan steered the truck in the direction of the ferry terminal and veered left across the pavement toward the entrance to Pier 39. The security chain that was stretched across the terminal entrance snapped like cotton as the vehicle struck it at speed and hurtled toward the waiting crowds.

The waiting area at Pier 39 looked like a car lot. The dock itself made a square, one edge was the sea wall where the ferries docked, two sides were made with old tramcars that tourists could sit in to shelter from the freezing bay winds and the final edge was the entrance from Bay Road. The centre of the square was cordoned into a long zigzag queuing area where people waited in line for the boats to take them to 'The Rock'. A ferry had just docked; the pier was full as one ferry load of passengers waited to board, while another was disembarking.

Petur Petersson was an Icelandic national; he was blonde-haired and blue-eyed, as was his wife Ingrid, his son Petur Jnr, and daughter Anna. They stood huddled together in a line waiting to board a ferry that would take them to Alcatraz. They were shifting their weight from one foot to the other, as cold people do. They all wore the same style fleece jackets with San Francisco embroidered on the front. The two men wore black jackets and the women pink. They laughed as they counted how many people had the same style fleece tops as they did.

Mark Twain said, 'The coldest winter I ever spent was a summer in San Francisco.'

Never a truer word was spoken, Petur thought as he had paid for the four garments earlier that morning. Even though the sun was shining, and the sky was blue, it was bitterly cold, the sea breeze caught out many tourists who had arrived in the bay wearing shorts and T-shirts. By lunchtime most days, hundreds of tourists had been forced to buy fleece coats from the market traders to hide them from the bitter bay winds.

Petur heard the loud, 'Thwack' as the security chain snapped; he tried to make sense of the scene, a large gas truck appeared to be out of control, it ploughed through the crowds at speed. The vehicle crushed everyone in its path as it headed toward the ferry which had just docked. Most of the crowd had nowhere to run, hemmed in by the sheer number of people on the dock. Petur turned and grabbed his family, pushing them out of the path of the truck, which showed no sign of stopping. He looked into the cab as it neared; the driver seemed to pull some invisible cord. Petur was thrown clear as the concussion wave from the grenades hit him; his ears were ringing from the blast when the gas truck exploded, turning Pier 39, the ferry, and hundreds of people into a fireball.

CHAPTER 7

Grand Canyon – Hank

Hank Lyons stood in front of a low stone wall at the edge of the Grand Canyon. He was in a resort called the Bright Angel Lodge. The Canyon view in front of him was truly awesome to behold. *People use the adjective awesome too much,* he thought.

'You don't know the meaning of the word until you've seen this,' Hank said to himself.

If you stand in the cold Arizona morning, waiting for dawn at the edge of the Grand Canyon, you would have no comprehension of the enormity of the landscape in front of you. As the sun rises and the canyon is revealed, rock formations sculpted by years of erosion are illuminated, long convoluted shadows are cast onto giant screen-like cliffs. It is only when you notice details such as tiny trees, or people walking on the trails below, that you can truly put the size and scale of the canyon into any context.

Hank stood alone and watched the sunrise; a man approached the path that he was on, heading toward the accommodation lodges, he was coming from the rim trails; the rim trails were the narrow gravel footpaths that hugged the edge of the canyon's south rim. It was a little early to have finished walking the rim trails, Hank pondered, but he thought nothing of it. Tourists often started their walks as dawn broke in the Grand Canyon, taking advantage of the cooler temperatures in the mornings. 'Morning, sir. Isn't that a sight?' Hank said to the dark-skinned man as he approached.

'What? Oh, yes. Yes, it is,' Muktar replied without stopping to continue a conversation. As far as Muktar was concerned, Hank was just an old man in a cowboy hat. 'I was just being friendly,' Hank said after the man. *Strange foreign type,* he thought.

Hank was sixty years old today and this trip to the Canyon was a birthday present from his wife. His wife of forty years, Lizzie, had died six months earlier; the cancer that had ravaged her body finally defeated her after an eight-year struggle against the disease. Hank had worked around farms and horses all his life, a true wrangler and his ambition ever since he was a little boy was to ride down the Canyon to the Colorado River on one of the mule trains, but Hank and Lizzie never seemed to have the money to pay for his dream. In 1997, Lizzie had started collecting their waste aluminium cans with a view to selling them as scrap metal sometime in the future. After she had passed away, it had taken Hank four days to crush the cans and bag them up, he bought his wife a modest headstone with some of the money that he received for the scrap metal; the rest of the money he had used to take him to the Canyon on his sixtieth birthday. He had made it at last, and as he looked out over the natural wonder, he felt sad that he was experiencing it alone.

He missed his wife terribly. They had argued very little during their forty years together, Lizzie had been his sweetheart, lover, and his best friend. 'I wish you could have seen this, Lizzie,' Hank said to himself. A tear leaked from the corner of his eye and ran down his cheek. Hank looked skyward at two black Californian Condors that circled the rim using the thermals of warming air to float effortlessly. The huge birds flew down beneath the canyon's edge and landed on the outcrop of rock which was situated below the lodge. They looked like feathered guardians perched looking over the canyon. 'Sure, is some sight, Lizzie.' Hank turned and headed down the path toward the mule corral.

CHAPTER 8

Special Emergency Reaction Team

Trooper Bob Duncan parked the Hummer in an empty space on the car lot that serviced the Flagstaff Police Headquarters. There were officers from a myriad of different departments arriving at the same time. Bob spotted a large black van that would be carrying officers from the local SWAT team; the abbreviation was painted on the side of the vehicle in bold white letters. He entered the busy building and headed for the office where his men would be gathering, as an emergency call had been made to every available officer earlier that morning.

'What's the situation so far, Lieutenant?' Trooper Duncan asked as he walked into his squad room. The alarm call had gone out to all relevant response teams at 0300 hrs that morning. All Special Emergency Reaction Teams had to report for duty. America was under imminent threat of a terrorist attack.

'Okay, men, listen up, we've received reports of at least three dead terrorists in Orlando, along with at least a hundred civilian casualties. We may also have a live one. One bomb failed to explode, but it did ignite his clothing, so he's burned pretty badly.' A chorus of sarcastic comments rippled around the room. The men were edgy, and their nerves were jangling. 'Keep it quiet. From what we know so far, the terrorists are of Middle Eastern appearance, possibly al-Qaeda affiliates. We think that they're linked to a terror cell that fell off the radar six months ago. The surviving terrorist, we're calling him, The Duck, for now, was wearing a suicide vest rigged with explosives and ball bearings. It was a typical home-made system that's been used against the Israelis in the Middle East for years. The local guys down in Florida have pulled a wallet off the surviving terrorist, which had a credit card in it that links him with an extremist group known as 'Axe'. These people are linked to bombings worldwide, they're well-funded, well-trained, and well-organised.' A second murmur spread across the gathering, as snippets of information about the terrorist group were shared. 'Okay, quiet please. We have two possible links to these terrorists; one is a mobile phone message that was sent from a marked SIM card in Las Vegas. NSA electronic surveillance specialists have been tracking this mobile phone for two weeks now. We know that the phone was purchased with money from a suspect bank account. The National Security Agency has agents on the ground in Las Vegas as we speak. They are trying to trace whoever used that mobile phone, right now. The other link that we have is a credit card that was used to make a call from a phone bank at The Bright Angel Lodge in the Grand Canyon village. This means that we have a possible terrorist cell operating in the Grand Canyon right now and that's our problem. The targets do not know that we are watching their bank accounts and phone records. The bank accounts are linked to an Iraqi national called Yasser Ahmed, the leader of the Axe group. We have information that links Ahmed with several suicide bomb attacks, some here in America and others abroad.'

The mention of Yasser Ahmed brought more ripples of consternation from the elite law enforcement officers in the meeting. He was a well renowned terrorist suspect. 'The Bright Angel Lodge is our objective, that's where the telephone calls were made. This resort is on the edge of the Canyon and following the pattern of the attacks overnight, Washington thinks that tourist areas are their targets. We have two choppers en route to pick us up. I want full body armour, and full weapon dynamics. If you see these bastards, you shoot on sight.' The lieutenant clapped his hands together and his officers responded by checking equipment; the volume in the room reached fever pitch.

'What do you think, Trooper?' the lieutenant asked Bob Duncan as the other men dispersed to begin their preparations. The lieutenant had completed two tours of Afghanistan with Bob Duncan and he valued his opinion. They had dealt with many combat situations over the years and their service in the army gave them the experience they needed to lead the police SERT. The trooper was revered as one of the best snipers in the world.

During their last tour of Afghanistan, the lieutenant and Trooper Duncan had been leading a search and destroy mission into the mountains of the Helmand province. Their scouts had sighted and identified a Taliban warlord who was high up on the most wanted list; he was responsible for the manufacture of the majority of Improvised Explosive Devices that were commonly used to attack coalition personnel carriers; the blood of over thirty Marines was on the warlord's hands. When he was located and identified he was eating an evening meal with his followers, sat around a campfire one and a half miles away from where the lieutenant's squad were located. Trooper Bob Duncan had shot the warlord dead – using a sniper rifle and telescopic sight – with a single shot to the head, from over a mile away. The sniper shot that killed the Taliban warlord had become the stuff of army legend.

The trooper rubbed his goatee beard as he contemplated the threat of a terrorist cell operating at the Canyon. 'Well, I think it's busy up there at the Canyon at this time of year, but the crowds are dispersed. Maybe one or two men could place a couple of car bombs at some of the main viewing platforms like Hopi point.' Bob pointed to an area on the map that two SERT team men were looking at. 'This is the main viewpoint that most tour companies use. There are coach loads of people coming and going all day long. If someone decided to use a car bomb here, there would be no way of spotting them until it was too late.'

28

Trooper Bob was a combat veteran, and he had a sixth sense when it came to guessing the enemies plans. It had saved his life and the lives of his troops many times. 'I remember a guy in Chicago in 1984. He went on the rampage with a Kalashnikov machine gun. He took out fourteen people with the gun and then headed for the hills. We chased the son of a bitch in helicopters. The problem was this guy was not impressed by all our equipment and hardware. The helicopters did not intimidate him, and he was an accomplished marksman. He could shoot the spot off a domino. He was in good shape and motivated, and he kept on running through the woods up there. He shot three of my men down before we got him. We don't know what the terrorists have planned, but what I'm saying is that if I was a terrorist at the Grand Canyon, all I'd need is a rifle and a good spot to shoot from.'

CHAPTER 9

Liverpool

John Tankersley pulled up to a McDonalds drive-thru and pressed the button that would bring his window down; he ordered his drink, paid for it, and then arrived at the second window. He was greeted by a sulky young girl who was wearing a green uniform and a matching baseball cap. 'Did you order a large coffee? Do you need cream and sugar?' The spotty young girl in the baseball cap handed him a bag with enough cream and sugar to satisfy ten people. 'Cheers,' he replied laughing. As he drove away, his phone rang. 'Is that you, Tank? You had better get your ass into the office fast. Have you seen the news?' The familiar voice of his colleague Faz sounded flustered.

'Yes, I've been following it on the radio all morning. Have we had any Intel from the boys across the pond?' Tank asked. Communications between American and British secret services had improved since 9/11, but he wondered how much could be known at this early stage. 'The boss has got a file of information on this terror cell already. They seem to think there's a European connection. It could be connected to the Madrid and London incidents. He's waiting for you to arrive before he briefs the troops.'

Tank drove out of the car park and headed for the dock road that ran beside the River Mersey. He glanced to his left at the dark bricks of the Albert Docks across the road. The docks were built in the seventeenth century, when Liverpool was the busiest port in Europe. The city became the stop-off point for the human slave trade ships that carried Africans from their homeland to the Americas. In the 1970s it was closed to shipping and the dock fell into disarray, leaving dangerous derelict buildings. Their riverside position and long maritime history led to them being restored in the 1980s. The Albert Dock buildings were built entirely from cast iron, brick, and stone, with no structural wood, they cover over a million square feet of land on the banks of the River Mersey. They were now a busy tourist magnet full of restaurants, shops, and hotels.

The car park that serviced the docks was filling up already, with tourists who came from all over the world to visit the historic site. The docks had become the home of The Beatles Museum; Liverpool's most famous sons, still attracted thousands of visitors of all ages. The docks and The Beatles Museum were a tourist trap nestled on the banks of the River Mersey. It was similar to any other tourist hotspots that attracted large numbers of people. They were all potentially 'Soft Targets'.

30

Tank had been stationed in Liverpool with the Terrorist Task Force since 1991. As a younger man he had completed a six-year stint in the British Army and was almost immediately sent to serve in Northern Ireland, where he was quickly selected for a position with Special Forces before joining a mixed taskforce that combined military personnel with civilian law enforcement officers. Tank joined the armed services as a seventeen-year-old boy, just out of high school. He was always a well-built young man, naturally bigger and stronger than most the boys his age, and he was picked for the army boxing team. Tank was a fit young soldier and he quickly became a talented pugilist. In his first competitive bout he had come up against a much older opponent from the Paratroops Regiment. British Paratroops have a fearsome reputation and the men that serve in those divisions are fiercely proud of their regiments. The boxing matches that were organised between different regiments hold a lot of kudos and regimental pride is always at stake. Despite his strength, Tank was not expected to win, because his opponent was bigger, stronger, and more talented. The fight was held over six, three-minute rounds, and Tank had stood toe to toe with his bigger opponent every round, not appearing to feel the blows from the heavier man. No matter what combinations the talented paratrooper hit Tank with, he couldn't make any headway against the younger soldier. 'It's like firing a pea shooter at a tank! I've hit him with my best shots and he's still standing.' His opponent had said after the third round. That was it. The nickname stuck, Tank.

The nickname suited him more now that he was older than before. Tank had become a keen martial arts exponent, trained in Thai-boxing, and Brazilian wrestling. The effects of combining the powerful kicks and punches of Muay-Thai kick-boxing, with the lethal chokeholds and lock techniques of Brazilian Jujitsu were devastating. John Tankersley was a one-man demolition squad. He had lifted weights three times a week religiously since leaving school and had increased his muscle mass since joining the Army. His shaved head and muscular physique had an intimidating effect on most of the criminals he encountered; his Glock 9mm scared the rest.

Now he was lead officer on a joint taskforce known as the TTF. They were based at a huge police station overlooking the docks on the River Mersey, where the civilian force that policed the city of Liverpool consisted of over four thousand uniformed officers. The building was designed to act as a fortress in the event of public unrest and its windows were tall and narrow, resembling the arrow slits of a medieval castle. It did not blend in with the city's historic buildings; it looked like a square concrete castle.

Tank parked in the car park and headed into the elevator using his taskforce pass key to activate it. He stepped out onto the top floor of the police station where the taskforce was based. The floors below buzzed with the daily activities of uniformed policing, and the

31

uniformed police were always busy in a big city like Liverpool. The top floor was exclusively the home of the Terrorist Task Force. When the doors opened and he entered the room, the office had a sombre feel to it. People were quiet, only nodding hello as he went by. *Nervous anticipation,* Tank thought. This was the calm before the storm. The events that had taken place in American holiday resorts overnight would have a resounding impact on security forces the world over.

There were thirty-two people assigned to the taskforce at any one time. Twenty-eight were here, two were on holiday, and two were involved in undercover operations elsewhere. 'Be quiet, please!' Stanley Timms the taskforce director shouted across the office. A large remote screen started to descend the wall next to where Timms stood. 'We have a satellite link-up with our people in the States. Now it seems to me that they have more information on the suspected perpetrators than we usually have at this stage of an investigation. Pay attention to what the FBI Agent is going to tell us. Jade, please could you record the communication and make sure everyone gets transcripts of it today?' Jade nodded. Everyone else made themselves comfortable and got ready to listen to the communication from American security services. 'At this point in the investigation, the only stupid question is the one you later wish that you had asked. Patch us through to Quantico, please.'

Director of Operations, Major Stanley Timms rolled up his sleeves and stood back a little to see the screen. A man with perfect hair and a dark suit appeared on the digital screen, he adjusted a small microphone in front of him. Special Agent Galvin introduced himself briefly as the coordinator of an ongoing operation involving the FBI and the NSA. 'The story so far as we have it, guys, is as follows. We have a dead Iranian national who failed to detonate his device in the Disney incident. This suspect is not in our system; however, he had a credit card on his person that was linked to a group of bank accounts that we've been watching since 9/11. We also have a dead Iraqi national; we'll refer to him as body V, for now, who was shot in a parking garage beneath a Las Vegas hotel. He was shot resisting capture by officers of the NSA and they were alerted by a text message that was sent from Vegas to a mobile phone that we know was last used in Florida. Body V also had credit cards on him that are linked to the suspect bank accounts and he had checked into the hotel using a fake passport. We've recovered three sniper rifles from the boot of the victim's car, and enough ammunition to start a war. In addition to that we have a Special Emergency Reaction Team heading to the Grand Canyon national park area. We've traced a call that was paid for through one of the accounts that we're monitoring, and it was used at a resort called the Bright Angel Lodge. We are anticipating some terrorist activity in that area. We do not know what type of attack, if any, is planned but we must play on the safe side.' Agent Galvin opened a thin manila file and looked at the information that was contained in it.

'Thirty minutes ago, we started receiving reports of a truck bomb that has exploded at Pier 39 in the San Francisco bay area. We have no definitive proof they are linked to the other attacks, but we have to assume that they are. The other problem that we have at the moment and the reason we are being so forthcoming at this stage, is that the last purchase made from this bank account before we froze it was an airline ticket. A woman called Yasmine Mina Ahmed, an Iraqi passport holder, made the purchase. She flew into Manchester, England this morning.' The room stayed silent as Galvin finished his summary.

'Why were these bank accounts that you have been monitoring not frozen sooner?' asked Faz, she was never one to stay quiet for long.

'We need to know where these terrorists and their suspected affiliates are at any one time. We've been following their movements undetected using this financial information since 9/11. These people think they're invisible. Therefore, we freeze some accounts and pretend that we don't know about others in order to track the movement of suspects.'

'What information do we have on Yasmine Ahmed?' Major Timms asked the FBI agent.

'We know that she is related to Yasser Indri Ahmed, his file has been e-mailed across to you. This guy is big trouble with a capital T. We've suspected him of sponsoring religious training camps in Somalia, Pakistan, Iran and Syria. He has also spent time in the Sudan and Afghanistan. This guy has been linked with most of the top Islamic Militant groups. We think he is the brains behind the group, 'Axe'. All our intelligence on the Axe organisation is with the Ahmed file that I've sent to you. The strange thing is that we have Yasmine Ahmed listed as dead. We believe she died two years ago in an American military air strike in Iraq.'

'Who bought the airline ticket and travelled on that Manchester flight then? Do we have CCTV footage of the passengers that boarded the aeroplane at all?' Timms prompted the American agent.

'All we have is a digital image of a female of Middle Eastern appearance, checking bags in at the airport desk. I'll have the film sent over to you immediately.'

'How many casualties do you have?' asked Tank.

'The explosions in Florida and San Francisco were so large that we are finding it difficult to recover complete bodies. I'm not sure we'll ever know the answer to that question,' Agent Galvin said.

CHAPTER 10

The Grand Canyon

Hank had been given the lead mule because he was an experienced rider; they headed down the winding trail. The trail was cut into the Canyon face and was only about four feet wide; it was a vivid orange colour made from stone and gravel. The trail was just wide enough to allow the mules to walk in single file or to pass safely beside the other tourists that were using it; the journey down into the canyon provides you with some idea of the scale of it. Distance becomes more real as you descend, the details of the scenery unfold around you. Hank looked up as the walls of the Canyon towered above him and he began to realise that the landmarks that looked so close from the rim would actually take hours to reach. He was excited and as the trail twisted down toward the Colorado River, the colours in the rocks changed. The awesome view that he had witnessed from above, changed to an equally awesome view from below. The Bright Angel Trail drops down some fifteen hundred feet before the first water stop is available at a rest site called the Indian Gardens and as they approached their first respite, Hank heard the distant pounding of helicopter blades.

Muktar had reached his primary sniper nest about half an hour before the mules approached the Indian Gardens; he had watched as they made their slow progress down the winding trail. The rim trails that he had used to reach his nest had been empty of prying eyes and curious tourists, his perch was invisible from the Canyon edge above him and anyone passing by wouldn't be able to see him from the path. The distance to the far side of the rim made it impossible for him to be seen from that angle too; it was at least a mile, but he was hidden from even the best binoculars. His only problem was that he was exposed from inside the canyon itself. Sightseeing helicopters could see him in plain view, but Muktar and Yasser had planned this well. No helicopter flights pass over this part of the south rim trails. The national park had imposed a no-fly zone in order to protect the giant Californian Condors. Trying to encourage them to nest and breed in the area again had been difficult enough and the frequent chopper flights that carried tourists into the canyon were restricted to the eastern edge which was fifty miles away.

Muktar looked through the telescopic sights on his M40-A5 sniper rifle and focused in on the lead mule. The M40 is manufactured to be less than half an inch in a hundred yards accurate. It's an American Marine Corps tactical weapon and has long since been the yardstick against which all precision rifles were measured. The old man on the lead mule looked vaguely familiar, but that didn't matter. *He looked like a cowboy in cowboy land*, Muktar thought. As the mules approach the rest stop, the trail bends sharply and narrows, and there is a vicious drop down into the canyon at that point. Groups of tourists stood huddled in their relative groups on the bend waiting for the mule train to pass.

Muktar lined up the cross sights on the chest of the old cowboy and tightened the pressure on the trigger. Just before he squeezed, he heard the pounding of the helicopter blades approaching and they were far too close to be an innocent sightseeing tour.

The Bell Jet Ranger helicopter flew low above the rim trails. The pilot was a two-tour Vietnam veteran, and he would need all his skill today to navigate the vicious thermals and air pockets that made flying in the Canyon so dangerous. Captain Scott Baker sat up front next to the pilot. The left side doors of the helicopter had been removed. Trooper Bob Duncan sat in the left rear seat, his feet resting on the skid facing outwards. Rifleman Mike Stout took a similar position in the front seat of the rear compartment. Both men wore seat harnesses that were tethered to a hard point on the floor for safety. Both soldiers were armed with M16-A1 sniper Marine rifles. The guns held magazines of twenty rounds; the initial three would be tracer rounds to aid the targeting of a suspect and the rest of the magazine was loaded with fat shells that could blow your head clean off from five hundred yards.

A second helicopter carried Trooper Jay Blithe and Lieutenant Armstrong, who was the leader of the ground team. The second helicopter began its descent to the Canyon rim opposite Muktar's position. The steel bird landed and dropped its human cargo in seconds, then quickly gained altitude and climbed steeply away from the Canyon. The two SERT men reached the cliff edge in minutes; crawling forward on their bellies, they scanned the trails leading down into the rock's abyss. Lieutenant Armstrong switched on his digital binoculars and looked through them. The image had a green tint, but the distance at which they could focus was greatly increased. 'Tell me what you can see. What have you got, Lieutenant?' asked Trooper Duncan from the SERT helicopter.

The pilot kept the helicopter low over the roads that follow the Canyon's edge, in parallel to the trails. The flying machine was hidden from view by the trees that lined the Canyons edge. They didn't want to announce their arrival to any potential terrorists just yet. They were still following the troopers gut instinct that a sniper attack here would be the most likely plan for a terrorist to try to execute. 'We have a big zero so far. I can see nothing out of the ordinary down below. I am scanning up and east, as we speak… wait! There is a shooter set up on a rock ledge approximately nineteen hundred yards from the Bright Angel Lodge. He is taking aim at someone on the Bright Angel Trail. If you fly west over the top of the lodge, you will have a chance to get a clear shot at the target, I repeat the shooter is nineteen hundred yards east of the lodge. Bring the helicopter over the top of the rim for the best shot!'

'Roger that. Hang on, boys, we're up and over. The shooter should be on your left as we come over the rim,' said the pilot of the SERT helicopter.

Muktar had heard both the helicopters' engines but in the Canyon the echoes confused the sound. He heard the second helicopter rotary engine climbing away from the Canyon, but it sounded like it was on the other side of the rim. Suddenly the engine noise increased from behind him. As Muktar turned to look, the SERT helicopter cleared the rim edge and hovered five hundred yards in front of his position. He held the rifle up to his shoulder and focused in on the helicopter using his telescopic sight. There were two soldiers dressed head to toe in black combat gear, positioned outside the helicopter itself. They were stood on the landing skids and taking aim in his direction. Muktar's fingers tightened on the stock of his gun, he squeezed the trigger ready to shoot and held his breath. A bead of sweat ran down the back of his neck.

Trooper Duncan sighted Muktar through his digital scope. The terrorist was aiming back at him and looked as if he was ready to shoot. The incessant pounding of the rotary blades seemed to fade as Trooper Duncan pulled the rifle tight into his shoulder. He saw a flash from the target's gun as the sun reflected from the barrel of the weapon and then the trooper pulled the trigger. Muktar, Trooper Duncan, and Rifleman Stout opened fire at the same time. Trooper Duncan fired a burst of nine shots, hitting Muktar eight times, in the legs, body, and head. Muktar's bullets hit Rifleman Stout in the face and neck, Trooper Duncan was sprayed with the rifleman's blood and fragments of teeth. Both Trooper Stout and Muktar died instantly, the soldier was left hanging limp from the helicopter suspended from his safety harness as they hovered above the Canyon.

Muktar spun on the orange rock outcrop, doing a macabre dance as the fat high velocity bullets smashed into his body. He twisted one last time and then fell over the edge, his body crashing to a halt two thousand feet below.

The noise of the engines had boomed from the Canyon walls as the helicopter had cleared the rim. The mules, which were not accustomed to the deafening sound, reared and snorted, their fear causing unease among the animals. The sound of rapid gunfire had made the animals bolt. The mule train guides had managed to control the beasts, all except one, the lead animal. Hank's ride had bolted toward the sharp bend. The old cowboy had used all his skill to bring the mule to a halt, but he had controlled the animal too late. The animal crashed into a group of Japanese walkers, knocking them over like skittles. Three of the oriental tourists had gone over the edge of the narrow trail to their deaths. As the animal reared, Hank pulled back on the reins, but the mule toppled backward off the path, taking the quickest route to the bottom. Hank would get to see his dead wife Lizzie today after all. This time there would be no parting them.

CHAPTER 11

Manchester, England

Flight 42 from Orlando, Florida to Manchester, England was on approach, the aeroplane was full to capacity with British tourists, many of whom were returning home from their holidays in Florida. Yasser Ahmed had listened to conversation after conversation about the atrocities that had taken place earlier that evening. Many of the passengers expressed gratitude to be leaving Florida behind, others told tales of how they'd been close to the bombings and had narrowly missed being caught up in them.

'Ladies and Gentlemen, we should be down on the tarmac in about fifteen minutes. We are to taxi a little to our gate, so you should have your feet firmly on the ground in approximately twenty-five minutes. The temperature in Manchester at the moment is fourteen degrees and it's raining,' the co-pilot said over the cabin's speaker system.

Yasser sat in a window seat still dressed as Yasmine, he had not moved from the chair since boarding eight hours ago, not even to use the toilet. The fewer people he had contact with, even visually, the better, as he knew that if the authorities were onto him, they would pounce here. Once he had disembarked from the aeroplane, he could disappear into the large Asian communities that live in Britain's cities. He was uncomfortable from the long journey that he had made dressed as Yasmine, but so far, he was still a free man.

The plane touched down and Yasser disembarked the aircraft without any incident. It appeared that the security services had not managed to trace the attacks to him yet. He knew that they would eventually, but by then he would be long gone. The attacks had gone well; the Americans would once again realise that there was a price to be paid for their leader's foreign policies and the invasion of Muslim countries. His people also owed Britain a powerful blow in repayment for their crusades in Iraq and Afghanistan. He was going to need some time to prepare his attacks, but the process was already in motion to strike at America's greatest ally. There were already many followers of Islam in Britain who were deeply offended by the government's decision to invade Iraq despite protests from the British public. The invasion had already provoked a violent response. Yasser had been aware of the 7/7 bombings of the

37

London Transport system in 2005, the attacks had confirmed that the UK was now a major target for Islamic fundamentalist terror groups. On Thursday, July 7, 2005 a co-ordinated attack of four bombs killed fifty-two people and injured seven hundred more in the county's capital city, London. Young men from relatively stable backgrounds placed the bombs; they were not people like Yasser, whose life had been shattered by war or poverty. None of them had been previously identified as violent extremists and in most cases their families and friends had expressed extreme shock and sadness that they'd been involved. Yet they'd been so incensed by the British government's policies that they chose to leave their families and condemned themselves to death by becoming suicide bombers. Yasser knew he could rally support in this country for his Jihad against the Christian invaders.

Yasser walked down the long air bridge that joined the aeroplane to the terminal building. He stopped and pretended to tie the shoelace in his pink training shoes. He spotted what he was looking for further down the long, carpeted corridor. He stepped onto a travellator while looking at the rain that was running down the windows to his left. *This country is so bloody miserable*, he thought. He saw the sign that identified the Ladies' toilets further up the corridor and he joined the next moving escalator.

Yasser stepped off the moving pavement and headed for the toilet areas. He walked into the toilets and entered the disabled cubicle. Locking the door behind him, he opened his hand luggage and started to get changed quickly, he removed the make-up that he was wearing from his eyes, using wet wipes. He changed into a pair of dark work pants that he had packed up in his hand luggage and removed his pastel coloured tracksuit jacket. He took out the bright yellow hi-viz waistcoat that he had placed into the side pocket of his bag and put it on over his plain black T-shirt. On the back of the yellow waist coat in big blue letters was the word 'Baggage'. Yasser tied up his long black hair into a tight ball on the back of his head and covered it with a baseball cap. The badge on the cap said 'Supervisor'. He clipped his mobile phone to his belt and hung a bunch of keys from his waist and then placed a fake plastic ID wallet around his neck. He left the toilets and headed in the opposite direction from which he had come, back toward the aeroplane; he pushed open the first fire exit door that he could find.

Alarms rang out all over the terminal because the fire door had been breached. Two unarmed security guards ran down the long terminal corridors toward the fire exit doors, to investigate what had happened. One of the guards was so fat, that he was out of breath by the time he reached Yasser. 'Hello, mate, did you see who opened this fire exit door?' he panted, thinking that Yasser was just another airport employee. The overweight security guard lifted his walkie-talkie to his ear. 'Do we have any idea what's going on with the fire exit alarms in corridor twenty-two, Mallory?' A static voice came over the air.

38

'A tall blonde man with a black leather jacket walked close by to where I was standing, and he suddenly bolted through the fire exit door. I didn't want to follow him until you guys got here, just in case he is dangerous,' Yasser told the guards.

'Mallory to control room, come in please, boss. We have a tall blonde male wearing a black leather jacket that has entered a fire exit on corridor twenty-two. It's an unauthorised area sir,' the fat guard said into the radio.

'No shit, Sherlock. Get your fat ass down there after him and arrest him. If you want to keep your job do not come back without him, Mallory,' the static voice shouted.

Yasser could see that the heavy man was starting to panic. The pressure on airport security guards had become intense due to the increased number of security checks that were now required at all airports. The increased number of immigrants entering the country illegally had also put pressure on an already stretched operation. Yasser saw his opportunity. 'You guys take the corridors and storerooms down there and I will take the exit areas and the exterior. I will give you a hand and get the baggage men to check our areas too.' Yasser pointed the flustered security guards in the direction that the non-existent man had run.

The guards headed off to chase the wild goose and Yasser slipped out of the airport terminal building onto the tarmac; he walked confidently around the boarding gate areas. He headed toward the perimeter fences, through the rain, which was starting to fall heavily now. Yasser had estimated that the walk to the employee car park would take him about twenty minutes. He went beneath a dozen large jets that were attached to the terminal building by air bridges, people were buzzing around loading and re-fuelling aircraft. Yasser was almost invisible with his yellow baggage handlers' hi-viz jacket on. He blended in perfectly, just another immigrant in a low-paid job at the airport. There were so many employees at the airport that pretending to be one of them was the perfect disguise. He walked along the edge of the terminal building and headed for the main bus route drop off and pick up point. There he took the bus which serviced the long stay car park out to terminal two. Terminal two had an employee parking section that was permanently full. Four shifts a day of baggage handlers, restaurant staff, cleaners, air stewards, pilots, and security guards all had to come to and from this section.

Yasser climbed off the airport shuttle bus and entered the employee parking lot. He pulled his waistcoat high around his neck to stop the rain from soaking him completely. Yasser pressed the remote on the plastic key card that he held in his hand, waiting for a vehicle to respond. He walked the full length of a second row of parked cars, but nothing happened. Yasser entered the third and final row and at last a red Volkswagen Golf flashed its headlights and beeped in response to the key card. Yasser climbed into the vehicle and started the engine.

He lit a cigarette and then opened the keep box, which was between the seats. He took out the mobile phone that had been placed inside, hit the recall button, and dialled the number that appeared on the screen.

'Hello, I have recently arrived in this country and I am looking for accommodation,' Yasser said. He was using a pre-prepared sentence that the person receiving the call should recognise.

'You will find our rooms very cold, my old friend. I see from the news that your business trip was successful,' replied the voice, recognition and excitement in his tone.

'Yes, the trip was a remarkable success; however, it is time to bring my plans for the British to fruition. How are my brother and sister? I hope that they have been well looked after. I would like to see them soon whilst we are working on our plans. They have been in exile too long. Their time for hiding from my enemies is over. We will meet at the cold room, the day after tomorrow. I would like to be able to meet with my brother and sister shortly after the meeting. You must tell no one of my arrival here in this country, I cannot trust anyone.'

Yasser pressed the call terminate button and headed the vehicle toward the exit barriers. He inserted the ticket and the automatic payment machine requested the exit fee. Yasser placed a credit card into the machine in order to pay. The machine illuminated a red light, which indicated that the card had been declined. An alternative method of payment was requested on the digital screen. Yasser placed an alternative credit card, which was linked to a separate bank account. The barrier lifted slowly. Yasser realised that the international security services had identified his bank account and had frozen it. He headed west on to the M56 Motorway away from Manchester Airport. He followed the signpost which directed him toward Warrington in Cheshire; that would be his home for a while.

As Yasser Ahmed was making good his escape, Tank and the Terrorist Task Force had desperately tried to contact Manchester Airport security. They had informed them that a Middle Eastern woman using an Iraqi passport was a terror suspect and that she must be detained. The control room radioed the instructions over the airwaves.

'Mallory and all units, we have a target female Asian national who has just disembarked from the Orlando, flight forty-two. She is to be considered dangerous, possibly armed. She should be between passport control and baggage collection. I want you to use a low-profile approach please, do not panic the other passengers but apprehend her immediately.' The static voice from the control room boomed through the security guard's radio.

'What a fucking day I'm having chasing bloody nuisances around the airport,' Mallory said to no one. The security guards and armed police officers searched all the way through the terminal walkways and found nothing. They searched passport control and went into the

40

baggage collection area but all the passengers from flight forty-two were gone. Mallory retraced his steps back to the terminal corridors and checked inside the disabled toilets; they found a pastel coloured tracksuit, pink training shoes, and some sunglasses. Armed police officers stood in the empty luggage collection hall where their owners had already collected the bags from Orlando. There was no sign of the Iraqi woman. Two lost and lonely cases went around on the conveyor belt repeatedly. The nametags on them indicated that they'd belonged to Yasmine Ahmed.

CHAPTER 12

Liverpool

Tank saw the punch coming and moved to his left quickly, he lowered his left shoulder and swung a vicious left hook toward his opponent's head. The punch landed, stunned the smaller man, and made him drop his guard. Tank moved swiftly for a big man and in seconds he had his opponent in a chokehold. 'I've got you, Chen, my boy. I've got you. Come on now, tap out, or pass out, it's your choice!' Chen was choking. The guillotine lock that Tank had applied across his windpipe could kill him in seconds. Mixed martial arts rules are similar to the rules in wrestling. If you tap your opponent, or the canvas, with your hand, then you lose but you live to fight another day. Chen hated tapping out to the big man. He knew that Tank would go on about it all bloody day when they got back to the taskforce office.

Faz stood ringside leaning through the ropes; a white sweat towel was hanging around her neck. She was watching the boys sparring, which they did three times a week. Faz was cooling down, having finished her session with Tank earlier. She loved sparring with him because it was such a challenge. He was big, strong, and very quick. Grace Farrington, who everyone called Faz, had been born in Liverpool but was of West Indian origin, her dark skin was shiny with sweat as she watched Chen choking in the boxing ring. Tank was applying even more pressure to the little Chinaman's throat. 'Come on, Chen, just tap out and it will all be over. A better opponent has beaten you. Tap out or pass out. Tap out or pass out!' Tank was talking through clenched teeth.

'Tap out, Chen, or none of your shirts will fit you anymore; your neck size will be three sizes smaller!' Faz shouted. 'You'd better let him go, Tank, he's turning blue.'

Suddenly Chen stopped struggling and went limp in Tank's arms. Tank felt the Chinaman stop struggling; his dead weight signalling the mental alarm bells in his head. Tank loosened the grip on Chen's throat and was straining his head round to look at Chen's face. Tank was worried that he had hurt his friend and colleague; panic was setting in. Chen's eyes suddenly snapped open and he pulled away from the big man's grip, moving like lightening. Tank was rooted to the canvas, confused and shocked. Chen ducked and threw an uppercut that hit Tank under the chin. Tank's knees buckled and he collapsed stunned, onto the canvas, his eyes open, staring at the ceiling. Chen stood over him laughing. 'You cheat, you horrible, nasty little man, I don't believe I fell for that.' Tank spat out his gum shield and rubbed his jaw dramatically for effect. He rolled over onto his belly, looking at Faz for sympathy or support.

None was forthcoming. Faz had her hand over her mouth mimicking that she wasn't laughing. 'Nothing wrong with that, he never tapped out. You're getting slow in your old age, big fellah!' She laughed and threw her towel over Tank's head.

'We'd better call that a day and get back to the office.' Tank stood and walked toward the shower room with his arm around Chen's shoulders. 'You know I'm going to have to get you back for the bloody liberty you've just taken, don't you?' Tank laughed.

The three Terrorist Task Force officers met in the gym car park and climbed into Faz's Jeep Cherokee. 'How's the research into the Axe group going, Chen?' Faz asked as she started the Jeep and turned the radio down simultaneously as the Arctic Monkeys blared out from the speakers. Chen was an expert on terror groups and their operational histories. What he didn't know, he researched. 'It's been very interesting so far. It seems our man Yasser Ahmed fell out of favour with the more mainstream leaders of al-Qaeda about the time of his sister's reported death. We don't know for sure, but it looks like he reported her death to cover-up that he was smuggling her and his brother out of the country. It would seem somebody threatened to kill his family if he didn't conform to the group's demands,' Chen paused.

'So, he reports that his brother and sister have been killed in an air strike and makes them disappear. He is obviously a smart boy. What's his relationship with al-Qaeda like now, then?' Tank asked.

'It appears they don't have one at all. Yasser's methods were extreme, and he was just as ruthless with his Islamic enemies; he wouldn't conform to the leadership, so he set up his own group, Axe. It seems he is very popular with the fanatics. All their funding comes from Saudi and Syria we think. We know he had recently been to Spain shortly before the Madrid bombings,' Chen said excitedly. 'The Madrid Bombings took place on March 11, 2004 and targeted the busy commuter train network that serviced the city, killing one hundred and ninety-two people and injuring over two thousand more. Although it was originally blamed on a Spanish terrorist group it had soon become clear that it had been carried out by members of a Moroccan-based Islamic group. Again, we can only assume that Yasser Ahmed was involved. We also know that he was in the Somali camps at the same time as Omar Khan, six months before he carried out the London bomb attacks on 7/7. We think the fact that the Spanish immediately pulled their troops out of Iraq after the Madrid attacks gained Yasser Ahmed a great deal of support and more financial backing.' Chen finished speaking and he wound down the window, still hot from his workout.

'So, what does a bloke have to do to be more extreme than the guys in al-Qaeda? How can you be more extreme than the extremists?' Faz asked exasperated.

'Yasser Ahmed and his cronies hijacked a minibus containing an Iraqi basketball team that were planning to begin a tour of America. They beheaded them on video with a kitchen knife. Ahmed sent the tape to Islamic news stations and Internet sites as a warning to anyone else wanting to play Western sport; enter the Olympics et cetera, et cetera. Ahmed did most of the cutting himself. He's a first-class psychopath. He also seems to be very good at recruiting other psychopaths to go and kill innocent people and themselves, in the name of his cause. Some incidents we can link to him directly, but there are plenty of incidents that we think he was the inspiration behind, rather than the logistical brains.' Chen knew that Yasser Ahmed had been linked to far too many terror attacks to have been physically involved in them all himself. However, he was definitely the inspirational motivation for thousands of extremists to follow. 'We've been told he takes his inspiration from some of the early Egyptian extremists. For instance, on November 17, 1997, six terrorists disguised themselves as security guards at a temple in Luxor. They were armed with automatic weapons and knives and they followed a group of Swiss tourists to the tomb of the Pharaoh Hapshepsut. They launched an all-out attack on the tourists, killing them all. By the time the Egyptian police arrived, many of the victims had been disembowelled or beheaded. All the terrorists were killed in the ensuing gun battle but the horror of their methods and the impact it had worldwide did not go unnoticed by the likes of Yasser Ahmed,' Chen added to enforce the point that the more terrifying the attack, the further reaching its effects become.

'Wasn't there some link with the Axe group and what happened at the university shooting in Virginia Tec? I seem to remember something about 'Axe' being mentioned in the SWAT team's reports,' Tank said.

'Surely that was one mentally deranged student who lost the plot?' Faz said.

'We will never know that for sure, but there are some interesting theories. This guy, Sueng Hui Cho, was a Korean Muslim. He was studying English literature at the University, but the building where he killed thirty of his thirty-two victims was the engineering department. People have speculated that he may have had a grievance against them in particular. On the day itself, he'd left the dorm room by 5.15 a.m. According to statements accredited to his roommates this was unusual, not his normal pattern of behaviour. No one seems to know what he did between leaving the dorm and 7.15 a.m., when he killed his first female victim. The resident caretaker of the building was killed next, they think that he ran to her assistance and was also shot by Cho. Then Cho takes chains and locks with him to the Engineering building and chains all three entrance and exit doors shut. He goes up to the second floor and manages to shoot fifty-five students and teachers. A total of thirty-two dead and one hundred and seventy rounds fired. He had enough ammo on him to cause mayhem. One man with two guns caused fifty-seven wounded and thirty-two dead. All caused by just one man on a mission.' Chen recounted the details demonstrating his enormous capacity for retaining information.

'That could have been just like the Las Vegas plot if the NSA hadn't stopped the perpetrator. The Grand Canyon could have been much worse too, if the SERT hadn't arrived when they did,' Faz interrupted.

'That's exactly my point. These attacks don't need to be complicated. We know that the SWAT teams that responded to the shooting in the Virginia Tech breached the entrance doors by shooting through the chains with 00-gauge shotguns. The noise of the shotguns tipped Cho to the fact that they'd arrived, so he put the gun to his head and blew his brains out. We don't know what was troubling this kid and we never will, but he sent a package to *NBC News* giving us some clues. The tape rants on about cruel students and criticises the Christian faith. The kid also has the words 'ISMAEL AX' written on his arm in red ink. Now there are two famous literary characters called Ishmael; one is from the novel, *Moby Dick* and the other is a religious character. Ishmael was one of the two sons of Abraham in the bible. He was eventually sent away from Abraham and his story is revered in the Muslim faith. There they tell the story of how Ishmael took plates of food to the statue idols in the mosque. He goes back later the same day and of course the food is still there. The statues have not eaten the offerings. Therefore, he determined that the idols are false. In the story, he took an axe and destroyed them all. Therefore, Ishmael's Axe was the destroyer of false gods.'

'You can't be implying that Cho was a terrorist?' Tank asked thoughtfully.

'No, of course we can't say that for certain, but beyond his mental stability what was his motivation? We can't dismiss that this could have been his own act of Jihad. Look at his videotape when we get back to the office. Compare that to the images of homicide bombers and other martyrs; you can't ignore the similarities. He displays himself with several weapons depicting himself as a warrior or soldier. He shows his willingness to commit acts of violence and to accept his own death. Look how long he took to plan this. You can't say the man just suddenly shot people in a fit of rage. The evidence shows he made videos; he bought weapons. He bought chains and padlocks to keep his victims in the building and the police outside. This amount of preparation is not the actions of a lunatic. It is all premeditated and planned. The connection to the Ishmael legend is just speculation but think about it. I'm convinced that the Axe group has taken their name from Ishmael's story.'

'Yasser Ahmed is a dangerous man. If he can persuade and motivate individuals or small groups of people to go out and kill indiscriminately in this country, as he has done elsewhere, then we have a serious problem. Question is what's he planning next and where is he now?' Tank said, more to himself than anyone else.

CHAPTER 13

TTF Office

Tank, Chen, and Faz stepped out of the elevator into the TTF nerve centre. The room was buzzing with excitement, but not the positive kind. The faces in the room showed real concern; some were almost white with fear. Major Stanley Timms waved a hand in the air. He was standing across the room signalling them into his office. 'What's the score, Major? What do you know that we don't?' asked Chen; his Liverpool accent had always made Tank smile.

Chen was born in the city centre in the sixties. Like most of the large cities in Britain, Liverpool had a large 'China Town' area. The Chinese restaurants and bars were always busy, acting as a magnet to those who enjoyed the oriental cuisine. It was in ghetto-like areas that Chen was most at home. His scouse accent enabled him to blend into the crowds and talk to the indigenous inhabitants without raising suspicion. His ability to speak Cantonese as though he had lived in China all his life meant that he could draw information from within the Chinese communities countrywide. His father had been a restaurant owner and a Wing-Chun Kung fu teacher. He had passed on his art to Chen beginning at an early age. Many a bigger man had made the mistake of thinking that Chen's small frame was a physical weakness.

'We have DNA results back from the lab. The suitcases left at Manchester Airport were tagged and barcoded as belonging to Yasmine Ahmed. The credit card used in Orlando was linked to the bank accounts frozen after the attacks there. Now we have the CCTV footage of an Asian woman fitting Yasmine Ahmed's description checking in her bags at Orlando. Now watch this.'

Major Stanley Timms was an ex-Royal Marine; he had a war record that Hollywood couldn't write. He had been involved in the famous yomp across the Falkland Islands that the Royal Marines had achieved, on their way to recapture Port Stanley. The Royal Marines had been sent to the islands to spearhead the attack when they were invaded by Argentina. The Marines had been airlifted to a point so remote on the islands, that the Argies never thought anyone could launch an attack across such harsh terrain on foot. They had underestimated the capability of a pissed-off platoon of Royal Marines and the Argentine army was defeated in days.

The Major's shoes were always like liquid black glass, the type of shine only an ex-squaddie can achieve. He sat back on the edge of his desk, keeping his back rigid and pointed to the screen with his pointer. Tank would have laughed at any other time; it always reminded him of old black and white war films when Major Timms got out his pointer. However, today it wasn't funny.

The picture on the screen was poor quality, but it showed passengers walking down a wide corridor, following visible signs to passport control. Timms pressed the pause button and slowed the film down. He pointed to the right-hand side of the screen. A female with long black hair, in a casual pastel coloured tracksuit, opened the door that led into the disabled toilets situated between the air bridges and passport control, next to the Ladies toilets. In what seemed like just a matter of minutes, what appeared to be a male baggage handler wearing a baseball cap and a hi-viz jacket, emerged from the disabled bathroom.

'The DNA on the bags that were checked in was male. Let me introduce Mr Yasser Ahmed. Not only is he on the loose in Britain, but he is also here right under our bloody noses.' Major Timms started to redden as he spoke. The implication of this mad man operating on their turf did not need to be spelled out. 'We know that he tried to use the marked credit card to get out of the long stay car park. The Yanks had already frozen the accounts while he was up in the air. If he had tried to pass through passport control, we would have had him. Someone had to park a car there, ready and waiting for him to use when he landed. We know that he has been into this country recently, therefore he already has supporters and contacts here. We have to assume that he is either stopping here on his way back to the Middle East, or he's here to carry out further attacks on British soil.' Timms turned, walked around the desk, and picked up a small manila file. He ejected the DVD that he had just played and inserted another. 'This is a copy of a statement sent to the *New York Times*, *CNN*, and the *BBC*,' he handed around copies of the transcript and pressed play on the remote. The screen came to life with images of the men involved in the recent attacks that had been carried out in American tourist centres. They were dressed in their Islamic Warriors' costumes in their suicide videos. The film showed the terrorists carrying machine guns, wearing headbands, and talking of their imminent death and glory. The scenes changed only briefly as one after the other, the now dead terrorists acted out their swan songs, their legacy. 'Home of the brave and land of the free, you shall be no more. Our glorious brothers will strike fear into the heart of your people. Your people will know the pain of death and destruction in their homes. You bring your crusades once again to our lands, now we return the favour and bring ours to you,' a now dead terrorist boasted from the screen.

'The fact that this bastard is here spells trouble. I want everything we have focused on this man. I want every mosque in the country visited and Ahmed's picture circulated. We must get the help of the Muslim communities if we are going to catch him. They're as worried as we are about the extremists. Order the uniform police divisions to help us. Let's circulate the pictures out there today. We need to contact all our undercover people working in those communities and get them asking questions. Someone is hiding this man and his cronies. Whoever is hiding Ahmed, it's not going to be a white middle-aged couple in Devon. It won't be Chen's uncle Woo in Brighton! There'll be no politically correct bullshit on this! I don't care who we upset, or who gets offended. We can pat them on the head and say sorry, once this man is either in jail or dead.' Political correctness had hampered many investigations in recent years, both in the civilian judicial systems and the military ones. The Major continued, 'Faz I want you personally to speak to every district commander in the country, starting with the obvious ones that have concentrated populations of Asian immigrants. Tell them TTF expects every armed response unit to be up to scratch about Yasser Ahmed. If they see him, they have the authorisation to shoot on sight.' Faz sprang into action and headed into a side office where she could make her calls to the country's police chiefs.

'Tank, I want you to organise your people into teams and send them out there shaking every tree we can find. You know what needs to be done. We will have a progress report at 7.00 p.m. this evening. I'm going to make a press statement to get the public's help to find this man without trying to cause panic. I just hope nobody asks me how he got into the country.'

CHAPTER 14

Holyhead

Mustapha was sat in his caravan watching football on the television when the telephone rang. There was quiet on the line and a tingle ran down his spine, he immediately knew it was them. Mustapha had been entrusted into the care of Yasser Ahmed's supporters, in the North-West of England, when he first arrived from Iraq. He had never met the people that had been given the responsibility to care for him and his sister, but they'd called him many times to check on his safety. They were placed into the care of a small Islamic community where their day-to-day needs were taken care of by surrogate Muslim families. The men that called Mustapha to check on their financial well-being were always very secretive and cautious. When Axe called Mustapha, they were always silent until he spoke a sentence containing the word 'Egypt', then they would speak. He knew that his brother was wanted by the authorities in many countries, including his own. He could only assume from the secretive behaviour they used, that the Iraqi men that contacted him were also fugitives.

'Just because my brother is a lunatic, doesn't mean that I live in Egypt!' Mustapha said as sarcastically as he could. He hated the way these men, whoever they were, had to use all these cloak and dagger tactics. It was because of Yasser and his antics that he had to leave his family and friends behind in Iraq. He hated his brother and his followers, for the turmoil they'd caused him and his sister. He did not share their religious convictions, but he did understand them. The Iraqi people had been invaded and conquered many times through history. The armies of modern-day Iran, then called Persia, to the east of Iraq were strong, as were the armies of the Turks to the North of the country. The huge Turkish Ottoman Empire, which was inspired and sustained by Islamic institutions, had taken Iraq under its military umbrella from the 1400s until the end of the First World War in 1918.

The British Army defeated what was left of the Ottoman Empire and colonised modern Iraq. France took Syria and Lebanon. Under British mandate, Iraqi King Faisal ruled over a smouldering religious time bomb. British rule was hampered by the minority Sunnis who were both influential and well-educated but were violently anti imperialist and believed that they should rule the country. The Shiite majority were equally determined that they wouldn't be ruled by the Sunnis or the British government. Thrown into the mix was the fact that the Kurds who lived in the north of Iraq wouldn't accept either Turkish or Arabian domination.

The British failed to control this religious and cultural nightmare and left the new nation of Iraq to its own devices in 1932. The new nation of Iraq in 1932 does not seem too dissimilar to the one we see today. Mustapha could understand his country's anger and frustration with the West, especially Britain. What made them think they could achieve by the invasion in 2003, what they'd failed to do in fifteen years of rule? Mustapha could understand his Muslim brothers' anger, but he did not agree with their methods.

'You are foolish and flippant, Mustapha Ahmed, and your words will be shared with those that should be told of your behaviour,' the heavy Iraqi accent on the line chastised him. Mustapha was five years younger than his brother Yasser. Yasser had smuggled him out of the Middle East by sending him to Ireland, via a container boat from Libya. Oil tankers from Libya had long been used by the Irish Republican Army to smuggle guns and ammunition into Ireland, to fight the British. The Libyan leaders had sympathy for the Republican Army and supported their struggle with money and arms. Finding Mustapha and Yasmine safe passage out of Iraq had been reasonably simple.

Mustapha hardly knew the man that was his brother and he resented the fact that he could still dominate his life from the other side of the world. He didn't even know where his brother was, and he didn't really care. What he did know about him, he hated. At school in Iraq, his friends often spoke of Yasser and the other men in the local militia, as if they were heroes. He had seen the video clip which showed sportsmen being beheaded by his brother and his affiliates. It had been part of a longer tape that glorified Islamic terrorism and included messages from Osama bin Laden. It had given him nightmares for years. The Mullah that had arranged the sick viewing made the mistake of assuming that all who watched it would be impressed and given inspiration from it.

The men that Yasser had entrusted with his siblings' education and safekeeping had taken a bizarre social lift within their small community, from the fact that they were asked to do so by such an infamous man. His brother was infamous for killing people. Mustapha was not impressed by this infamy. As Mustapha grew older in his adopted Islamic community, he had become so unruly and troublesome that they'd sent him to Wales, to Anglesey, out of the way. His constant running away and refusal to worship had drawn unwanted attention from the Muslim community, so this was the simple answer. Ordinarily the boy would have been disciplined into submission, but no one wanted to beat on the little brother of Yasser Ahmed.

'Your brother has bestowed his glorious presence upon us. He is here on these heathen shores. He requires that you be brought to meet with him, your exile appears to be ending, young Ahmed. You will be picked up tomorrow morning at 5.30 a.m.' The phone went dead.

What is Yasser doing here in this country? He surely hasn't just popped over here to say hello, Mustapha thought as he put down the handset.

Mustapha lived near to the town of Holyhead, the largest town in the county of Anglesey in the North-West of Wales. The town is not actually on Anglesey but is instead located on Holy Island, which is connected to Anglesey only by a man-made causeway. Holyhead is probably best known for its busy port, which sees more than two million passengers pass through each year. Europe's biggest ferry companies operate from the port sailing to Dublin and Dun Laoghaire in Ireland. The town is the principle link for surface transport between Ireland, Wales, and the rest of Europe. The passenger ferries that sail across the Irish Sea were the main source of industry for the island, apart from tourism. The beaches that surrounded Anglesey were famous for their breathtaking beauty, and they attracted tourists from all over the United Kingdom and Europe. Mustapha had made his home in one of the thousands of holiday caravan sites that peppered the coastline.

He turned off the football and threw the remote control across the room. Now he was annoyed. His greatest passion was Liverpool Football Club, but even watching the remainder of the game on the television wouldn't be able to settle him; he had too many questions going through his mind.

What was his brother doing here? Why can't he go and blow something up in Iraq? More to the point, why can't he just go and get blown up himself and do everyone a favour? Mustapha thought. Mustapha pulled on his jacket and opened the trailer door. He stepped out onto the grass, immediately feeling the sea breeze. He really needed to speak to his girlfriend, Sian. The caravan that he rented overlooked the Porthdafarc beach and was perched high up on the headland overlooking the stunning sea cliffs that encircled the bay. He looked across the golden semi-circle of sandy beach to the dark cliffs opposite. A huge wave crashed up the rocks, foaming white before it returned to the ocean.

The day was overcast, and the gloom matched his mood as it started to rain. Mustapha did not know why his brother was here or why he would want to send his followers to pick him up at five-thirty the next morning, but he knew that he wasn't going to be there when they came for him. He had to speak to Sian, she was at work, but he needed to see her. Mustapha pulled up his hood and walked toward the path that would take him to the road. The path hugged the cliff edge and he watched the surf pounding the dark rocks below him as he walked.

CHAPTER 15

Sian

Sian walked around the black Mercedes Benz. She indicated to the driver to lower the window of the vehicle. 'Turn off the engine and step out of the car please, sir,' she said with authority. The large customs shed echoed and boomed with the noise of the engines from passing cars and trucks, the ferry from Dun Laoghaire in Southern Ireland had just docked. Its cargo of passengers and vehicles had started their journeys away from the port by driving down the ramp of the huge catamaran ferryboat and through the customs sheds that belonged to the port authorities.

The port of Holyhead was the main thoroughfare for haulage goods to pass from the UK mainland across to Ireland. The journey from the Welsh town to the cities of Liverpool and Manchester, by road, would take less than two hours, London only an hour on top of that. In the times of the troubles between Britain and Ireland, the port's customs officers were always on the lookout for Irish Republican Army members. Weapons and explosives had arrived on the British mainland many times through this large port and had been used with devastating effect. Now that the terrorist threat from the Emerald Isle had ceased, drug smugglers were the new enemies.

Sian had been born and raised in the town, which despite being a busy European port was a very small tight-knit community. The population of about eleven thousand people rarely set eyes on the two million passengers that travelled through the port each year. Holyhead was a place most people passed through, on the way to, or from Ireland. Small towns such as Holyhead are awash with tales and stories of generations gone by, stories that became exaggerated as they were passed from person to person; eventually they become an urban legend and local folklore. Sian had heard many a tale from her family and friends over the years of how the shores of Anglesey were dangerous for passing ships. Stories of pirates and smugglers had fascinated her as a child. In the 1980s as she grew up, several large black plastic containers had been washed up on a part of Anglesey called Treaddur Bay, they'd contained hundreds of kilos of cannabis. The general consensus was that the drugs had been dropped into the ocean from a smugglers boat with the intention of it being picked up by a second craft and brought ashore at a later date. The unpredictable tides and rough seas had scuppered the plan before the contraband could be retrieved of course, the tales of how much of the drug had been salvaged for personal use, by a friend of a friend, of a friend, still echoed down the years, even now becoming urban legend. She often wondered if that's why she had joined the police force. After joining, she had decided to become one of Her Majesty's Customs squad, that way she could remain in the community that she had grown up in and still realise her ambition of a career in law enforcement.

Everyone in the town knew everyone else's business. Sian had gained a lot of valuable information over the years from listening to idle gossip. The people of Holyhead knew her as Sian 'Coch'; 'Coch' in the Welsh language meaning red, which applied to her hair colour. The name also distinguished her from any other Sian that lived in the town. Her father, Joe, called her Sian 'Bach'. 'Bach' being an affectionate term for small or young.

The man in the black Mercedes wound the window down and said, 'Are you having a laugh, love? We're in an awful hurry here now'. The accent was a harsh Irish tone; she identified it as being from Belfast, in the north of the country. Sian pressed the red button on her remote control and the huge custom shed roller shutters descended in seconds. They were a precaution to stop any possible escape from the customs sheds and were activated at the first sign of aggression. It was standard procedure to close the shutter doors immediately if there was sign of a problem, especially if the engine of the suspect vehicle was still running. The Belfast man's face reddened as he turned off the engine and opened the car door. He stepped out of the black Mercedes and slammed the door shut; looked down at his feet and leaned against the rear door. 'Your face has gone red. What's the matter? Have I made you mad, or have you done something wrong?' Sian was well aware that she had annoyed him, but she liked to use her female sexuality to unnerve suspects. Many men did not react kindly to being told what to do by a woman in uniform, especially men that patronised females in general. 'We've done nothing wrong, my dear woman. We are in a rush you see. My mother's very ill in hospital and we need to get there quickly, my darling,' he spluttered, trying to lie as convincingly as he could. His strong Irish accent had a somewhat charming effect. 'Best not keep you here too long then had we? Can you step out of the car too please, Sir. I mean right now.' Sian opened the passenger door as she spoke and signalled to her nearby colleagues to move toward the boot of the vehicle. The passenger was an Asian man. He stepped out of the car and looked at her, she sensed his fear immediately. He looked stressed; his eyes darting around looking for an exit.

'He doesn't speak English very well, so he doesn't,' said the Belfast man. He pointed at his Asian passenger and moved around the car away from the customs men.

'Your English isn't great to be honest. Now both of you stand still, put your hands on the car and shut up.' Sian and the other customs officers knew these men were not clean, the fear and panic in the voice of the Belfast man, combined with the silence of his Asian friend, were clearly signs that they were carrying something that they shouldn't be. Both men complied and put their hands onto the roof of the black Mercedes. There was sweat running down the Asian man's face as the officers opened the boot of the car. Sian walked toward the boot and looked into it as it opened. It was empty.

One officer patted down the Irish man looking for a weapon or illegal substances. Two more of Sian's men opened the rear doors of the Mercedes and searched beneath the seats. 'Nothing here, Ma'am, it looks clean,' a voice from inside the vehicle said. Sian looked into the boot again. Something wasn't right. The back of the rear seats appeared to be too close to her. There was too much space unaccounted for between the boot and the rear passenger seats. 'Cuff them and read them their rights, suspicion of drug smuggling will do for now. Let's get this thing ripped to pieces, starting with the rear seat. I don't think you're going to make visiting hours at the hospital, gentlemen. In fact, I think you'll be about ten years too late!' Sian stared at the men, looking for a reaction as she spoke. The Asian man bolted in a vain attempt to escape. Sian took a step back and pointed her Guardian Angel at his face as he approached her. The Guardian Angel can stop a man at a distance, before he does any harm to anyone. It looks like a small handgun; it has a powerful pyrotechnic charge that accurately fires two concentrated blasts of a potent liquid irritant into the face and eyes of an attacker. The effect is like a pepper spray on steroids, it sprays the liquid at 90 mph; way too fast to avoid. The effect on the Asian man as it struck him in the face was instant. He collapsed in a heap at Sian's feet, screaming. The solution caused an incredibly painful burning to the eyes, nose, and throat. He writhed on the floor screaming and choking. 'You fucking bitch! You fucking bitch, I can't breathe,' he said pausing to vomit.

'There doesn't appear to be anything wrong with his English now, does there?' she said to the Belfast man, as he was led away in handcuffs.

The two men were taken and placed in the holding cells. The result of the vehicle search would determine how long they stayed there, and which agency they would ultimately be handed over to. The Asian man moaned and wailed for about an hour in his cell, but sympathy was not forthcoming.

Sian called the local drugs squad and told them that they had a suspect vehicle that was being searched in the customs sheds. She knew from experience that there was a false panel that had been placed between the seats and the boots storage space. the majority of secret compartments were used for the transportation of drugs. Sian was sat talking to the drug squads leading officer, the Detective Inspector, when the results of the preliminary search came in. A customs officer handed Sian a clipboard across the desk.

'We've evacuated the customs shed, Ma'am and the bomb squad are on their way to remove the substance,' the officer said as he handed Sian the results of the preliminary search.

'Oh, my God!' Sian said almost whispering.

'What have we got, Sian, cocaine, ecstasy, heroin, crack?' the DI said, alarmed by the concern on her face, she was one tough woman, but she looked visibly shaken.

'I wish it was. I really do, it would be your problem then. The car is packed with what looks like Semtex explosive. It's not assembled, so it looks like they were just transporting it somewhere else. We've always been concerned what the IRA would do with its arms once the troubles ended. It looks like some of them are up for sale. We need to get the bomb squad to check it over though. The IRA always booby trapped their weapons piles, in case they were discovered. We have to be certain that it's been made safe before we move it.'

Sian thanked the DI as he was leaving, and he left her in the office alone. This was beyond his remit; he was in charge of drug crimes only. She locked the door behind as he left and switched on the videophone. She picked up her mobile phone and checked the screen; she had received a text message from Mustapha. 'I could do with a chat, what time do you finish?' The message read. She placed the mobile phone back onto her desk. She would answer it later. She turned back to the videophone and dialled the number of the Terrorist Task Force in Liverpool. The digital image of Tank's head appeared on the screen. Sian had been recruited by the TTF six years ago when the troubles in Ireland were still very much alive. She was one of their undercover team, her position at the customs office required that she was permanently undercover. The government had never really believed the Irish terrorists would actually stop their terror campaign on the mainland of Britain, they also believed rogue elements would turn the use of their weapons toward crime, or sell them on the British mainland. Sian was in the ideal position to relay any sighting of the now redundant Republicans, or their surplus weapons, directly to her bosses at the TTF.

'Hello, Sian, I need you to set the phone to receive a digital picture of a suspect that we need to catch very quickly. I don't think it's likely that he'll come your way, but could you please distribute his picture among your men?'

'I'll do it now, Boss.' She switched the receive button to the on position. 'Tank, I have two men in custody here, one is definitely Irish, and he is from Belfast we think. The other is a young male of Middle Eastern appearance. They have no identification on them, or their vehicle, which just happens to be packed full of Semtex explosives.' Semtex had been used successfully by the Irish Republican Army for many years. It was originally from a factory in a Czech Republic province called Semtim, where the plastic explosive gets its name from. Sian had learned during her taskforce training that the popularity of Semtex explosives with terrorists was because it's extremely difficult to detect. Recent international pressure had led to the manufacturers adding ethylene glycol dinitrate, which gives it a distinct vapour signature. This had made it easier for security services to detect its presence.

'Fucking hell, Sian when did this happen? Why haven't you called it in?' Tank sounded angry and his face darkened on the small digital screen. 'I'm calling it in right now, Tank. Five minutes ago, I was handed the results of the preliminary search of a black Mercedes. That's why I've called you now, to inform you of what's happened,' Sian replied, feeling the anger rise in her.

'I see. I thought you were contacting me in response to the e-mail I've sent you about this suspect Yasser Ahmed. His picture is on the way to you now. Is this Asian man that you have arrested talking yet?' Tank seemed flustered.

'I haven't checked any e-mail yet, Tank. My hands have been full with these two jokers and their car full of explosives; and no, he's not said a dickie bird since we pulled them in.' Sian downloaded the e-picture as they spoke.

'Sian, I want you to instruct your guys to interview them all night long if necessary. No sleep, no cups of tea, make sure that they get nothing until we get there. Then I will want you and myself with the Asian, Faz, and Chen with the Irish man.' Tank suspected that there could be a link between Yasser Ahmed's arrival in Britain and this attempt to smuggle Semtex into the country. 'We think that the brain behind the Disney bomb is here in the UK and we think that he has plans for us. If your arrests are linked to Yasser Ahmed, and I believe that they are, then this is the first mistake that these people seem to have made. How did you rumble them, Sian? Was it just a random check?' Tank seemed more animated than she had ever seen him before.

'No, we got an anonymous tip last night. We received no detailed information, just that two men in a dark Mercedes were carrying contraband. The caller didn't even say what they were smuggling. We've pulled every dark Mercedes that was travelling on the midnight, three o'clock, and six o'clock ferries throughout the night. Then we've searched the nine o'clock and midday boats today. We knew from the two men's reaction when we stopped them that they were dirty. Tank, we were expecting to intercept a shipment of drugs, that's why I didn't call it in any earlier. Are you connecting these people to your suspect?'

'Not until you called me, before that we had nothing. Now I'm getting a very bad feeling about your anonymous caller. It's the oldest trick in the book, Sian. I think that the two men that you have in custody were sacrificed. I'm thinking that they were sent as decoys to cover an even larger shipment. It could have been a diversion to get your attention. You were busy looking for the dark Mercedes while a lorry load of Semtex was driving by you. I want every articulated truck, van, container, and suitcase traced to his or her destinations. Get on to

56

the local uniform guys and get them to set up a roadblock on both bridges off the Island. We might be able to intercept them before they get to the mainland.' Tank was speaking faster than his rational mind could think.

'The last truck off that ferry left here two hours ago. They could be in Manchester by now, Tank; it's too late for roadblocks.' Sian knew it was useless. The road across Anglesey was a two-lane dual carriageway. She could reach the first town on the Welsh mainland, Bangor, in twenty minutes. 'What time are you going to arrive here with the others?' she added.

'I want your guys to soften them up for a while, so we'll be there about 6 a.m. tomorrow. Sian, I want you to instruct your forensic boys to take that car to pieces before I get there in the morning. I'll see you tomorrow. If you get anything at all from them beforehand, then please call me.' The picture of Tank turned to grey as the call ended and a digital image of the suspect that Tank had sent started to download. Sian looked at the picture and received her second nasty shock of the day. Although older, the man in the picture could have been her boyfriend, Mustapha's twin brother.

CHAPTER 16

Mustapha and Sian

When Mustapha was taken from his home in the Middle East, he was a frightened little boy, the journey across the oceans to Ireland on the Libyan vessel had been traumatic; heavy seas had constantly rocked the boat making him feel sick from dusk until dawn. They had not been allowed to leave the small cabin in which they were stowed, there was no porthole in the steel walls to see the sunrise; he only knew it was night time when his sister switched the light off. The cabin, which was deep in the bowels of the ship, was plunged into darkness so deep that he couldn't see his hand in front of his face when the light was extinguished. The men that brought them food and water were from all over the Middle East and North Africa. Most of them stank of body odour and diesel oil. All of them leered at his sister when they entered the cabin, making rude comments in strange languages that he couldn't understand, the words were alien to him, but the expression on their dirty faces translated the sexual intention behind them.

The fresh air he breathed as they disembarked, when they finally arrived in Ireland, was the best he'd ever tasted. They were met at the docks by two Irishmen. The men had gruffly introduced themselves as friends of their brother Yasser and led them to a black Range Rover. He did not understand their accents, at the time, even though his knowledge of the English language was perfect. They travelled across Ireland in silence to the port of Dun Laoghaire. There they were handed tickets for the ferry that would take them across the Irish Sea, to the Welsh port of Holyhead.

Mustapha spent the entire three hour ferry voyage outside on the viewing deck; the memory of the long voyage from Libya was still too fresh in his mind, he never wanted to venture below decks on a boat ever again. The ferry approached Anglesey from the Irish Sea and he watched Holyhead Mountain come into view. It stood like a giant monolith on the horizon. Mustapha stood leaning over the rails staring at the craggy coastline, the waves crashing against the huge sea cliffs that formed the base of the mountain. One giant rock stood away from the cliff wall, it formed a small island that was alone in the sea. Perched on top of the small island was a white building with a high white tower; on top of the tower was a huge revolving light, he could see a little suspension bridge, which joined the island to the base of the mountain. There was a narrow stone path, which snaked up the cliff face into the distance. 'Look, Yasmine,' he'd shouted excitedly. 'I can see a lighthouse. Isn't it beautiful? This is where I want to live, Yasmine, by the sea in a lighthouse!'

Unfortunately, it had not quite worked out as the young boy wanted it to. When they arrived at their destination, and disembarked from the ferryboat, friends of Yasser, who had been sent to meet Mustapha and Yasmine, were waiting at the ferry port of Holyhead. They had driven them across Anglesey onto the Welsh coast road and then north to the town of Warrington in England.

Mustapha and Yasmine were taken under the roof of the local Mullah and integrated into the small Muslim community there. Mustapha knew almost immediately that he was not like these people. Their lives revolved around religion, but he did not share their conviction. He was constantly battling with his guardians about listening to pop music and enjoying his new-found love of football. He especially enjoyed watching Liverpool Football Club play; Yasmine often took him to Anfield, their stadium, to watch their games. They would lie about where they were going to their surrogate families because football was not seen as a suitable pastime for devout Muslims. A friend at school had given Mustapha a Liverpool Football Club replica team shirt to wear. He was so excited that he ran all the way home to try it on. His guardian had beaten him and destroyed the football shirt.

After consulting with the other elders in the community, his guardian decided that it was time that he knew the truth about why he had come to this country. After prayers one afternoon, he and three other young men his age were taken to a small anti-room. The room was at the back of a community centre. Once there, they were told the stories of great heroes from the Jihad. They had been lectured about the struggles in Iraq and Afghanistan. The Mullah told them about groups of Muslims all over the world that were physically and spiritually at war with the West. Mustapha was shocked to hear of his brother's past. It was revealed to Mustapha that his brother Yasser was the leader of a group they called Ishmael's Axe. They showed them a video, which contained speeches from bin Laden and footage from the attacks on 9/11. There was also a brief clip of his brother cutting the heads off men who were wearing tracksuits. This attempt to turn young boys into young extremists failed miserably. Mustapha rebelled completely, even refusing to attend prayers. They tried separating him from his sister in an attempt to isolate him and break his will. When this failed, they sent him from the community. Mustapha was to be exiled from the Islamic community, but not wanting to anger Yasser Ahmed, the Mullahs asked Mustapha where he wanted to live. The wish that he made as a boy on the ferryboat journey from Ireland to Wales had finally come true. He would live near the seashore, by the lighthouse that he had fallen in love with years before. He told them that he wanted to live near the ocean, and he decided that Holyhead would be perfect.

After looking at several apartments, which were available to rent, he chose the caravan park because of the views. He could walk from his door to the cliff edges in less than a dozen paces. The sea bewitched him. The coastline that Mustapha chose to live on was only a short twenty-minute walk along the Pordafarc Road, to the small town of Holyhead. The town centre was built around St Cybi's church, which was built inside one of Europe's only three-walled Roman fortresses; the fourth wall was formed by the sea. Mustapha realised quickly that Holyhead had only a few Asians living there. The locals stared at him if he went to the small town centre shopping. The sight of a stranger was gossip enough, but an Asian stranger was big news.

In an attempt to integrate and find friends, Mustapha found a local Liverpool FC, fan club; he found the address on the Internet and discovered that the members met at a bar in the town centre. Mustapha eventually plucked up the courage to go and join. The initial shock of a Middle Eastern man walking into the Welsh Fusilier pub had soon worn off and he was welcomed into the group and soon made new friends. The club organised coach tours that made the two-hour journey to Anfield. The group watched the games that were played too far away to travel to on a big screen in the pub. It was here, while watching one of the away games with his friends, that he met Sian. She had saved his life.

The day that they met, Mustapha had gone to the bar to order some drinks for his friends. He approached the bar and felt an uncomfortable gaze coming from the man that was standing next to him. 'Are you letting Pakis in the bar now, Gareth? What's the world coming to? That will devalue the price of my house if you let Pakis in the pub,' Jarrod Evans said to the red-faced proprietor, Gareth. Gareth was scared of Jarrod, but then so were most people that lived in Holyhead.

'Jarrod, there's no need for that kind of talk, and I don't want to hear any racist nonsense in my pub. Is that clear?' The landlord tried to sound as assertive as he could, but he only succeeded in annoying Jarrod further.

'Fuck you and your Pakistani mate then, Gareth. If you don't like it, then why don't you come around here and do something about it?' Jarrod shouted, silencing the entire bar.

Jarrod was notorious for starting fights. His reputation in Holyhead was as a troublemaker. The problem was that he was as hard as nails, so no one messed with him. In a small town like Holyhead, reputation was everything. Jarrod had once been involved in a fight outside a local nightclub, when the police were called. A police dog handler had been deployed to the incident and he tried to arrest Jarrod at the scene. By the time police backup arrived, Jarrod had already knocked the police dog handler unconscious. He had also bitten the ear off a large Alsatian police dog. No one messed with Jarrod after that. At the time of the incident he was just seventeen years old.

'I am not a Pakistani,' Mustapha said quietly trying to calm the racist down.

'You are not a what?' Jarrod hissed through clenched teeth, moving toward the small Asian man in a threatening manner.

'I said that I am not a Pakistani. My name is Mustapha, but everyone calls me Musty. I'm from Iraq.' Mustapha stepped forward a little and offered his hand in a gesture of friendship. At this point, most reasonably intelligent people would have calmed down and backed off. Jarrod was neither intelligent nor reasonable. He had spent some time in Borstal as a young man. Borstal is a young 'offenders' prison and it had a brutal reputation for delivering discipline to its inmates. When sentenced to a spell inside Borstal the inmates had to complete an assault course daily, as part of their physical training regime. Jarrod had twice broken the course record time for completion during his sentence. Two months after his release from prison word had spread around town that another local lad had beaten the course record, while serving a sentence for burglary. Jarrod had gone ballistic; he got drunk and then smashed a window in the shopping centre that belonged to the town chemist. When the police arrived, he was sat waiting for them; it had taken four officers to cuff him and put him into the van. He had to make sure that he was arrested, so that he could go back inside Borstal to regain his record. He was quite prepared to serve more time in prison, just to remain the top dog holding the prison record. Jarrod was not the sharpest tool in the box.

'Leave him alone, Evans and back off,' Sian interrupted. She was watching the incident from a few feet away. Sian was well aware of Jarrod's history, as she had attended the same high school as him; he had always caused trouble even back then. Sian liked to relax in her spare time and loved watching football games with the men in the pub. Although she was not in uniform today, everyone knew that she was a serving officer in the police force. She was very popular with the inhabitants of Holyhead, but she also had a formidable reputation of her own.

'Fuck off, you ginger bitch. Why are you sticking your oar in? What are you protecting him for? Don't you know that Pakis hate pigs?' Jarrod turned quickly toward Mustapha and pulled out a vicious looking blade. Sian's intervention had left him no option now but to defend his violent reputation. Sian had been given her new pepper spray gun just that morning; The Guardian Angel had been deployed to the security services to be used for just such an event. Sian didn't think that she would ever need it while she was watching a football game, but Jarrod had a knife. She reached into her bag when Jarrod pulled out the blade. 'Gareth, I think you should call the police station, now!' She instructed the landlord who was already on the telephone. Sian had known Jarrod Evans for many years, and she knew that it would be pointless trying to reason with him. She stepped in front of Jarrod, pointed the Guardian Angel, and pulled the trigger. Jarrod collapsed, choking in a blubbering heap onto the floor. He dropped the knife as he thrashed around like a drunken break-dancer. The people in the bar started cheering and shouting words of encouragement to Sian. 'Nice job, Officer. It's about time somebody shut him up!'

The local police arrived and carted Jarrod off to his favourite jail cell. Mustapha watched, feeling a little embarrassed, as Sian told the local officers what had happened. The police exited the bar leaving Sian and Mustapha together in the doorway of the pub. Sian turned to face Mustapha. 'I hate it when people call me ginger, he always called me that at school.' She laughed. 'Let's go and watch the end of the game. You can buy me a drink for that!' Mustapha had spent the rest of the football game spellbound by this beautiful policewoman with auburn hair. Sian in turn was attracted to this quiet, dark-skinned man, especially his piercing olive green eyes. It wasn't long before they became friends and lovers.

CHAPTER 17

The Truck

Majid drove the white transit van over the Britannia Bridge, leaving Anglesey behind. The view from the bridge was beautiful and he slowed down to look at the Menai Straits, which was below him. The stretch of water separated the island from the North Wales mainland. The treacherous rip tides that flowed between the two landmasses made the water look dark and fast flowing. He looked up to his right and saw the enormous peaks of the Mount Snowdon range. The view of the sea and the mountains soothed his nerves.

In the back of the van he was carrying eight cardboard cartons containing denim jeans. Next to them was the disassembled metal structure of a market stall. The stall was made from one-inch square metal bars and they banged and rattled about against the metal of the van body. Plastic market stall covers were rolled up into huge white bundles covering everything beneath them from view. The rear body of the van had been lined with wooden panels, hooks, and brackets attached to the wood held an assortment of clips and bungee cords. They would be used to keep the market stall dry once it was erected. If anyone had stopped him and searched the van on his journey from Ireland, he would have looked like an innocent market trader going about his business.

The Semtex explosive that he carried had been packed into the spaces between the wooden panels and the van's sides; the explosive was then covered in sawdust and coffee grounds, to disguise the scent from sniffer dogs. He had not been stopped. His journey across the Irish Sea was uneventful so far.

His destination was a large industrial park in the town of Warrington. Warrington had become home to many of the large companies and brands that operated telephone support centres in the United Kingdom. The town was surrounded by motorways, which are Britain's main distribution arteries, leading to every part of the UK, for distribution purposes it was an ideal location to base a business, it was geographically central and because it was in the north-west of England, the rent and rates were considerably lower than the cities in the south. The town was home to a dozen large industrial parks, retail parks, call centres and science parks, and they were all situated conveniently next to the country's major road networks.

The unit Majid was heading for had been rented the year before and comprised an office reception area with a large warehouse at the rear. The van would be parked inside, invisible among the hundreds of white transit vans that buzzed around Warrington night and

63

day. Once it was there, its deadly cargo could be unloaded and stored without the fear of interruption or capture. Majid chose to circle Warrington using the M6 motorway avoiding the busy town centre. The last thing he needed was to be involved in an accident or to be stuck in a traffic jam. He pulled off the motorway and just a mile further on, he approached the big steel roller shutter of the unit. The shutter clattered as it opened, and he drove in nodding a greeting to the men inside. One of the men that stood in the doorway of the office was surrounded by the elders of the group. He recognised his face. His name was Yasser Ahmed.

He felt honoured to be in the presence of a man so revered and his face flushed; he followed the hand signals of his friend Tariq. Tariq guided him through pallets of cardboard cartons that were scattered about as he was directed toward the rear of the unit. The unit had been empty when he had left three days earlier, but now there were two strange vehicles parked in the spot next to where he was instructed to park the transit van. Both the vehicles were old and scruffy looking. Two men were sanding down the paintwork and applying new cartoon decals to the two old ice cream vans. Majid didn't know what they were doing parked in the unit, but he knew that it was none of his business to ask.

CHAPTER 18

TTF Interviews

Tank stood on the huge concrete police station roof with Faz and Chen. The station was situated two hundred yards from the River Mersey and the wind whistled through buildings from the Irish Sea. Tank crouched down as the chopper approached and touched down onto the landing pad. The big yellow Wessex helicopter had flown from the Royal Air Force base on Anglesey. It would take them just twenty-five minutes to fly to Holyhead. Faz had a plastic folder under her arm and she had to cling tightly to it, as the downdraft from the rotor blades grew stronger. The three taskforce officers climbed aboard the noisy machine.

'Morning, sir. Make yourselves comfortable and strap yourselves in if you would be so kind. Flight time should be about twenty-five minutes, so we won't be serving any breakfast and there is no movie being shown. We don't have any toilet facilities so we'll just get you there as fast as we can!' The pilot spoke with an Oxbridge accent that even the Queen would have been proud of. He sported a large moustache that wouldn't have been out of place on the face of a First World War flying ace. 'A comedian at this time in the morning is just what I need. All these Royal Air Force types are the same. They're a bunch of bloody big puffs,' Tank said, leaning over to Faz so that she could hear him over the engine noise. Tanks time in the Army had made him biased about the RAF and the Royal Navy's service men. Competition between the separate armed forces had always been fierce. The bias had stayed with him.

'Bring me up to speed please, Faz. What do we know about the two men that Sian is holding?' Tank said, straightening his tie. He always looked uncomfortable in a suit; his neck was thick and muscular, making collars restrictive to wear. Faz had spoken to Sian at the custody suite in Holyhead just ten minutes earlier so she knew that her information was current. 'We've run their pictures through the digital profile system. The Asian man is a blank. The other man is one Patrick Finnen, a former member of the IRA, current member of Sinn Fein. He served time in the 'H-blocks' for murder and conspiracy to commit murder. Finnen was also arrested on a Libyan Tanker called the Claudia on 28 March 1973 in Irish territorial waters off the coast of County Waterford. The boat was found to be laden with five tons of Libyan arms and ammunition, including 120 SA-7 shoulder mounted Surface to Air Missiles and fifty-six Rocket-Propelled Grenade launchers. He was released from prison as part of the Good Friday Peace agreement three years ago. We have him listed as living at a Belfast address; the Irish police are getting a search warrant this morning. The car, a black Mercedes has false plates, but the chassis number matches a vehicle stolen in Manchester six months ago. The engine number, however, matches a silver Mercedes stolen in London three months ago. It's probably been created from several other stolen cars in a chop shop. The hidden storage compartment had forty kilos of military grade Semtex hidden inside. The explosive has been matched with a manufacturer in the Czech Republic. It's part of a shipment that was sold to Libya on 23 December 2002. We are checking to see if this batch matches any that has been used elsewhere outside of Libya. Right now, it looks like the Republicans are selling off their assets to the highest bidder.' Faz closed the thin plastic file as she exhausted the information in it.

'That is just bloody marvellous! Forty kilos of Semtex for sale, just one careful owner; how long is it going to take the Irish force to search his house?' Tank asked angrily. 'Are they looking at any of his known associates?' Faz shrugged her shoulders and explained that a progress report should be available to them when they reached Holyhead. 'Ask them how much of this stuff do they think the IRA has left. I want to know everything they know, and I want to know it today. I want their best men on this, and I want to know what explosive capacity the Republicans had. I want to know what type of weapons they are selling. Is there any possibility that they still have Surface to Air missiles at their disposal?'

Tank knew that just one Surface to Air Missile in the wrong hands could lead to any civilian passenger aeroplane being shot down. Most of the commercial airports in Britain were built in suburban areas. Finding a position to launch a missile at a passenger jet on take-off or landing wouldn't be difficult. 'We don't know how many Libyan arms shipments actually arrived successfully in Ireland. We know that the Royal Navy intercepted several Libyan vessels in the late 1980s that were all laden with arms and munitions for the IRA.' Grace Farrington had the exact details in her file, and she scanned them for anything that would be relevant. It was extremely difficult to make her voice heard in the speeding helicopter. 'Do they have access to sniper rifles, machine pistols, RPGs at this moment in time and if they do, how is it being sold to these lunatics over here? We know what Yasser Ahmed is capable of. If he gets his hands on this stuff, we'll be clearing up bodies for years. I want this route from Dublin to Holyhead shut tight.' Tank had to shout now to make himself heard. He pulled at his collar again, trying to make his shirt feel more comfortable. It didn't work.

They landed twenty minutes later, and it was a short drive down London Road to the detention suite. Faz looked through the two-way mirror at the Irish man that sat handcuffed at the table. He looked tired and dirty. Two of Sian's customs officers sat opposite the man asking the same questions over and over again. The Irish man sat silently and stared at an imaginary spot in front of him. It was a classic military interview technique, turn off and say nothing. Faz looked down the corridor for the others; they were walking down the sterile looking hallway toward her. She felt the eyes of the customs officer that stood next to her looking her up and down. Faz was a sexy black woman, tall and lean with an ass to die for, she was wearing tight black jeans and a white high-necked top that accentuated her breasts. She was a very rare specimen in a town like Holyhead.

'How long have they been interviewing Finnen for?' Faz asked the customs officer. His eyes snapped away from her body and he reddened with embarrassment. He had been caught in the act.

'About four hours, ma'am. He's given us a false name and address and that's it. The Paki's said nothing at all so far,' he replied as Sian and Tank entered the room with Chen following behind them, talking on his mobile phone. 'He is not a 'Paki', Officer Jones. In fact, we don't know what he is just yet, and until we do, I would suggest you keep your racist remarks to yourself. Do I make myself clear or would you rather hear it from a white female superior officer?' Faz had suffered from racial discrimination all her career and she relished the opportunity to slap down a racist junior officer. 'Make yourself useful, go into those interview rooms and take both of the prisoners a cup of hot tea.' Faz had virtually castrated him in a sentence.

Sian and Tank leaned against the two-way glass trying very hard not to burst out laughing at the embarrassed customs officer. 'Stop causing trouble with the locals!' Sian gently slapped Grace on the arm in jest. The two female taskforce officers laughed. 'All right, boss, how do you want to do this?' Sian said to Tank, still laughing.

'Sian, I want your officers pulled back to the custody suite. No one is to be in these interview rooms except us. Tell your people that if we need them, we'll call them. No interruptions under any circumstances. Chen and Faz, you take the Irishman Finnen. No bullshit, tell him that we know who he is and that with his record he is looking at life behind bars. He is no longer a member of the IRA; therefore, he is a civilian, not a political prisoner. The interviews are code black. They may have information that could stop an imminent attack. Make him talk. Sian, you're with me. Get your people out and give me a five-minute head start before you join me with the Asian. Let's go,' Tank spoke quietly, not wanting the customs men to hear too much before they were ushered out of the interview rooms.

Tank walked into the interview room and closed the door. The Asian man looked up at the big man in the suit and he knew that he was no customs officer. He had just picked up the cup of fresh, hot tea that Faz had ordered for him. His mouth and throat were still burning from the effects of being shot by the Guardian Angel pepper spray the previous night. He was so thirsty; he had not had so much as a drink of water all night, and he was feeling very scared. The Asian man had heard the officers that were interviewing him repeatedly asking questions

67

about explosives. He knew that being accused of smuggling explosives was a very serious situation to be in, but he said nothing, because he didn't know anything.

He had been ordered to pick up the Mercedes from Ireland, and to drive it back toward Manchester. The influential members of his small community had told him that he would be called en route with instructions and a final destination. He had not been in the country long but had found a room to stay in and temporary agency work in Warrington. The Asian shared a house with six other men, two Egyptian, one from Jordan, and three Pakistanis. They found him work at one of the huge distribution warehouses in the town's industrial area. They picked and then packed sandwich orders in a refrigerated cold room from midnight until midday. The work continued throughout the night. The sandwich deliveries then headed all over the country in refrigerated vans. It was dull, but the work force was predominantly Asians, so there was a community atmosphere among the employees. There were always rumours being passed around the cold room at night. Talk of Mujahidin soldiers of God and unrest among the more extreme young Asian men. Despite living and working in Britain, many young Muslims felt the urge to commit violent protest in response to the British government's policy in Iraq and Afghanistan. He worked with the men every night and prayed with them at their mosque every day. It was in the cold room that he had been recruited to drive the Mercedes from Ireland. It was part of a bigger plan he was told. It would be an act of faith, a demonstration of commitment to his new community. He did not think that driving a car from Ireland could be dangerous or difficult.

Now this big man with a shaved head had come into the room and he had brought a feeling of malice in with him. The Asian man had just taken a sip of his tea, when without even speaking; the big man slapped him hard across the back of his head. The hot tea fell into his lap scalding his genitals, and he stood quickly, trying to escape the burning sensation in his groin. Tank threw a powerful roundhouse kick into the man's midriff as he stood up from his chair; his shin bone sunk into the soft flesh and muscle, knocking the wind from his lungs. The Asian man fell heavily onto his side, gasping to get air into his body for the second time in twenty-four hours. Tank dragged him up from the floor and slammed him into the chair. He was struggling to breathe, still winded from the powerful kick that he had received. Tears filled his eyes and he felt more afraid than he had ever been. 'What's your name? You have been caught carrying bomb-making materials into my country. I take that very personally. I'm a little pissed off about it in fact.' Tank leaned over the table and glared into the frightened man's tearful eyes. He could tell that he was nearly broken already. The Asian man looked at the empty table and said nothing. His bottom lip was quivering slightly.

'My name is Tankersley; I'm head of the Terrorist Task Force. I'm the one who gets to decide which prison you will go into. I'm going to put you into a jail full of National Front boys. Real live skinhead Nazi bastards. Have you ever heard of Combat 18? They like young Asian boys to be put into their prison. They get to work off all their aggression.' Tank watched the Asian pale, his eyes widened, and tears flowed freely down his cheeks.

'Right now, that's where you're headed. What is your name?' Tank slapped him again knocking his head forward viciously. The Asian man started to cry, openly sobbing and blood was running from his nose.

'You have been set up. You're the fall guy. Whoever you think you're protecting has used you to smuggle explosives through this port into my country.' Tank hit him again, this time with the back of his fist across the bridge of his nose.

'They waited until you and that thick Paddy next door, were on your way, then they made a phone call.' Tank tossed a telephone record sheet onto the table in front of the man. The man rocked backwards and forward in his chair, blubbering like a child. His nose and throat were still raw from the pepper spray he had encountered earlier. His eyes screwed tightly closed, saliva and blood dripped onto his shirt. Tank took a cassette from his pocket and placed it into the machine on the desk. He grabbed the Asian man by the back of the head, pulling it back sharply. 'Listen to this. This is the sound of your boss, dropping you from a great height, into a great big pile of shit.' Tank pressed the play button.

The voice on the tape was muffled. The caller had tried to disguise their voice but there could be no hiding the accent. It was Arabic. The man opened his eyes wide in disbelief. The pain of betrayal didn't lessen the pain of the beating. 'Usef. My name is Usef Mamood. I did not know about any explosives, I swear upon my Lord I did not,' Usef whined, spittle mixed with his blood and tears as they dripped from his chin. The reality of his situation had finally hit home.

Sian entered the room with shock in her eyes as she looked at the sobbing man. Tank walked away from the broken man toward Sian. 'He has spilt his tea, slipped and fallen over I am afraid. However, he has managed to tell me that his name is Usef Mamood, and he wants to tell you everything that he knows. Get it all on tape please, Sian. I want to see what Paddy Finnen next door is saying.' Tank opened the door as he spoke; he nodded at Sian and loosened his collar as he passed her.

The Irish man, Finnen was lying on his back on the floor. His chair had been upturned and Chen had his foot across Finnen's throat when Tank walked into the room. Finnen was shouting abuse at the Chinese officer but it was mostly very garbled due to his predicament. Chen was responding with a kick every time he heard the word 'Chink' in the abuse. Tank reached down and picked up the Irishman, correcting the chair beneath him as he did so. 'Get this mad Chink off my throat. He can't treat me like this. I want a fucking lawyer right now.' Finnen grew a little more confident as he was brought vertical again. The ferocity of Chen's interrogation had taken the IRA man by surprise. Finnen began to think that he was in big trouble this time. Tank stepped behind Finnen, who was now seated, and quickly forced his forearm beneath his chin, around his neck. He tightened the guillotine lock, applying pressure to the man's windpipe, choking him. 'We don't need any solicitors, Patrick; you're a terrorist suspect. You are mine for twenty-eight days before I even need to tell anyone that you're in custody.' Tank squeezed tighter. 'You have two choices. Tap out or pass out. You can tap your hands on the desk if you want to talk to us, or you can choke to death. I don't give a fuck personally because your mate next door is singing like a bird.' Tank squeezed the lock harder. Finnen's face was now a purple colour and his eyes were popping from his head. 'Tap out, or pass out, Patrick, it's your decision. However, while you're deciding what to do, have my friends here told you that you were set up? Big hard Provo boy like you, set up by a bunch of camel herders. What would the boys in the 'H-blocks' make of that Patrick?' Tank applied more pressure. Finnen started to twitch as he tried desperately to tap his hand on the desk. His face was the colour of a ripe aubergine and the veins in his forehead were pulsing rapidly as his brain struggled for oxygen. 'Do you think he wants to talk to us, or do you just think he's dying?' Tank asked sarcastically, ignoring the Irishman's attempt to give up.

'I think he probably wants you to let go of his neck. You could always do it again later if he changes his mind,' Faz added with a wry smile. Tank released Finnen and he crumpled onto the desk gasping for breath. Sian opened the door and looked at the man prone on the desk.

'I know,' she said, looking at Tank, 'He spilt his tea and then slipped.'

CHAPTER 19

Yasser – Warrington

Yasser Ahmed sat behind a large leather-topped desk in a black leather chair. It was very rare that he called a meeting, but the situation required one. He couldn't allow himself to be exposed by a traitor or a fool with a loose tongue, so no one knew of his whereabouts. He looked at the faces around the room wondering who, if any, could be a traitor to the cause. He had called only the most senior men to meet and discuss his plans.

'What do we know about this man that has been captured? Is his name Usef? Why was he chosen for this task?' Yasser asked the oldest man in the room. It was a mistake to entrust a relative stranger with an important task. Yasser trusted no one at all, especially a newcomer.

'He is a relative newcomer to us, but we were concerned about the integrity of the Irishmen, so we chose him to make this journey in case something went wrong. We didn't want to risk losing any of our Mujahideen. We know someone is leaking information to the police. The car bombs that we sent to London and Edinburgh, last year were intercepted before they could be detonated. One of our Mujahidin was captured on M6 motorway with his wife in the vehicle just outside of Warrington. There were six police cars and a helicopter involved in the arrest, it was not a random incident. Someone had tipped them off. We were concerned that we could have an informer, so we picked Usef to drive the car with the Irish man in it. We told no one about the van and its cargo. The only person outside of this room that knew of the Mercedes was Tariq.' The bearded old man spoke very quietly trying to keep the situation calm. He respected Yasser Ahmed, but he also feared him.

'I cannot believe Tariq would betray our plans to the police. I made the journey to Mecca last year with his father and his uncle before they were killed by the American Infidel, they are an honourable family.' The old man was justifying his decision as forcefully as he could without riling the violent young Caliph.

'The Irishmen that sold us the merchandise have assured me that only the driver of the Mercedes knew what was in the vehicle. They are adamant that the information did not come from their side of the business.'

Tariq was a second-generation Pakistani immigrant. His father and grandfather had travelled to live in Britain during the partition of India in 1947. After years of being a part of the British Empire, India became as unstable as the Iraq we know today. The unrest was mainly caused by the large Muslim population that felt that they were both neglected and underrepresented politically. The British government decided to leave India to rule her own people; however, they also decided to partition the country religiously before they left it. The North-East of India was separated into the independent Muslim state of Pakistan. All non-Muslims were forced to move to the new Indian state.

During partition fifteen million people were displaced from their homes forcibly. The resulting riots and ethnic cleansing caused the deaths of over one million people. It was little wonder that Tariq had little tolerance of the British government. The pain and death that their policies in India had caused left a lasting legacy of religious hatred. Tariq was angry at the West, but he wanted no part in killing innocent people. Yasser thought about the Irishmen and their assurances. He did not trust them.

'What happened to the weapons we bought from the Irishmen? They don't appear to be on the list of goods that arrived in the van?' Yasser enquired. He had expected to receive two tons of weapons including Russian made AK-47s, Rocket-Propelled Grenades, and Armalite rifles.

'They were never sent to us by the IRA men, Yasser. We are having a dispute with them over the price. Twice we have agreed a price and twice they have reneged on the deal. Each time they increase the price and demand more money.' One of the younger Imams interrupted. The old man that had been answering Yasser's earlier questions stared at the younger man to try to silence him but without success. The younger members of the group had wanted to take action against the double-crossing Irishmen, but the old man knew that it would lead to further violence. Their Jihad was more important than petty squabbles over a business deal. The old man believed that half of the problem in modern Iraq was this culture of infighting between Muslim factions. He had seen the destruction that this had caused, and he did not want sporadic violence erupting between the redundant Irish Republican Army and his Mujahideen.

'I have a plan for our Irish friends, and they will learn a very harsh lesson. We have all the explosives that we need for the time being. Source some weapons from our contact within the Manchester Somali gangs,' Yasser instructed. The city of Manchester had a gun culture. Drug gangs in the city were always able to supply arms if the price was right. Large groups of Muslim Somali's inhabited the city and they could be a source from which to buy firearms.

'We will deal with our Irish foes with the force of Ishmael's Axe.' Yasser finished speaking to the young Imam and turned his attention back to the elder.

'What is the news about my brother, Mustapha? When is he arriving?' Yasser asked sipping his Indian tea.

'Your brother has been somewhat troublesome to say the least, but we are having him brought here today. Some of our most trusted men have been sent to collect him. They should have telephoned us by now, to say that they were on their way back here with Mustapha. He has chosen to live in a caravan on the cliffs at Porthdafarc beach, near Holyhead. He was very unsettled when he arrived here, and we thought it best that he lived wherever he wanted to.'

The old man's telephone rang interrupting him, as he tried to explain the awkward situation surrounding the Caliph's brother. Yasser waved at the old man frustrated at him and told him to answer it.

'Hello, do you have Mustapha? What do you mean you can't find him? Look again! Have you been inside? No, do not ask anyone, we do not want to attract any more attention to that boy! Wait nearby; he can't have gone far away. Don't return without him.' The old man shook his head slowly and looked at Yasser.

'I am afraid your brother has gone. He has disappeared from his caravan and taken some of his belongings with him. There is not a trace of him there. Our men will wait nearby to see if he turns up. It is a small town.' The old man was nervous because he had failed the young Caliph Yasser Ahmed and he could see the anger on his face. His piercing olive green eyes seemed to bore into his own. Yasser thought for a few moments. The room remained silent. No one dared to interrupt his deliberating.

'Bring Tariq in. We must speak to him. My brother can wait for the moment; he will surface when he needs some money.'

The younger Imam opened the door and returned with Tariq. Tariq stood, his shoulders hunched, in the middle of the room wearing a black hooded tracksuit and white training shoes. He was tall and slim, almost skinny and his hooked nose made Yasser think that he was Pakistani of origin. Like Yasser his hair was kept long, and he had tied it up into a neat ball on the back of his head. He looked nervous in the company of this gathering of his leaders. Yasser stood and walked around the desk toward Tariq and smiled.

'Tariq, I have a special gift for you that your Imams and Mullahs, think that you deserve. You will be rewarded for your actions both here and in heaven. You have helped us to get as far as we have today. I need to know if you told anyone about Usef driving from Ireland.'

Yasser did not wait for an answer. He swiftly pulled out a thin box cutter blade from his sleeve and slashed Tariq across the throat. Tariq grabbed at his wound trying desperately to keep his lifeblood from leaving him. His eyes looked around the room pleading for help, but none came. Blood sprayed from his severed jugular vein splattering the beige office walls in sticky red arcs. Tariq made a gurgling sound as blood poured into his lungs down his windpipe.

73

His legs buckled at the knees and he fell forward. His body stayed kneeling; his forehead was pressed on the carpet as if in a final prayer. A dark pool of blood widened around him.

'Get rid of this pig and make sure the others know of his fate. This will be a lesson to them all, I will not tolerate treason. You will tell no one of our plans. I will tell you who needs to know the facts and when they need to know it. Put the word out at the cold room and through your contacts that I need more people for the next glorious attacks. I need more Mujahideen. Now move this body.' Yasser kicked the dying man as he spoke.

'How is our acquisition of ice cream vans progressing?' Yasser stepped over the prone body and continued to ask questions as if nothing had happened.

CHAPTER 20

Sian and Tank – Holyhead

Sian sat opposite Tank in her office at the customs suite. The interviews with Finnen and Mamood were going well; both men were now answering whatever questions were asked of them. A little gentle persuasion from her superior officer had speeded things up. Sian was concerned that what she had to discuss with her boss would affect her career with the Terrorist Task Force.

'What's so important that it can't wait until we are finished with the interrogations, Sian? I hope you're not going to express your distaste at the way we dealt with them. You are part of this squad, Sian.' Tank was starting to rant incoherently. He wrongly believed that Sian had not approved of his interview techniques. Sian raised her hand to stop him in mid flow.

'It's got nothing to do with that, sir. It's very important. I have to discuss this with you urgently, but I'm not quite sure where to start,' she said.

Tank looked at her. *She never calls me sir*, he thought. They had a good working relationship and Tank knew that the use of the title Sir, usually meant trouble was coming.

'What's the problem, Sian? Just spit it out. Contrary to popular belief, I won't bite you.' He tried to lighten the atmosphere; he knew something was very wrong.

'No, but you might try to choke me to death, boss. I'm only joking, please take a good look at this picture.' She placed a Polaroid photograph on the desk in front of him. Tank picked it up and studied it closely. It was a picture of Sian stood next to a male of Middle Eastern appearance. The sea was in the background; it looked like a holiday snap. It took Tank's brain several seconds to register the relevance of this snapshot. He looked again at the man, then at Sian.

'I can see there is a striking resemblance between this man and Yasser Ahmed but it's not him, is it?' Tank had to ask just to reassure himself. The man in the picture looked very much like the terrorist Yasser Ahmed, but he was too shocked and confused to make the connection.

'He's my boyfriend, Tank. His name is Mustapha Ahmed. He's been living here in Holyhead for three years now. When I went home last night, he was waiting for me at my house. He was upset and in a real panic. He told me that his family had contacted him and that they wanted to come and see him today. They wanted to pick him up and take him to see his older brother. He has never spoken about having a brother before. He was scared, Tank, so we

75

drove in my car to his caravan and we took some of his things. I still haven't told him that we're looking for Yasser Ahmed, and he hasn't seen the picture that you sent through to me yesterday.' Sian paused and took a sip of mineral water from a bottle of Evian.

'He's never talked about his family, Tank; he told me they were all dead. That picture of Yasser Ahmed, and the way he was so scared last night, I think he is related, Tank, I think that Mustapha is his brother.' Sian exhaled. The stress of the events over the last twenty-four hours was now taking its toll.

'Where is he right now?' Tank asked. He was thinking at a million miles an hour. He remembered the information about Ahmed's sister and younger brother. Yasser had smuggled them out of Iraq when they were younger. Out of harm's way. Opposing members of the warring factions had threatened Yasser's family's safety.

'He's at my house on Holyhead Mountain. What are you thinking? We could really use this link to get to Ahmed. I think Mustapha would help us,' Sian said.

'I really don't know what to think just yet, but I want him here under detention while we think it through. Get him picked up and get Faz and Chen in here. Let's find out who your Mustapha is.' Tank stood up and reached for his mobile phone.

'Better still, you and I'll go and get him. I don't want him to panic. You can tell me all about him on the way.'

They left the building and climbed into her car in silence. Tank was deep in thought as Sian drove out of town and headed down Porthdafarc road. The route would take them past where Mustapha had been living, before zigzagging up the mountain toward South Stack Lighthouse. She pointed out Mustapha's caravan to Tank as they passed.

'Do you know who telephoned him and arranged to pick him up?' Tank asked as he looked across the sandy beach at Mustapha's caravan, which was perched up on the cliffs overlooking the sea. Sian turned right at the end of the beach approach and the flat road changed into a steep gradient.

'No, I don't know who called him, but I know that before he moved to Holyhead, he spent a few years in Warrington. I can only assume that's where his family live. As I said earlier, he won't talk about his past to me. I do know that he was brought up by very religious people and that he doesn't share their convictions. I always get the impression from him that he wasn't welcome at home, I've never heard him talk about his religion; he doesn't even pray.'

The vehicle reached the crest of the hill. Sian had to use the lower gears to keep the vehicle climbing the steep road to her house. They stopped and she parked the Jeep on a gravel path. They climbed out of the vehicle and walked toward the front of the house. Tank looked across the grassy headlands that surrounded Sian's home. In the distance he could see the white bricks of a lighthouse. The sea looked dark and angry from this distance, huge waves crashing on the rocks, the spray almost reaching as high as the lighthouse tower itself.

'I think this is a nice place to live, Sian,' Tank said.

'Thanks. I think so. There he is, in the window.' Sian pointed to the silhouette of Mustapha. She waved at him and smiled. He waved and smiled back at her.

'He could be Yasser Ahmed. Looking at him from here, Sian, he is identical.' Tank was correct; he could almost be his twin.

Mustapha opened the door and kissed Sian on the cheek as she entered the house. He turned and looked at the big man in the dark suit. It looked like his muscular shoulders would rip through the stitching of his jacket if he wasn't careful.

Sian spoke first. 'Mustapha, this is my boss John Tankersley. You can call him John, but he prefers to be called Tank. We need to ask you some questions. We have some questions about your family. Let's go inside and sit down.' She indicated that they should follow her into the living area. The room was large and reached all the way to the rear of the house. Patio doors opened out onto a wooden deck that overlooked the coastline and the lighthouse.

Mustapha sat down in silence. He had never heard Sian talk about this big man. He was very distinctive; he would have remembered him if she had. He always remembered men with shaven heads because he found them scary, they made him nervous. Tank stood close to where Mustapha had sat, and he leaned over and passed him a photograph of Yasser Ahmed. Tank didn't speak. He just watched Mustapha's reaction. Every movement that Mustapha made gave Tank an indication of what he was thinking about. Every twitch of the eyes told Tank a story. Mustapha looked at the photograph. He looked up at Sian and then at the big man.

'This is my brother, Yasser,' he said slowly, almost in a whisper.

'I was told yesterday that he was in this country. They called me and told me that he wanted to see me. I knew that he would bring trouble with him for me. He always does.'

'Mustapha, we need to talk to your brother urgently. He was responsible for the recent spate of terrorist attacks in America. If you know where he is, you must tell me.' Tank tried to disguise the tension in his voice.

'Who called you and what did they say about your brother?' Tank pushed a little more.

'I don't know where he is precisely, just that he's here in Britain. I can believe he has caused all those deaths in America. He's a monster. He caused many deaths in my country too, that's why we had to leave. I've never met the people that support him. I never know who it is that calls me. When I speak to them, there is never a name used, never a number given. They speak in code to make sure that it's me that they're talking to. They won't speak until I say a sentence with the word Egypt in it. I am not welcome in their circles… I don't hold with their views. They only ring me to see that I'm safe and have enough money to live. They feel that they have a responsibility to Yasser to look after me.' Mustapha stood up and continued to ramble.

'I don't really know who my brother is. I remember nothing of my brother until he arranged for my sister and me to be smuggled from our home. We have lived with strangers ever since. Am I supposed to be grateful to this man? It's because of his actions and his belief that we have been running and hiding all our lives. I hope you catch him. I hope you kill him. I don't have a brother anymore.' Mustapha wept and threw the picture across the room.

CHAPTER 21

Dublin

Billy Finnen lifted the glass of dark liquid from the wooden bar and studied it for a moment. The white froth on the top of his Guinness had the pattern of a shamrock poured into it.

'What's the news on your brother Patrick, Billy? Are the police still holding him at Holyhead?' Shamus asked the question. He was trying to expand on what he already knew to be true. Billy Finnen wasn't a man that you wanted to irritate, and he didn't appear to be in the mood to talk. He was once the main enforcer for the Republican IRA.

The IRA did not only fight a war for independence against the British Army, they also took it upon themselves to police the Catholic communities, they took a very dim view of anti-social behaviour of any kind especially drug dealing, burglary, and car theft. It seems ironic that these brutal killers deemed such ordinary crimes as unacceptable. If there was a thief identified within the community that needed to be punished, Billy would arrange for it to happen.

The Provo's favourite punishment was to kneecap their victim. A pistol would be placed against the back of the victim's knee joint and then fired; the bullet would exit the front of the joint taking most of the shattered bone and cartilage with it. The result was to permanently cripple the criminal leaving them with a limp. The resulting crippled limb would then be a stigma that the criminal had to carry around his community for the rest of his life. A visible warning to anyone that contemplated going down that path.

Though he had pulled the trigger many times himself, the Catholic community knew Billy as a fixer nowadays. His henchmen however were as brutal as he had ever been. Since the troubles with the British Army in Ireland had subsided, the IRA's gangster networks had turned their hands to other business. Drugs were the number one profit maker closely followed by the booming trade of importing young girls for the sex trade. Eastern European girls were given promises of great jobs in the UK, prospective nannies and nurses flocked over Europe's borders in their hundreds, only to end up being sold into prostitution. The arms trade was also lucrative. The Provos had smuggled guns in and out of the country for years during the troubles, why waste an opportunity now?

'It's all about supply and demand, Shamus boy! We supply and then we demand the money!' Was one of Billy's favourite sayings. It was usually followed by a hearty slap on the back from a big hand that resembled a spade.

'He's been moved to Liverpool we think, to the new Terrorist Task Force lock-up on the River Mersey.' Billy leaned forward toward Shamus and lowered his voice. He didn't want anyone to overhear his conversation. The Republicans had fallen foul of informers for years. There were many people in Ireland who did not condone the Provo's methods and were only too keen to sell vital information to the British Intelligence agencies.

'I'm not a happy man, Shamus, my friend. I think that the Arabs have tried to fuck me over. They had the nerve to ask me if one of our men had tipped the fucking customs with information about the explosives that my own brother was smuggling. The nerve of them, I ask you…? I have a van full of guns and grenades that belongs to them mind you, but I'm not so sure they'll ever see them now. I'm sure that you get my drift, Shamus, I don't think that the Arabs understand exactly who they're fucking with, Shamus.' The Irishman took a long drink of his beloved Guinness before continuing.

'They think that we're a bunch of stupid Micks. They think that we're just thick Irishmen. Well now, we'll just have to show them the error of their ways now won't we, my friend?' Billy had a very strict code of justice. If you crossed him, it would generally cost you your life.

'What have you got in mind, Billy?' Shamus felt the rush of adrenalin in his veins. It sounded like Billy meant business. That would mean that someone would get hurt; and that would also mean a big cash bonus for Shamus.

'The Arab from Kilkenny that arranged the deal is on his way to the farm now. I want you to go and meet him there, Shamus. My brother is sitting sweating his balls off in a Liverpool prison because these fuckers have pulled a fast one. I want him hurt, Shamus, but I need him alive. He will need to be able to pass the message back to these bastards that we need some kind of compensation.' The IRA had experienced the power and wealth that governments and affiliated organisations from the Middle East possessed. The Republicans had received over two-million pounds sterling in aid during their struggle against the British Army from Arab nations. Billy's greed was taking control of his best interest.

'Financial compensation for the imprisonment of my brother is what we need. I am thinking the name of the bastard who grassed them up and about a million pounds should cover the damage, lovely.' Billy took a gulp from his Guinness. Shamus swallowed his whisky and nodded in agreement.

'Is there anything that you need to know from the Arab apart from the informer's name?' he asked as the burning Irish whiskey warmed his stomach.

'I need an address in Warrington. That's where the money for the guns came from. I'm planning to send a little parcel through the post just as an incentive, you understand. I'll need an address, Shamus, my friend. Bloody hell, this is just like the old days!' Billy finished his pint and headed to the bar for another.

CHAPTER 22

Sanjeet – Ireland

Sanjeet slowed the vehicle and turned onto the gravel track that would lead up to the farm. Both he and his passenger had been here before to meet the Irishmen and arrange the arms deal. He had received an angry call that afternoon from Billy Finnen. Sanjeet had never met the man, but he had spoken to him in negotiations on the telephone. The Irishman always sounded drunk, his voice slurred and his temper volatile. Billy had demanded a face-to-face meeting to discuss the vanload of guns and grenades that had not yet been delivered; and he was demanding information as to the reasons why the deal had gone wrong at customs. He was placing the blame for the arrest of his brother firmly at their doorstep. The Irishman insisted that the information must have been given to the police by the Axe group. Billy Finnen told Sanjeet that he had an informer working for the customs office at Holyhead. He said that his informer was positive that the anonymous tip off had come from a man with an Arabic accent.

Sanjeet slowed the vehicle down as they approached the empty farm buildings. He was worried about what the leaders of Axe would think of him. They had warned him not to go to the meeting with the Irishmen, but he felt that he had failed and let them down. He decided to meet with Billy Finnen at the farm, taking just his cousin, Ida, as support. He wanted to try to negotiate a refund of the monies paid, or to take delivery of the weapons. He drove the vehicle slowly into the empty farmyard.

Suddenly the windscreen exploded inwards. A shower of shattered glass hit Sanjeet in the face. He felt the warm trickle of blood running into his eyes. Sanjeet looked at his cousin in the passenger seat as he slammed on the brakes and brought the vehicle to a screeching stop. The bullet which shattered the glass, had entered his cousin's face just below the eye; the rear of his skull had exploded as the fat AK-47 ammunition exited, spraying the ceiling of the car red. Two more bullets smashed through the ruined glass, ripping Ida's jawbone from his skull. Teeth and bone hit Sanjeet in the face and he wrestled with the door handle trying to escape. The door flew open and he scrambled away from the bloody scene and fell to his knees.

Shamus brought the rifle butt down onto the back of Sanjeet's head; Sanjeet fell forward and lay still.

'You two get rid of the car and the dead Arab. I want it wiped down and cleaned before you torch it, now Sanjeet, you and I need a nice long chat inside!' Shamus had used the old farmhouse many times for interrogations. Several high-ranking IRA informers had eventually confessed to their betrayal inside the damp mossy walls of the farm. Many more had confessed to things that they hadn't even done just to stop the pain.

Sanjeet had been trained for just three months in a terror camp in Somalia. When he came to the West, he moved first to London and then after a visit on holiday, he had chosen Ireland as his home. The men that captured him had been republican soldiers all their lives. The British Army occupied Northern Ireland for thirty-eight years causing a whole generation of men to grow up never knowing peace. The men involved in the Irish conflict, both the Catholic and Protestant paramilitaries, were hardened soldiers. When it came down to business, they were brutal men with no mercy. Sanjeet had trespassed into their world and he was well out of his depth.

He awoke with a start. Cold water had been thrown from a bucket into his face. He was tied to an old wooden chair in the middle of a derelict room and his hands and feet were bound tightly with plastic clip ties.

'Wakey, wakey, Sanjeet, my friend. My name is Shamus, and I work for Billy. Now Billy is a little pissed off right now, as he feels like you're insulting his intelligence. He has the decency to sell you some guns, and what do your lot go and do? You only go and get his brother Patrick arrested. Now that's not polite or friendly. So, what I need to know from you is where exactly your friends are, so that we can go along and sort this little problem out.' Shamus emphasized the vowels as he spoke, his Irish accent almost sounding friendly. It was as if he was speaking to a child or an elderly relative.

Sanjeet remained silent. He looked at the floor, but he couldn't disguise the fear in his eyes. He noticed that the old wooden floorboards were stained dark red with old dried blood.

'I am a very patient man, but we need this information as a matter of urgency. I am sure you understand. Where can we find your friends?' Shamus coaxed, his voice was still far too jolly for this situation. Sanjeet looked at Shamus and shrugged his shoulders. Shamus nodded to the man standing behind Sanjeet. He stepped forward into Sanjeet's line of vision, leaning his weight slightly on a woodcutter's axe, holding it as if it were a walking cane. He had an almost inane grin on his face.

'Now, this here is Martin and he's got no patience at all. In fact, I would go so far as to say he's mad. Now I wouldn't want to be upsetting Martin, if I was you. The doctors have told Martin's family not to let him have anything sharp. He is not a full shilling we would say. He's one sandwich short of a picnic. So, I'll ask you one more time, where do we find your friends?' Shamus was starting to scare Sanjeet now with his jovial tone. He was enjoying this far too much. Sanjeet wished he could go back home to his family. He decided to try to cooperate.

'I don't know where they are. I only speak to them on the telephone. I only do as I'm asked. I'm sorry about your friend's brother being arrested but I don't know anything.' Sanjeet now had sweat mingling with the blood that ran into his eyes.

Shamus nodded toward Martin. Martin picked up the sharp weapon and held it above his head. He smiled at Sanjeet as he swung the big axe. The blade arced down and smashed through the end of Sanjeet's right foot. The big toe and the two next to it were completely severed. Sanjeet screamed and almost passed out. The pain seared through his brain. He thought about how he had become involved in this nightmare. He had known that the weapons deal that he procured would result in the deaths of many people. Now he was reaping what he had sown. He screamed again as he watched Shamus approaching him holding a blowtorch in his hand.

'I told you he was mad now didn't I. You wouldn't listen. Now we don't want you bleeding to death here when you still haven't told me where your fine friends are now, do we?' Shamus placed the blue flame of the blowtorch on to the bloody stump that was once Sanjeet's foot. The flesh burned and blackened as the intense heat cauterised the wound. The bleeding stopped but Shamus held the flame on his wound, this time he passed out.

Sanjeet woke up in agony when Martin stood on his mangled foot. He screamed but found that they'd stuffed a rag into his mouth to muffle the sound.

'I'm going to leave you with Martin for a while. He thinks he can cut bits off you and then stop you bleeding from now until midnight. It's only six o'clock so I've bet him that you're dead by seven thirty. He's convinced that he can keep you alive until twelve o'clock though; but as I've already told you, he is bloody mad.' Shamus lit a cigarette with the blowtorch.

'No! No, please don't hurt me anymore. I'll tell you what you want to know. Please don't let him hurt me again. I just want to go home to my family.' Sanjeet wasn't sure if the Irishmen would let him go or not. He started praying that they would. Shamus pulled up a chair and sat opposite Sanjeet.

'I thought you might just do that.' Shamus smiled.

CHAPTER 23

Holyhead – Sian's House

Tank walked over to the patio doors and looked at the view. He watched the waves crashing against the rocks beneath the white lighthouse which looked tiny from this distance. Sian and Mustapha were in the kitchen making coffee. Mustapha had become upset during their discussion, so Tank suggested that they made some coffee to give the Iraqi man a break.

He had a major situation to control and he tried to arrange the pieces in his mind. He heard a car approaching and turned to see Chen and Faz come to a stop outside. He waved at them through the glass and signalled with his hands for them to come in. They walked in silence toward the house gazing out past the building to the sea. Tank was playing mental chess with the information that he had gathered in the last forty-eight hours.

The most wanted terrorist on the planet was in the country and had tried to import explosives from the now redundant, but still dangerous, Irish Republican Army. Sian and her team had apprehended two men who were in the process of smuggling the explosives from Dublin to Holyhead, but Tank was convinced that it was a decoy to cover a larger shipment.

Chen walked into the room with Faz at the same time as Sian and Mustapha walked in from the kitchen carrying their coffee cups. Chen and Faz simultaneously reached for their guns. Mustapha froze like a rabbit in the headlights of an oncoming truck.

'Whoa! Put the guns away. Put the guns away please, guys! He is not who you think he is.' Tank moved between his officers and Mustapha and the two agents lowered their guns.

'Meet Mustapha Ahmed. He is the brother of Yasser Indri Ahmed.' Tank took the coffee cup from the shocked Mustapha, whose hands were shaking, spilling the hot liquid onto the wooden floor.

'As you can tell, my guys are quite keen to catch your brother.' Tank led Mustapha to the couch, and he sat down next to him.

'What did we get from Patrick Finnen?' Sian asked referring to the interrogations at the customs suite.

'It's pretty complicated but the gist of it is that he thinks he was set up by the Axe group. Finnen and his cronies, all ex Provos, were approached by Axe, who wanted to purchase guns and explosives.' Faz started to explain.

'I am sorry but what are Provos?' Mustapha interrupted. If this was really all about his brother, then he wanted to understand.

85

'Provos is the slang name for Provisional IRA members; they were the Catholic paramilitaries, terrorists. Anyway, the contact came from a man called Sanjeet, who was based in Kilkenny, he handled all the negotiations for Axe, and he had insisted that the cargo be split into three loads. The black Mercedes we already know about, there is a transit van somewhere full of AK-47s, Uzi submachine guns, and grenades. In addition, the icing on the cake is that there was also a van containing Semtex, twenty-two RPGs, and two Surface to Air Missiles. We don't know where that is. Finnen seems to think that the guns are still in Ireland.' Grace Farrington shrugged her shoulders and raised her hands as if baffled by her own story.

'Do we know where this stuff is headed?' Tank stood up and walked over to the patio doors. He unfastened the top button of his shirt and loosened his tie.

'Warrington, Finnen said that his brother, Billy, had traced the money to Warrington. The second prisoner is Usef Mamood. He says that he was just picking up a black Mercedes. That's all. He was to let the previous owner drive it onto the ferry across from Dublin to Holyhead, and then he was to drive it back to Warrington. He's been working in a sandwich distribution warehouse at a place called Kingsland Grange. We have his address he shares a house with six others, all Middle Eastern nationals, they all pray at a mosque in Appleton. He is insistent that he knew nothing about any explosives. He says that he's new into the community where he lives and that he was set up. One more thing, we've traced the SIM card from the phone that made the anonymous tip off. It is an unregistered prepaid SIM card, we can't trace the owner, but we've triangulated the whereabouts to guess where, Warrington.' Faz smiled, her white teeth seemed to gleam against her dark skin.

'Warrington is where I was sent to as a young boy. My brother has many sympathizers in that community, but I cannot believe that those people would make bombs.' Mustapha stood and walked toward Tank.

'What will happen to me now? I am related to him, Mr Tankersley, that is all. I have done nothing wrong. I do not believe in their Jihad. I'm no threat to anyone.' Mustapha was beginning to fear for his liberty.

'Right now, you're in as much danger as everybody else. They have tried to take you to your brother; they have contacted you regularly by telephone. I'm afraid that you are very much in trouble; you're a link to your brother. Financially we can find out where your money is coming from and who is giving it to you. We can get closer to Yasser as long as we have you and Yasser will be thinking the same thing. He's tried to reach out to you, and you have rebuked his approaches. You've now become a liability to him, which means that you're in great danger. We will put you into protective custody for now. It's for your own good.' Tank put his big hand onto Mustapha's shoulder trying to reassure him.

'Chen, get the crime lab boys to Mustapha's caravan, tell them to dust for prints. I want to know who was looking for him. I want the electronic team to rig that telephone line to divert. If they call him again, I want it bugged. Let's have Finnen and Mamood transferred to Liverpool and tell Timms to put our best men on that. I want to know that everything that they've told us is correct.' Chen turned and pulled out his mobile phone, he was already dialling when Tank turned to Faz.

'Grace, have a full Armed Response Team prepared to hit the Warrington address that you have. We'll hit the distribution centre, the mosque, and Mamood's home address simultaneously. You and Chen take a team each and I'll take the other. Run all this by Major Timms immediately and tell him that we have Yasser's brother in protective custody.' Faz moved toward the front door. She started dialling before she had gotten outside.

'Sian, if Patrick Finnen thinks that those machine guns are still in Ireland then that's where I want them to stay. Make sure that your people are checking everything that passes through that port. I want you to go over to Dublin to coordinate with the Irish Police. Find Billy Finnen and find those guns.' Tank stopped and took a mouthful of cold coffee.

'And, Sian, don't worry about Mustapha, I will make sure he is safe.' Tank felt strange giving that assurance to Sian and a shiver ran down his spine.

CHAPTER 24

Leaving Holyhead

Tank sat in the back seat of Sian's Jeep, next to Mustapha. Chen and Faz had left earlier to organise the raids that Tank had ordered. Sian steered the Jeep down the steep gradient toward Porthdafarc beach. They drove by Mustapha's caravan, men from the crime labs and technical departments were already swarming all over it like ants. They headed straight back toward the heliport avoiding the town centre, opting to take the coast road through Treaddur bay. The road snaked around the coast, rising and falling frequently as it hugged the headlands. Sian could have driven the treacherous road blindfolded; she was so familiar with it. The road turned sharply to the right and dipped down steeply past a farm track. The farmer that owned the track used it as the main route for his cows to travel from their fields, to the milking sheds. The bend had become affectionately known as 'Cowshit Corner' by the locals. Many a young motorbike rider had taken a tumble on this sharp corner, as a layer of excrement stopped their motorbike tyres from gripping the road. Sian slowed the vehicle, knowing the dangerous reputation of the corner well.

Suddenly from the farm track came the dazzling headlights of a dark BMW-X5. The lights blinded Sian for a moment. The BMW lurched forward at speed and slammed into Sian's Jeep. The broadside sent the vehicle into a spin; the manure on the road was making it like an ice rink. The car span round twice and then slammed into a stone wall, a chunk of sandstone the size of a football smashed through the side window, it stuck Mustapha on the side of the head rendering him unconscious. Sian was slumped over the steering wheel; the impact from the air bags had stunned her momentarily. Tank instinctively pulled out the Glock 9mm and tried to get out of the vehicle, but his door was sandwiched against the wall, it wouldn't open. He looked at the BMW and saw it reversing, the wheels skidding and spraying cow manure into the air, the two rear doors opened, and three masked men climbed out carrying Uzi submachine guns.

Tank turned and fired four shots through the rear window at the masked men. The glass exploded, clearing his view and he watched as one of the men fell backwards, knocked off his feet by the high calibre bullet that blew the top of his head off. The two other gunmen pulled their dead colleague behind the back of the black SUV. A volley of bullets from an Uzi smashed into the stone wall; fragments of stone and hot metal exploded near Tank's face. He ducked and aimed again firing three shots toward the windshield of the BMW. The driver was rocked backwards as the bullets smashed into his chest destroying his lungs and turning his spleen into pulp, he fell forward his head resting on the steering wheel. The two men behind the BMW broke cover and opened fire with the submachine guns. Tank was still trapped in the back seat of the vehicle by the stone wall. He jumped across the unconscious Mustapha, grabbed the door handle and rolled out of the vehicle onto the road as the machine-gun bullets peppered the space he had just left, showering Mustapha with broken glass. Tank tried to stand and return fire, but he slipped in the fresh manure, he fell, face first onto the road, the thick green liquid sticking to his clothes and his skin. He wiped his eyes clear of the green excrement with his sleeve and saw one of the masked men taking aim again; he knew he didn't have time to fire before the man with the machine gun opened fire. Tank heard the familiar boom of a Glock 9mm behind him. The masked man who was pointing an Uzi at Tank suddenly twitched violently as Sian's bullet left a dark circular rent in his forehead; he toppled forward as if in slow motion. Cow manure splattered as his face hit the road. Sian aimed the weapon at the remaining assailant and fired as he dived behind the BMW. The last gunman ran around the X5 to the driver's door, he opened it and dragged the dead driver out onto the road.

The engine roared as the gunman put the vehicle into reverse, the wheels finding no purchase on the slippery road. He stopped revving and put the vehicle into first gear, it lurched, wheels spinning toward Tank and Sian. Tank grabbed Sian and pulled her behind the car as the BMW screamed past them; they both raised their weapons and emptied their bullet clips into the back of the escaping X5. It rounded the bend at the crest of the hill and disappeared from sight.

'I'm covered in shit and I'm not a happy chappy. Sian, we can't leave Mustapha here. I'm going after him, get in.' Tank took off his jacket and quickly used the inside to wipe his hands and face, simultaneously starting the Jeep. He pressed his foot to the floor and the Jeep fishtailed up the hill in pursuit of the escaping gunman.

'You really don't smell too good, Tank,' she said reloading her Glock. She reloaded and then took Tank's weapon and did the same. She turned to the back seat and pulled out her first aid kit from underneath it. She assessed Mustapha's wound and placed a swab dressing on to the gash in the Iraqi man's head.

'It looks nasty, Tank. He will need stitches and he will definitely have a headache, but I think he will be okay.'

Tank followed the tail lights of the X5 as it headed back toward Porthdafarc beach; he was gaining on it as it swung right taking a turn at a dangerous speed.

'Where does this road lead to, Sian?' Tank asked as he accelerated after the BMW.

Sian was talking into her mobile alerting the customs suite that they had an armed confrontation in progress.

'It's Porthdafarc Road. It heads straight to the town centre. If he doesn't know his way around here, he'll miss the turning for the exit road off the island. If he doesn't take that, he'll be trapped between us and the Irish Sea.' Sian continued to give details of their pursuit on a shared frequency. All on duty agents would be listening in and reacting to try to help.

'He's missed the exit road; he's headed past the fire station toward the bridge. He's going north past the Kings Head on Lands' End road heading for the Newry Beach.'

The Newry beach was essentially a wide promenade road that overlooked a marina. Wide grassy areas sloped gently down from the road to the seashore. Yachts floated in rows tied to bright orange buoys, moored safely behind the protection of the breakwater. The breakwater was a huge stone sea wall built for ships to take shelter from the treacherous storms of the Irish Sea. It had a road that ran along the top of it that was easily wide enough for two vehicles to pass side by side and it reached two-and-a-half miles out to sea. The Newry Beach road was a dead end, but it gave access to the breakwater road. The BMW accelerated down the promenade; the road was wide and straight. The Jeep lost ground as the faster vehicle utilised the wide road. Tank looked into the rear-view mirror and saw the flashing blue lights of the local police joining the pursuit. The brake lights on the X5 illuminated as the driver neared the end of the promenade and smoke came from the tires as he braked hard swerving the vehicle onto the breakwater road.

The road weaved through a small wooded copse. Stone walls were on either side. In the headlights a large derelict building stood out from the darkness. Once painted white and built in the style of a mock castle it had been a beautiful hotel. The once white walls were now covered in green moss, the windows dark and empty, it was an eerie sight.

'We are in pursuit following the X5 past the old Soldiers Point hotel. He is trapped now,' Sian said as she switched the safety off her weapon. The vehicles burst free from the wooded road and roared onto the open breakwater. The BMW sprayed gravel from beneath its wheels, the stones bounced off the windscreen of the Jeep behind it as it drove along the top of the giant sea wall. Tank lowered his window and leaned out pointing his Glock 9mm at the vehicle in front. He fired three bullets and sparks shot up from the back of the X5. The rear tail lights on the driver's side exploded into a cloud of coloured glass. He fired again. This time the rear window smashed and three large holes the size of a melon appeared in the glass, but the vehicle sped on.

Across the marina, Tank saw the flashing emergency lights of the police vehicles as they drove down the Newry beach. A spotlight appeared on the BMW from above. A voice boomed from the loudspeaker mounted beneath the helicopter that had joined in the chase. Sian couldn't hear what the voice was saying, but she figured he was telling the driver to pull over and stop. *Just like that! We've been chasing and shooting at the bloke for twenty minutes and that dickhead in the helicopter thinks he'll stop if he asks him nicely*, she thought.

She leaned out of her window and fired three shots aiming at the rear tyres of the BMW. Sparks flew from the sea wall and a lump of plastic bumper material was blasted off the vehicle, it veered viciously to the left slamming into the crash barriers, sparks flew as metal ground against solid rock. Then it veered right just as violently, and the BMW careered toward the sheer edge of the breakwater wall. The X5 seemed to take off for a second as it left the road, its speed and velocity kept it horizontal for just a moment. Then it nosedived down and was almost vertical when it hit the dark water with a huge splash. The black sea turned white as the vehicle hit it and it floated, bobbing on the surface. The driver made no attempt to escape from his watery grave as the vehicle sank and the water turned dark becoming still once more. Tank and Sian stood on the edge of the breakwater some thirty foot above the sea looking for any sign of life as the screaming sirens and flashing lights approached.

'I could do with a bath myself,' Tank said as he turned and walked toward the arriving police cars.

CHAPTER 25

Billy Finnen and Shamus

Shamus climbed up into the lorry's cab and shut the door. Billy Finnen sat in the driver's seat smiling as he put on his seat belt and pulled the truck out of the Post Office car park.

'I've sent our little message to the Arabs by first-class delivery. It's on the way to our foreign friends in sunny Warrington, I thought it was only right and proper to pay the extra bit of money, just to make sure that it arrives tomorrow morning,' Shamus said laughing, his soft southern Irish accent exaggerating the sarcasm in his voice.

'You know what, Billy; it's a dying art now. What we've done today will certainly keep a dying art alive.' Billy laughed. Shamus was right. He couldn't remember the last time they'd made and sent a letter bomb. During the troubles, especially in the '70s, letter bombs were sent frequently from Irish Paramilitaries to targets on the mainland with some success. Newspaper editors who printed unfavourable opinions of the Irish Republican Army were a favourite target for the bombers. Politicians, police stations even the government were sent these lethal parcels via Her Majesty's Royal Mail. They were simple and devastatingly effective, especially to the unsuspecting recipient.

Eventually anonymous tip-offs that a letter bomb had been sent were commonplace. The fake warnings were enough to shut down whole sorting offices, empty post rooms, and clear entire office blocks with just a call. By the time the bomb squad had looked for the alleged package, thousands of pounds worth of business could be lost.

This was not a fake though and there would be no warning. Billy had used the address of a mosque in Warrington. Shamus had extracted the information from the Arab's Irish contact Sanjeet, at the farmhouse. The poor man had also told them that there was some big shot Iraqi terrorist on the scene; and that he was sending more of his people over to Ireland. Sanjeet had told Shamus that members of Axe had chartered a private aeroplane to fly to County Cork in southern Ireland. They had been sent to get the guns that they'd paid for and not received.

Apart from that, his information had been pretty useless and rather vague. Shamus and Martin had brought an empty jam jar containing the remains of Sanjeet's bloody teeth; and a carrier bag with most of his fingers and toes in it. Billy knew that whatever information the man possessed had been passed onto Shamus. He had probably screamed a lot as he parted with most of it. Shamus had packaged up Sanjeet's teeth and digits and sent them to his family in Kilkenny. It seemed like the right thing to do since Sanjeet had repeatedly kept asking if he could be allowed home to see his family.

'I hope everything arrives safely in the post tomorrow. I always think Warrington has been a bad omen for us, don't you think?' Billy mused as he spoke thinking about Warrington's history and its unfortunate links to their struggle. The IRA history with Cheshire's main town is a sad one for all concerned.

Warrington's main through road, the A49, runs from the west side of the town straight across the middle, to the east side, halfway across the town on this main road is a huge gas storage depot, surrounded by residential housing estates. The towns planning committee must have been on pretty strong drugs the day they allowed it to be built so close to so many homes.

For reasons that can only be known by the IRA bombers themselves, on Thursday 25, 1993 the town of Warrington and specifically the gas works were chosen as a target. Three IRA terrorists broke into the gas storage depot and planted several Semtex devices. During the attempted escape, the Irish terrorists were spotted by a patrolling police officer. The officer gave chase and was shot during the arrests. The devices that the terrorists had attached to the gas storage tanks, some four stories high, failed to detonate; all bar one, which caused a huge fireball. This stroke of bad luck for the IRA probably saved hundreds if not thousands of lives. All three men were captured and eventually jailed for twenty and thirty-five years, respectively.

Unfortunately, some months later their colleagues returned to the town again for revenge. On Saturday 20 March, 1993, the day before Mother's Day, the IRA placed two bombs into litterbins on the high street. Bridge Street was busy with hundreds of excited young children, clutching their pocket money tightly in sweaty little hands, hunting for a present for their mothers to open the next day. At around midday a coded message was received by a charity help line of the Samaritans. The message said that a device would explode outside Boots the Chemist, in the City of Liverpool fifteen miles away. It was a devious trick.

The first bomb exploded outside of Boots the Chemist, in Warrington. Just a few minutes later, the second device exploded outside of a catalogue shop, which was 150 yards away on the same street. People had fled in panic after the first explosion, only to run into the path of the second blast. The bombs were placed inside two cast iron litterbins that contained aluminium liners. The bins effectively became large fragment grenades. They sent a deadly spray of shrapnel across the busy street and two little boys never made it home alive that day. A total of fifty-six people were maimed and injured.

The deaths of the two young boys from Warrington started a backlash of public opinion against the IRA that was unprecedented. Support for their cause at home and abroad started to dwindle. It was to start the long process of negotiations that eventually led to the Good Friday Peace agreement.

'Now, you know I'm not the thinking type of man that would let superstition bother me. Nevertheless, that town is a jinx for us.' Billy shook his head as he spoke and pulled out a cigarette.

'I hope you cleaned up here after your interrogation last night. I don't want the place to start smelling any worse than it does already.' Billy lit the cigarette and turned onto the track that led to the empty farmhouse.

'I left Martin to tidy up. He seems to like blood an awful lot more than a normal man should. I keep telling you he's not all there, Billy. He's away with the fairies most of the time. In fact, he's totally mad.' Shamus opened the door and stepped down from the cab. Billy jumped down onto the gravel and they walked toward the old barn. The truck they were driving contained all the guns that the Axe group had ordered and paid for. Billy now did not intend to hand them over and the barn had a secret storage cellar beneath it, where the IRA had kept weapons on and off, for over forty years.

An Asian man with a mask wrapped over his nose and mouth, wearing dark glasses stepped from the darkness of the barn. He was aiming a silver Mossberg 12-gauge shotgun at them. Billy held his hands up in a gesture of surrender and was about to speak to the man when the shotgun roared. Shamus, his jeans tattered into bloody shreds, fell to the ground holding onto what was left of his knees. Billy turned to run, but the shotgun roared again. The shot hit him at waist height, tearing a chunk of muscle the size of an orange from his buttocks.

Two more masked men joined the gunman and together they dragged the Irishmen kicking and screaming into the old barn. They stood them back-to-back and tied them together with an old rope. Shamus could hardly stand as his legs were so badly damaged. They tied their hands above their heads. One of the masked Asians placed an old tractor tire over their heads and then pulled it down their bodies toward their waists until it stuck fast. Then they fastened the rope, which bound their hands to a wooden beam above them.

It was only the rope that held Shamus upright now. The loss of blood was making him weak. The damage to his knees left them unable to bear any weight without bending in the wrong direction. He screamed as his legs buckled and the left knee joint collapsed backwards. The man with the shotgun rammed the butt of the gun into Shamus's stomach knocking the wind out of him and rendering him silent.

'Where are the guns that we have paid for, you thieving Irish pigs?' The man with the shotgun spoke through clenched teeth. He spoke with an Arabic accent.

'I told you Warrington is fucking unlucky for us, didn't I?' Shamus's voice was weak but his ability to use sarcasm stayed with him, even as he was bleeding to death.

'Will you shut the fuck up, Shamus?' Billy said. 'Hang on there and I will try to get us out of this shit.'

Billy tried to compose himself. He was usually the man with the gun, asking the questions. He had to use all his negotiation skills if they were to live. The dark-skinned men with masks had shot first though without even a thought.

We are in deep trouble, he thought.

'The guns my friends, are in a safe place. We had to hide them from the police. Now if you cut us down from here, I'll take you to the guns myself. A deal is a deal. We've been keeping them safe for you. That's all we've done. This is all a misunderstanding. If we had let the guns go onto the ferry, they would be with my brother in the bloody police station in Liverpool by now.'

'Burn them,' the man with the shotgun said to his accomplice. The man moved and picked up a green plastic petrol carrier. He turned the nozzle once and poured fuel all over the tyre and then over Shamus and Billy. The liquid ran into their eyes stinging as if it were acid. Billy closed his lips tight to stop it entering his mouth, but the noxious fumes filled his nose and throat making him retch.

'Okay, for Christ's sake, I'll tell you where they are. They are in the fucking van there outside the barn. Now take them and let us go for Christ's sake.'

Shotgun man lit a match and showed it to Billy turning it slowly between his fingers.

'Go and meet your Christ, Irishman,' he said tossing the match on to the tyre. Billy and Shamus screamed in unison as they turned into a human inferno. It was a full two minutes until they stopped moving.

The three Axe members left the barn and closed the doors, the fire inside was spreading quickly through the old barn. They took the keys from the truck's ignition and walked to the back of the vehicle. They needed to check that the load was complete before they headed for the small airfield at Cork. Axe knew they would never get their arms cache through the ports now that security had been increased and had arranged for a small aircraft to be chartered. One of them with pilot training would land the cargo safely at a private airfield on the British mainland.

Shotgun man put the key into the lock that secured the back doors and turned it. The booby trap bomb beneath the van exploded, turning the three men into a red vapour. When it came to booby traps and bombs, the IRA were masters.

CHAPTER 26

Liverpool – The Top Floor

Tank showered in the men's changing room facilities on the top floor of the Liverpool police station. He eventually managed to remove the stench of excrement from his skin. The flight on the helicopter back to the office had been short. Mustapha Ahmed was taken into protective custody when they landed. He was to be taken into the intelligence team's interview suite first where his life would be dissected. The information gleaned from his bank accounts and mobile phone activity alone could lead the taskforce directly to the group Axe. Forensic teams and systems analysts were working at light speed on the bodies left from the gunfight in Holyhead. Two mobiles had been found, all the men had wallets and identification on them, and two of them were known to MI5 as being politically active. At any one time, MI5 were watching over two thousand individuals belonging to over two hundred different Islamic terror cells in the UK alone.

Tank knew that in reality this was a tiny proportion of the Muslim community that proposed a danger, but the danger was prevalent, nonetheless. Tank finished showering and dressed in black combat pants, he pulled a white T-shirt on, which stretched against his muscular frame. He searched for his deodorant and sprayed himself from head to toe. The stench of cow manure was still in his nostrils.

As Tank walked through the office, he could feel and hear the buzz of activity as the preparations for the forthcoming raids were well under way.

'Moo! Moo! What's that smell, boys? Can anyone smell poo?' Faz, who was stood across the room, called to him.

'Do you fancy a pint of milk, Tank? Don't you worry about a thing… we have everything udder control!' Tank raised his hands in surrender, as laughter filled the top floor office.

'Okay, let's get all the bullshit jokes out of the way!' Tank walked into the glass office that they called the goldfish bowl. Major Stanley Timms was sat down at his desk. He gestured to Tank to sit down and continued listening to the voice on the telephone; his face looked like the conversation wasn't going very well. He replaced the receiver without saying a word and stood up. He looked out of the window into the night, toward the Pier Head and the river beyond. The Liver buildings stood illuminated across the dock road from the police headquarters. The granite bricks glowed under the harsh halogen spotlights. He looked up at the two huge bronze Liver birds that were permanently perched on top of the building. A ferry drifted toward the Pier Head, lit up like a Christmas tree in the dark.

'Let's get everyone together, John. I want to make sure we do this one correctly. That was Whitehall on the line, they say that everyone from the Americans to the Zulus, wants Ahmed extradited. It looks like we would have to give the Americans first bite at him because of the Soft Target bombs. Between me and you I'd rather like to have him and his friends here for a while before we turn them over.' Timms walked out into the crowded office. He clapped his hands together loudly to gain the team's attention.

'Okay, before we go kicking in doors and upsetting people, I want full updates on what we have so far. The surveillance and technical teams are going to brief us on the three sites that we're planning to hit tonight. We have helicopter spy drones above the targets already. They have infra-red X-rays and voice scanners on the buildings as we speak; so, we should know who and how many targets we have, well before we leave. Can you share the intelligence so far, what do we have?' The Major stepped back a little to allow the next speaker room.

'I'll start with the Emerald Isle and the situation as we understand it. We have a group of ex-IRA members who have now turned their skills to several different trades. They are involved in prostitution, drugs, protection rackets, and the sale of the surplus Republican arsenal. We know that two vehicles were sent from Dublin, Ireland, to Holyhead in Wales. They were carrying explosives and detonators. One we apprehended, one we didn't. One Ford truck was loaded with AK-47s, Uzi submachine guns, Mossberg 12-gauge shotguns, and a selection of fragment grenades. The weapons originate from the former Soviet Union, Kosovo, Bosnia, and North Africa. They entered the Irish Republic via ships from Libyan ports.'

David Bell paused for effect, he loved holding court in front of the whole team; tonight, he was in his element. The intelligence gained in the recent week had been unprecedented. From the day Yasser Ahmed entered the country he'd felt like he'd been on a roller coaster. The team called him the Fat Controller, his chubby face and high waist trousers gave him an odd round shape. To the team he was an information guru.

'Customs at Holyhead received a tip off which led to the arrest of Patrick Finnen. He's an ex-IRA member. They also arrested Usef Mamood who is linked with Yasser Ahmed's known associates in Warrington. We've traced the call to an unregistered mobile phone purchased in Warrington. So, we have to assume that the group Axe made the call, to detract our attention from the mother-load.'

The fat controller paused for a second and took a sip of water from a bottle of Evian.

'Now we have an arms deal that's gone bad. The Provos feel they've been double crossed by Axe. Axe on the other hand, think they've been ripped off by the Provos, who now

97

have their money, but did not deliver their guns to them. We have our forensic teams working at a derelict farmhouse on the outskirts of Dublin, as we speak. They have two white Caucasian bodies. They appear to have been tortured and then burnt to death in a barn. We think one of them is Billy Finnen. We also have some unidentified DNA from a person, or persons unknown, but definitely Middle Eastern origin. The remains were found next to the wreckage of an exploded van, which contains the remains of several dozen machine guns. We know from experience that the IRA liked to booby trap their weapons caches. We think someone tried to take the guns and walked into a trap.'

'It sounds like we have a war going on here and I want it stopped.' Timms stepped forward as the fat controller pulled his trousers up around his waist and sat down.

'Grace, what have we got from Holyhead?'

'The calls made to Mustapha's mobile phone were made via satellite link. We can't trace them unless they ring again. The prints we found on the caravan match one of the dead guys from the BMW. The three men recovered were all carrying identification; wallets, money, and two of them had their mobile phones. All of them were members of known extremist Islamic groups under MI5 scrutiny.' Faz explained to the team.

'These guys weren't expecting to encounter any problems,' Tank interrupted. 'They were armed, yes, but they wouldn't have been carrying their IDs and telephones if they thought for one minute they'd encounter armed police. That means they were there trying to find Mustapha Ahmed. They were probably waiting for him near to the caravan and then spotted him in the Jeep with us. They had no reason to think that we were police. They were just unlucky. They'd been sent by Yasser Ahmed to take Mustapha to him and the guns were there in case he needed any persuasion.' Tank was speculating, of course, but it seemed to be the most obvious explanation.

'So, as far as Yasser Ahmed is concerned Mustapha could be anywhere?' Timms asked.

'All he knows is that his men went to Anglesey with guns, looking for his brother and they never came back. Sian and her team are dealing with the Irish connection or what's left of them. Everything is pointing us toward the fact that Axe and Yasser Ahmed are in that town.' Tank pointed to Warrington on the digital map. It was just twelve miles away from their office as the crow flies.

'Chen, please could you give us the run down from the technical guys,' Tank said as he walked over to the water cooler and filled a plastic cup with cold liquid. He filled another and handed it to Faz, standing next to her as Chen dimmed the lights. He picked up a remote and stabbed at a button with his finger. The digital map flashed, and the picture changed to a close-up aerial picture of Warrington. Three red circles pulsed on the map indicating where the house, the mosque, and the food distribution centre were. He tapped his finger on the circle around the mosque and the picture changed again, zooming in on the building.

'This is the mosque at Appleton. We have six people on site; heat sensors show four more people are in the rooms at the rear of the building. Audio surveillance is giving us what sounds like a prayer meeting from the main body of the mosque, and a poker game at the back. Nothing subversive has been overheard so far and a pair of kings won the last hand!'

He tapped the second red circle and the picture zoomed down onto a detached, brick-built house with a black slate roof. The picture changed to look like the negative of a photograph. Amber blobs appeared in the image of the building, two moving and two still.

'Heat sensors show us the shapes here of four of the five men that Usef Mamood shared a house with. We know from audio surveillance that they are leaving for work any time now. They will be at this distribution centre until 0900 hrs tomorrow. We are going to abandon the raid on the house in exchange for breaking into and bugging it. We will be implanting a full portfolio of surveillance equipment. Video, audio, all shoes, bags, clothes, and luggage will be bugged a half hour after they leave for work.'

Chen touched a magic finger to the map again, this time the picture was an overhead of a large industrial park. Warehouses filled the picture top to bottom, but there was only one illuminated.

Focusing the view from a significant distance away, the entire area could be seen. Chen pointed to two large buildings with unusually shaped rooftops.

'These two are Brinks security money counting houses. Any monies that go into ATM cash machines anywhere in the north of the country, enters here to be counted first. You can see from the roof designs that they're conscious of being attacked from the air by helicopters hence the roof design to make it impossible for an aircraft to land on them. We have intelligence that this food distribution centre, which is next door, has a large cold room storage area staffed by around sixty staff. The bulk of the staff members are immigrants, mostly Asians, and the rest are a mixture of Eastern Europeans. We have suspicions that this cold room and the mosque are where Axe and other groups are recruiting their members. Audio is no use to us in there, as the condenser fans on the refrigeration units are blocking the signals. This is where we'll need most of our people and local police backup. Recent air reconnaissance of the area shows nothing out of the ordinary. We haven't seen anything unusual. Articulated lorries, panel vans, transits even a couple of ice cream vans.'

Chen switched the lights back on and stood to the side as the large map reappeared.

'Any questions so far?' Tank walked to the front.

99

'Sir, are you going to join us?' Tank directed the question to Major Timms.

'I will lead the raid on the warehouse with Chen and teams A, B, and C. Grace will take the mosque with the D and E teams.'

'I will help Grace and her teams at the mosque.' Timms nodded to Faz and smiled. He wagged his finger at her laughing. No one wanted the boss looking over his or her shoulder and he knew it. He had backed Tank up only once but found his methods too risky to condone. As the senior man in the taskforce, he had learned that what he didn't know wouldn't hurt him.

'We will be leaving in one hour, people. Everyone meet, suited and booted, back here for final checks, in one hour. Let's go!' Tank and his squad sprang into action.

CHAPTER 27

Yasser – Warrington

Yasser Indri Ahmed stood alone in the empty storage unit. He opened the door of the ice cream van and climbed inside, passing between the front seats he moved into the back of the van. He stood where the ice cream vendor would normally sell his wares. He opened the freezer compartment by sliding the black plastic lid, thus exposing the empty stainless-steel storage box. He smiled as he imagined the storage box crammed full of Semtex and ball bearings. There were three such storage containers, one on each side of the van and one beneath the back window. If this mobile truck bomb disguised as an innocent ice cream van was to be detonated among milling crowds of unsuspecting passers-by, the result would be sheer carnage.

Yasser had ordered the search and purchase of these vehicles some six months before. His followers across the British Isles had scoured the local papers and auto-marts. Some were bought for just a few hundred pounds, nothing more than rotting shells their equipment broken beyond repair, the refrigeration and road worthiness were of no concern to Yasser. They had fixed any damaged engines and repainted rusty exteriors. New cartoon decals were added to put the finishing touches to the disguise. He now had a fleet of six, complete and ready for service. They would be weapons in the fight against the infidel. His holy Jihad was soon to be unleashed on the British people.

President George Bush had been mistaken, when he had pointed to Osama bin Laden and the Islamic fundamentalist group al-Qaeda as the architects of all terrorist destruction. It is more realistic to describe them as a small group of extremists that were bankrolled by the son of an oil millionaire, who has little support among the majority of Arab nations. It had been proven by the 9/11 bombers in New York, and by the 7/7 bombers in London, just what scale of destruction can be achieved. They were devastating attacks planned and executed by small independent groups of extremists, armed only with box cutter knives and home-made bombs.

There was no evil mastermind sat in a secret hide out that took control of planning every terrorist attack, only in James Bond movies do such evil masterminds exist. Yasser was a great planner, but his resources were limited. The attacks he had planned and executed in American tourist attractions had been simple but effective. All he really needed was a man or woman with enough conviction to die for their belief; the rest was cheap and simple.

Few people knew of his current plan or its existence; he couldn't trust anyone with the full details of his evil plot. He had thought about his potential targets for hours and the choice was endless, shopping centres, parks, concerts, and sporting events were all potential targets. His mobile bombs could wreak havoc anywhere that there were crowds of people.

He climbed back out of the van and shut the door. Two pink pigs waved at him from a decal below the handle on the door. 'Pinky and Perky' he thought they were called. He walked across the unit, passing the silent ice cream vans that were parked there. He passed the last vehicle and stopped beside what looked like a large metal box on wheels, he lifted a stainless-steel lid and the smell of old onions hit him, he lifted the lid from a second container and the smell of hot dogs drifted toward him, he opened a stainless-steel door beneath the empty pans and looked inside, the storage space contained an old rusty gas bottle and some empty plastic ketchup and mustard dispensers.

'Hot dog stands and ice cream vans that explode, what a genius idea,' he said. Others would soon join the dirty old hot dog stand that stood by itself. They would be cleaned and then stripped of their innards; the old ketchup bottles replaced by a far more deadly cargo. All he needed was to pick the perfect venue. He wanted all his machines of destruction to attack simultaneously to amplify the effect of the carnage.

Yasser walked toward the front entrance of the warehouse, he unlocked the door and opened it allowing the cold night air to rush in. He only came to see the progress that had been made at night when the unit was empty of his followers. Most of his supporters had heard a rumour that he was in the country, but only a chosen few had actually seen him, he trusted no one. He glanced at his growing fleet of ice cream vans and smiled; the plan was progressing well. He extinguished the light and closed the unit door then he locked it behind him. Yasser looked up at the night sky toward the full moon. About a mile away on the other side of the industrial park he saw the silhouette of a small helicopter against the silver light of the moon. He gauged it was somewhere above the area of the cold room, but he could hear no engine noise. He knew immediately that it was a spy drone. The flying machines were almost silent, unmanned, and packed with high-tech surveillance equipment, they were flown by remote control and used to search for, and observe, military targets. He had seen many of them flying over the mountains of Pakistan and Kashmir, searching for the hideaway of Osama bin Laden.

A single headlight appeared on the corner close by, and he heard the high-pitched whine of a Japanese motorbike engine approaching. The rider pulled up close to the curb and put the bike onto its stand. The rider looked Yasser up and down. It had been some years since they'd met in the flesh. Yasser looked good in his dark-blue denim jeans; he had a simple white T-shirt beneath a tan leather jacket; the jacket matched his cowboy boots. He hadn't put on an ounce of weight since the last time they'd met, and he still wore his long hair in a bun tied tightly to the back of his head.

The bike rider turned off the engine and approached Yasser and he smiled as she removed her helmet.

'Yasmine, you have grown into a beautiful woman. How are you my sister?'

'Yasser, you look so well! I've been so worried about you. I miss you terribly. Mustapha has left us and his faith behind, he was so upset and disturbed leaving home that he just couldn't cope,' Yasmine blurted, only stopping for breath when Yasser placed a finger on her lips lightly.

'Shush, shush, Yasmine, now is not the time, you can tell me all about it when we get to where I am staying. We have much to catch up on little one.' Yasser smiled and took the spare helmet from her. Yasmine mounted the Honda Blackbird and started the engine. Yasser climbed on behind her and clung to the bar on the back of the bike.

'Where are we going to?' Yasmine shouted over the noise of the engine as she revved the machine excitedly.

'Do you know your way to Anfield in Liverpool, next to the football stadium?' he asked putting his boots up onto the footrests.

'Yes, I used to take Mustapha to watch them play when he was younger. Hold on tight it will not take us long.'

Yasser looked up at the drone again. It hadn't moved from its position above the cold room. *I think they are looking for me*, he thought smiling and pointing to the remote helicopter. They both laughed as the bike pulled away from the unit.

CHAPTER 28

Mustapha

In the seventh century AD, the Prophet Muhammad established Islam. He was believed to be the last prophet in the line that included Moses and Abraham. Within a century, Islam had conquered and spread across an area greater than the Roman Empire had been at its height. Now it remains the primary religion of the Middle East and most of North Africa, also spreading into huge parts of Asia. Major groups within Islam include the Sunnis, who constitute about ninety per cent of today's Muslims. Iraq and Iran are the homelands of the Shia Muslims, where it's the majority faith. History tells us that the two groups formed because of disputes about who the next Caliph would be early in the religion's formation.

Mustapha was born and raised as a Sunni Muslim. This meant that because they lived in Iraq, he and his family were in the minority. His brother Yasser had become involved with a small group of Sunni militia whose primary aim was to protect the Sunni community from the Shia. Tribal conflicts had raged for centuries, the violence and mistrust had been passed from one generation to the next. Saddam Hussein and his ruling party mostly belonged to the Sunni Muslims. Poor policy decisions that favoured Saddam's own people and added to their strength and wealth were met by a backlash from the Shia majority on the streets of Iraq. Small militia groups were set up to protect individual communities from religious sectarian violence. Saddam was a ruthless leader with an appalling human rights record, especially relating to the Kurdish people of the north. The Kurds themselves are the largest population of people on the planet that don't actually have their own country. The tribal tensions that were part of everyday life in Iraq began to boil over as the threat of an invasion loomed. The British and American forces along with a 50,000 strong army of Iraqi Kurdish militia, invaded on March 20, 2003. Mustapha saw his brother less and less as the young political activist turned into a terrorist psychopath. Yasser's popularity and fame became legendary in his small community, but his antics also angered the Shia militias. Mustapha and his family were in grave danger within eighteen months of the invasion rule of law had ceased to exist.

Mustapha's uncle was a schoolteacher before the invasion, but the schools had closed down soon after Baghdad fell. He had gained employment with the coalition armed forces as an interpreter. In the first three years after the invasion of Iraq, over 250 Iraqi interpreters were kidnapped, tortured, and killed by their own compatriots. When Mustapha's uncle was found, he had had holes drilled into his hands and knees, his legs had been broken, and he'd had acid poured over his face before he was finally shot in the head. Anyone who collaborated with the invading Western forces could meet a similar fate.

The days in Iraq all seemed so far away now as Mustapha sat in an interview room on the top floor of a police station in Liverpool. He stood up and walked to the window taking in the view of the river. He had been questioned for hours it seemed, his interrogators pressing him for as much information about Yasser and his supporters as they could. He didn't think he had been much help, really. He knew nothing of his brother's evil plans and even less about his associates.

The door opened and the fat controller, David Bell walked in. He had a suit jacket over his white shirt and his blue tie was loosened at the collar. He carried a thick white file of papers, which he placed onto the table.

'Sit down, Mustapha, please. This will not take long now. We need to put you somewhere safe for the time being. We have a safe house where you will be staying that is not far away from here. You will have two agents with you at all times. There is another thing that I need to ask you. We want your help to bring Yasser and his associates in.' The fat controller took his glasses off and cleaned them with his tie. He didn't look at Mustapha; he left the question hanging in the air.

'How can I help you to bring him in? I don't know where he is or what he is planning to do. I don't agree with his methods, but my brother thinks he is fighting a war, Jihad. It is the policies of the American government and its lapdog allies like the British that have caused people like my brother to retaliate. He thinks that he is a freedom fighter, a soldier of god, he is very wrong in what he has chosen to do but you need to understand the reasons why he chooses that path. I may not agree with his actions, all life is precious to me, but I will not help you. I don't know anything.' Mustapha stood and walked to the window again. A tall wooden sailing ship was moving slowly through the water to his left, making its way to the Albert Docks.

Mustapha thought about what he had been asked to do. He didn't hold with the use of violence especially when it was directed against innocent civilians. His brother was a lunatic he knew that, but he had his beliefs. It was not that long ago when Muslims from all over the world went to Afghanistan to help the Taliban fight against Soviet invasion. The Western alliances, including Britain and the USA had armed and trained the Muslim Taliban in their struggle against the evil of communism. Now they fought against them.

France and the West had armed and backed Saddam when he fought against Iran, again the table had turned, and these so-called freedom fighters were now terrorists. One man's freedom fighter is another man's terrorist. His brother and people like him wouldn't be

105

eradicated until the causes of Islamic anger at the West's perceived crusades into Muslim lands were removed. He hated his brother's actions, but he did not want to be involved in betraying him.

'Mustapha, we think that Yasser is with your sister Yasmine. She hasn't been seen for a year now, but we think that she is here. I don't know how she feels about your brother's campaign, but he is a very persuasive man.' The fat controller walked to the window and stood next to Mustapha. He spoke to the reflection in the window.

'I understand that this is difficult for you, but we think he is here to kill people. He is in possession of a large amount of Semtex explosive. We know he has been involved in the deaths of at least two men in Ireland, that we are sure of. He is planning something big Mustapha and it will involve the deaths of innocent people who don't know anything about his Jihad, al-Qaeda, the Mujahidin, the Axe group, or anybody else for that matter. Quite frankly most people don't really give a toss, but that doesn't mean they need to be blown to bits. Help us stop him, Mustapha, and I give you my word we will try to bring him and your sister in alive.'

Mustapha thought about what the fat man had said. He was right. He was involved in this whether he liked it or not. 'Yasser is a lunatic and he must be stopped,' Bell said.

'What do you need me to do?' Mustapha asked with a sigh.

CHAPTER 29

The Raids – Warrington

Chen looked at the house through his night sight binoculars. The body heat scan showed that no living person was in the house; everyone had gone to work at the cold room. Chen opened the car door and gave the thumbs up signal to a man in a dark van that was parked across the road. The side door of the van slid open and four men dressed head to toe in black exited. Each of the four men was carrying a black carbon suitcase in their hand. The men looked like modern-day Ninjas as they headed toward the front door of the house where they met Chen.

Chen removed a small piece of wire from the side of his watch and inserted it into the keyhole. The lock made a clicking noise as it opened. Once inside, the four men headed upstairs and then split up into the four bedrooms. All four bedrooms were bugged in minutes. Spy cameras were fitted to lampshades or curtain rails wherever they could be hidden. Chen moved from room to room as the surveillance team planted their equipment. He noticed that none of the rooms had beds in them, the occupants preferred to sleep on thin mattresses on the floor. The house smelled of strong cooking spices and body odour. The smell of curry had permeated through the building, tainting the fabric of the carpets and curtains with its noxious spicy scent. The content and belongings that the surveillance team searched appeared to be innocent enough.

Chen entered a room that had two mattresses on the floor. There were pictures and scriptures on the wall that appeared to be written in the Saudi dialect of Arabic. The Saudis had every reason to be angry with the Western governments. When the British Army tried to suppress Iraqi rebels during its occupation of the Middle East, following the First World War, they'd enlisted the help of King Ibn Saud of Hejaz. King Saud had used the British mandate to camouflage his own mission of destroying the Iraqis in the south of the country for his own end. In 1927, Britain signed the Treaty of Jeddah, recognising the independence of Saud's kingdom, known today as Saudi Arabia. He declared himself King and his family have ruled the country ever since, siphoning millions of pounds into personal wealth. The British government's policy of colonisation rarely seemed to benefit those countries or their peoples.

The next bedroom that he entered had a large flag pinned up on the wall. The flag had a deep red background with one white stripe that ran diagonally across it.

'What country does that flag represent?' asked a young technician. He was busy planting tracker devices in some shoes that he had found in a closet.

'It's a Padi scuba diving flag,' Chen said. 'It's used all over the world to attract scuba divers to their diving centres. Two of the men that live here are Egyptian, we believe. The East coast of Egypt borders the Red Sea. The reefs there, like Ras Mohammed are world famous. It's the best scuba diving in the world. The diving schools in Sharm el Sheikh tend to use local people as instructors because they expect to be paid less than foreign instructors are. It looks like our friend here is a diver. That worries me too. Semtex is just as deadly underwater.' Chen opened another closet door and looked inside. He found what he was looking for.

'There is a full set of diving equipment in here; make sure you put tracers on all of it.' Chen walked through the other rooms and told his team to be on the lookout for any other scuba equipment. There was none. It could just be an innocent hobby, but it's better to be safe than sorry when you work in the terrorist industry. He walked back to the scuba gear that he had discovered and picked up the wet suit. The technician had already placed a tiny transmitter in the material of the suit. It felt damp as if it had been used recently. A chill ran through Chen as he contemplated the possible scenarios. The most likely, was the manufacture of limpet mines. Limpet mines had been used to great effect by both sides in the Second World War. It would be relatively easy to attach a large explosive device to the hull of a ship and then swim away undetected. To be successful all that the plan would require was a target and a competent diver.

Chen called the control room of the TTF and reported his concerns. The control room would then inform the port authorities of the possible danger of a terrorist attack from beneath the sea. Chen told the control room to request a copy of the port's manifesto for the coming months. It would give them details of all the ships that were due to dock in the port and could help them to identify a potential target.

The docks in Liverpool were still very much a working deep-sea port. They handled millions of tons of cargo from all over the world every month. The city's historical maritime heritage also made it a popular destination for naval events, and the armadas of ancient wooden sailing ships that competed in round the world competitions.

Chen checked his watch. The four surveillance men appeared in the hallway downstairs. They were all finished exactly on time. Chen shut the front door behind them as they left. The four men in black climbed back into the side of the dark van and the door slid closed. Chen started the engine of his vehicle and headed in the direction of the cold room distribution centre. The black van waited for him to pass by and then pulled out behind him. They were to follow the Chinese man to the cold room and set up surveillance equipment there too. It was going to be a long night.

CHAPTER 30

The Raids – The Cold Room

Tank looked at the huge white doors of the cold room. They stood open and were held in place by a red fire extinguisher. There were long strips of clear plastic that hung from the ceiling to the floor keeping the cold air inside the huge refrigerator, and a small man in a white coat was standing next to Tank. He was shaking with fear. Ten minutes earlier Tank had arrived at the factory with forty armed agents who were dressed like Robocop.

'Could someone tell me what this is all about? We just pack and distribute sandwiches. Is there any need for all these guns?' said the little man.

'Shut up and get in the cold room with everyone else. If you are in charge here, one of my agents will come and speak to you shortly.' Tank gestured to an armed police marksman to take the man away. The officer pushed the supervisor through the clear plastic curtain into the cold room.

Tank followed them through the clear strips into the refrigerator and quickly assessed the situation in front of him. There were approximately sixty men dressed in heavy thermal jackets, gloves, and hats, they were lined up along one of the walls with their hands above their heads. The Armed Response Team stood menacingly in front of the frightened men with their guns pointed toward them. The brave one or two that questioned them about what was happening were silenced quickly.

'Anyone of white European appearance can be taken outside. The officers outside will take your details and then you can leave. You will not be working tonight so go home.' Tank waited for a reaction from the men, but none came.

'Most of them are Polish,' said the supervisor. 'They don't understand English very well.' The little man repeated what Tank had just said in Polish and the men started to file through the doors still looking frightened until they got outside. A heavily built man from Estonia stopped beside Tank.

'You are a fascist pig. Police officers in my country are like you also. They are fascist pigs too.'

Tank took half a step forward and drove his knee into the man's groin. The Estonian man crumpled at the knees and grabbed at his injured testicles, groaning in agony. Tank stepped closer to the man and swung his elbow into the bridge of his nose, and the Estonian man crashed onto the floor backwards, his face was covered in blood. An armed agent moved over the injured man and pointed his machine gun at his head. The injured Estonian raised his hands in surrender, pain and shock making him less confrontational.

'Has anyone else got any comments to pass on to me? Any feedback you can give, no matter how negative, is always welcome.' The room stayed silent apart from the noise from the big condenser fans and the man groaning on the floor.

The Eastern Europeans were escorted from the room, leaving the workers that were of Asian or Middle Eastern persuasion behind. The long slow process of checking the identities of everyone in the refrigerator began. Many of the men in the room shared identities. False passports and duplicate national insurance numbers were commonplace among illegal immigrants. This did not mean that all illegal immigrants were terrorists, or that all terrorists were illegal immigrants, but it was a start.

The lessons learned by the British security services from the 7/7 London Bombs indicated that the opposite was true. All the bombers were well integrated into the British community, most had employment, wives, and children. Their conviction, however, was strong enough for them to leave their families behind and become suicide bombers, nevertheless all the evidence that Tank had, was pointing to this Muslim community. The TTF agents interviewed the men thoroughly one at a time and if any of them had incorrect documentation, or if they couldn't be found on the electoral roll, they were handcuffed and taken into custody for further questioning. There was only half a dozen left to be spoken to when Chen arrived.

'The house is wired completely. I'm concerned about the scuba gear that we found; it has definitely been used recently. I can't tell if it was used in saltwater or fresh water yet. We've taken a sample to indicate which, but we won't know until tomorrow.' Chen noticed two of the suspects that were waiting to be spoken to, were arguing, their voices were hushed but tempers were fraying.

An armed response member moved toward the two men. He directed them to be quiet. The two Egyptian men moved as if they were one. One of them tackled the armed officer around the legs while the other grabbed his machine gun, a Panther AP4 Carbine, and he fired a volley of shots into the refrigerator ceiling. Then he pointed the gun at the head of the disarmed officer.

'Please point your guns at the floor and your colleague will not be hurt.' The two men pulled the officer close to them and slowly made toward the doorway. No one moved. Tank gestured to his team to stay cool; he did not want to lose a man during an operation, ever.

The two men walked through the plastic thermal curtain and headed outside toward the car park. They kept the officer as a human shield between them and any potential sniper. The gunman handed a set of keys to his accomplice and he climbed onto a blue Yamaha motorbike. The gunman climbed behind him; the gun still pointed at the head of the policeman.

Tank and Chen edged slowly toward the men knowing that there was nothing that they could do without risking their officer's life. The motorbike roared to life and the driver kicked the pedal, engaging first gear. As the bike pulled quickly away, the gunman squeezed the trigger. The hostage toppled forward as the bullets ripped through his chest. He lay very still on the floor as the people around him sprang into action. Two men rushed to the aid of their injured colleague, but the proximity from which the high velocity bullets were fired had rendered the Kevlar vest almost useless.

Bullets crashed off the road all around the escaping Yamaha, blasting chunks of concrete and hot metal all over the two Egyptian men as the racing bike screamed away from the scene. Tank and Chen sprinted toward Chen's car; both men were shouting angry instructions as they opened the doors and jumped into the vehicle.

The motorbike skidded onto the Kingsland Grange at high speed; a rolling barricade of police vehicles with blue lights flashing and sirens blaring, followed it closely. The remote spy drone helicopter moved from its position above the cold room and joined in the chase. Chen drove the car in pursuit of the two men as fast as the traffic would allow. Tank wound down the window and pointed his gun at the speeding Yamaha. He fired twice but the oncoming traffic made the risk of innocent casualties too great. He banged his fist on the dashboard in frustration.

The motorbike increased its speed as it hit the wide lanes of the Birchwood expressway, heading toward Hilden traffic island at over a hundred miles an hour; it doubled the gap between the Egyptian men and the taskforce officers in just seconds. The unmanned drone was directly above the motorbike; it was the only pursuit vehicle that was fast enough to keep up with the machine, the slower police vehicles were losing ground as the bike approached Orford Park.

The entrance to the park was only wide enough for pedal bikes and push chairs to access the wooded area beyond. The perimeter of the park was ringed with spiked metal railings. The Yamaha screamed through the narrow entrance without slowing and disappeared into the dark, only the tail lights could be seen.

'We can't follow them through there; we are going to have to go around.' Chen took the vehicle around the corner on two wheels as they tried to stay parallel with the speeding motorbike. They were two hundred yards from the park's exit when the motorbike emerged from the dark tree line and banked sharply back onto the highway heading toward the town centre down the main Winwick Road. The bike screamed by the railway station as it neared the town centre and took a sharp bend heading into the market multistorey car park. The driver killed the motorcycle's headlights and took the bike up the concrete ramp to the second level. It was late and so the car park was empty.

The pillion rider jumped off the bike and headed for the concrete stairwell. He opened the door and turned to his accomplice.

'Get to the safe house in Liverpool. I will meet you there if God will allow it to be so,' he shouted as he disappeared into the darkness of the stairs.

Tank and Chen had lost sight of the racing bike minutes before they rounded the bend outside the multistorey. They did not see it turn into the dark building.

'Where is that drone? Don't tell me we've lost these two bastards,' Tank said into the radio. It was broadcasting on an open channel. A static voice came back.

'The drone has lost them completely. There's no body heat or engine registering on the instruments. The only way this can happen is if they have gone underground. Could they have entered a tunnel?'

'The multi-storey car park, they must have turned into that. The layers of concrete will have the same effect as being underground. They must be in there.'

Chen slammed the car into reverse and spun the vehicle around to face the dark car park entrance. Tank opened the door and got out. He ran across the road and vaulted the low wall into the empty car park. He peered into the gloom trying to adjust his vision to the dark. He could see only a few abandoned vehicles, their owners probably drunk in the nearby pubs and clubs. Tank could hear the bass lines of a dozen music systems coming from the town centre bars.

Police cars screeched to halt forming a semi-circle of steel and coloured lights around the building. The officers got out of their vehicles and drew down their weapons on the multistorey.

The Egyptian pillion rider had dropped the automatic weapon when he dismounted the bike. He had entered the dark concrete stairwell and headed down. The fire door at the bottom of the stairs, which exited the rear of the building, had resisted him only briefly. The door splintered and burst open with the third kick. The Egyptian removed his thermal jacket and crossed the road slowly, trying not to attract any attention. He walked toward the sound of music and laughter that was coming from nearby. He walked down a narrow alleyway and found himself on Bridge Street. He laughed as he stepped into the bright lights of the town's drinking area. He mingled into the crowds of drunken revellers that staggered up and down the street going from pub to pub. The street was packed with people. There was no way he would be found now. He was free.

112

CHAPTER 31

The Mosque

Grace Farrington pulled the Jeep she was driving to a halt. She turned to her superior officer, Major Stanley Timms who was sat in the rear of the vehicle. Timms was monitoring the information that the spy drone was sending to his laptop computer. There were four people in the building's main body and two in a smaller room at the rear. Sian squeezed Faz's wrist in a nervous gesture of support from the front passenger seat. Sian had returned from her mission in Ireland just a half hour before the Armed Response Teams left the station in Liverpool. There had been little benefit from the trip to Dublin. The people that she needed information from were dead, and their associates had all gone to ground. The culture of silence that surrounded the paramilitaries in Ireland was still as strong today as it was during the troubles. No one dared speak to the authorities for fear of dreadful retribution.

'How do you want to play this, sir?' asked Faz.

'You and the troops go in and see who we have in the mosque. I will take two men around the back in case anyone decides that they would rather be somewhere else.' The Major opened his door, climbed out, and checked his battle vest. Happy that everything was in order he walked around to the rear of the vehicle. Sian and Faz followed him. Faz popped the lock with the electronic key. Sian opened the locked gun box and took out a Remington 870 pump-action shotgun. Faz picked up a similar weapon for herself and passed the third shotgun to Timms. The Remington 870 would stop a charging elephant at 200 yards. In a situation where a target may be in control of explosives then the target had to be neutralised quickly so that they couldn't activate any detonators. A wounded bomber could still possibly activate his explosive charge in theory. The Remington's destructive power lessened the chances of a potential target still being capable of causing any damage.

Timms cocked his weapon and indicated to two uniformed officers from the taskforce to follow him. They headed through a small gateway that ran along the building to the rear exit. Sian and Faz headed toward the front door of the mosque followed by their team.

They entered the unlocked mosque quickly and without any resistance. A startled cleric was sat in the centre of the large area facing three young Muslim teenagers. The three young girls were wearing the traditional robes of Islamic women. They were obviously receiving some religious instruction from their shocked teacher.

'This is a house of God. How dare you enter here with weapons in your hands? What possible reason can you have for this outrageous behaviour?' The Muslim cleric spoke in a quiet voice trying not to scare the already worried young girls. His accent was that of a local English man.

'We don't want to frighten you, sir, and your students can leave. Officer, escort these ladies from the premises please.' Faz smiled at the girls trying to calm them. She could see them staring at the silver pump-action shotgun that she carried before her.

'We need to search the building, Sir. We have a warrant. We are investigating the whereabouts of an Iraqi man known as Yasser Ahmed. Do you know him?' Sian led the team further into the building while Faz dealt with the holy man. Faz saw the flash of recognition in the man's eyes when she mentioned Yasser's name.

'I know of a man by that name, but he would not be welcomed into this house of God. We are peaceful people, Officer; the man you are looking for is a terrorist. You will not find him here.' The holy man stood and looked to see where Sian and the armed men had gone.

'We've received information that some of his supporters use this mosque for prayer. Do you know of anyone who might be giving shelter to this man? We know that he has bought explosives and is planning to use them in this country.' Faz pressed the old man. His expression was one of concern.

'Where in this country does any man go to buy explosives? Why do you think that we are connected? The community here is made up of bankers and doctors, lawyers and teachers; we have no bombers here.' The man gestured around the empty room as if his congregation were standing in front of them.

'I'm afraid that terrorist cells don't have 'Bomber' tattooed on their foreheads. We have one of your congregation in custody. He was stopped driving a car full of Semtex from Ireland when we arrested him. His name is Usef Mamood. Do you know him?' Faz could tell that the man did know Usef from the reaction on his face.

Sian appeared from the rear of the building followed by the officers in her team. They were leading two men in handcuffs through the buildings.

'The building is clear apart from these two. They have no identification and they are refusing to talk. Take them to the station we can interview them later on.' Sian walked toward Faz and the cleric. Major Timms entered through the front door with his two men.

'I think we should finish this conversation at the station. You are not being honest with me, are you?' Faz indicated to the two men who had entered with Major Timms, to take the cleric away with the others.

Sian said, 'There's an office and some living quarters through the back of the building. We might as well have a quick look around before forensics get here.' They walked toward the rear of the building. Sian led the way down a narrow corridor. There were two doorways leading off the corridor to the left.

Sian opened the first door and stepped into a small dormitory. There were six thin mattresses laid out on the floor. Two looked like they'd been slept in recently.

'This is where we found the two unidentified men. They were sleeping when we came in,' Sian said.

The three TTF members pulled on latex gloves and started to sift through items in the room. There were a few small sports bags containing socks and underwear but nothing of any great interest. At the far end of the dormitory was a small cupboard door. Faz opened it and looked at the two metal cylinders that were inside.

'There are two Scuba diving tanks in here. Chen found some diving equipment at the house, there must be a link.' Faz turned the metal valve on the top of one of the tanks and compressed air hissed out noisily.

'They are full too. They have not been used yet.' Faz checked the tanks to see if there was a supplier's name anywhere. There was a small sticker on the side that displayed the date on which the tanks were last filled. There was also a company name and telephone number.

'Carpenray is the name of the suppliers I think; there is a contact number on this tank.' Faz punched the number into her mobile phone and dialled the number she had found. A voice answered on the other end and she left the room to take the call, she pulled out a pen and paper as she walked through the doorway.

Sian and Major Timms finished the initial sweep of the dormitory and then headed down the corridor to the second door. The door opened into a large office space. There were three desks positioned in the room, all of them crammed with paperwork. Sian walked to the nearest desk and started to sift through a wire letter tray that was filled with unopened envelopes.

Major Timms moved across the room from Sian and searched through an untidy pile of papers. He found a receipt for payment that related to the charter of a small aeroplane from a private company in Cheshire, for a flight to County Cork in Southern Ireland. The bill related to a plane which had not been flown back to England when it was supposed to be.

'This is very interesting. It could explain how the men who died in the explosion in Dublin were planning to get home with their weapons. It certainly links this institution with the events in Ireland.' Stanley Timms stopped reading as Faz came into the room. The pretty black woman looked flustered.

117

'It turns out that Carpenray is a flooded quarry in the Lake District. It's a busy diving centre about sixty miles from here. They have apparently put old aeroplanes and cars into the quarry for divers to swim down to. The manager on the phone said that he has hundreds of members from all over the country. Many of them are Asian. He said that he doesn't remember specifically if any of them were from Warrington, and he can't check their files until they open tomorrow.' Faz shrugged her shoulders and walked over to the third desk.

Suddenly the phone on the desk next to Sian rang. She put the envelopes that she had been scanning back down on the desktop. She picked up the handset and listened. She didn't speak, waiting for the caller to announce himself or herself. There was nothing, just silence on the other end. She looked at Major Timms and shook her head. Timms rushed over to her and took the phone from her. He put it to his ear quickly and placed his hand over the mouthpiece.

'Hello, I am expecting a call from a friend in Egypt.' Timms remembered that Mustapha had told them the calls from satellite links were all coded. The use of the code word Egypt might work. The line went completely dead. It had not worked.

'Oh, bugger me. Well it was probably a sales call, anyway. Ask the tech guys to put a trace on it just in case.' He walked back over to the desk he had been searching.

Sian picked up the bundle of envelopes that she had been studying earlier. She looked thoughtful as she considered the possible connotations. There was no end of disaster that Yasser Ahmed could inflict with Semtex and qualified scuba divers. The River Mersey flowed by Liverpool on its way to the Irish Sea. The river had a fleet of passenger ferries, oil tankers, cargo ships and naval vessels; every type of sea going craft could be a potential target.

Sian's thoughts were disturbed for a moment. There was a thick brown manila envelope with an Irish postmark stamped on it. It had been posted in Dublin.

Major Timms' mobile phone rang, the caller ID showed Tank's number. He nodded and paced the room, the two female agents watched him in silence; the look on his face told them that this was bad news. He said a few brief words with Tank and arranged to continue the conversation back at headquarters.

'I am afraid that I have to be the bearer of bad news. We've lost a man at the distribution centre raid. It appears two Egyptian men disarmed him and took him as a hostage. They shot him during the getaway. One of the Egyptian men is dead and one of them is missing. Chen shot the dead man after they had cornered him in a car park however Chen has been injured in the process. His vest took most of the damage, but he has a bullet in his shoulder, and he has lost a lot of blood. We will not know if he will pull through for a few hours yet, he is in surgery now.' Timms knew how close his team was. Chen was a valued member of the Terrorist Task Force and a good friend to Sian and Faz.

'That has to be the final proof that Yasser Ahmed is here somewhere. Why would two men risk being shot to escape, if they had nothing to hide?' Sian tapped the envelope marked with the Dublin postcode on the desk as she spoke.

'The fact that they have shot a policeman together with the receipt you found; connects them with the explosives in Ireland. This envelope has a Dublin postmark on it.' She tapped the envelope on the desk again emphasising her points as she spoke.

Major Stanley Timms was an old school Royal Marine. He had more experience fighting the Irish Paramilitaries than any man still alive. He understood how they worked. He knew how they thought. Revenge attacks were swift and brutal.

'Put that envelope down, Sian. Put it down on the desk and back toward the door.' Timms never took his eyes from hers. He had seen enough unexploded letter bombs in the army to recognise this as one immediately.

Realisation hit Sian in an instant. She knew now that Timms thought the envelope was a bomb sent in retaliation by the IRA, payback for the arrest of Patrick Finnen. She also knew that they'd killed for far less. She looked at Faz, she was edging toward the door; her black skin shiny with perspiration.

Timms edged slowly toward Sian. She had frozen with fear. He reached his hands out very gently and grasped one edge of the letter bomb. Sian didn't release her grip on the other side, so he guided the letter gently toward the desk. Sian was staring at the letter as they moved it slowly to the desktop; both were holding one side each, as if it were an incredibly heavy object.

Faz reached the doorway and grabbed her mobile phone as she ran up the corridor.

'Get me the bomb squad quickly. Meet me at the mosque in Appleton.' She was about to speak again when the bomb exploded.

Grace Farrington was knocked off her feet by the blast. Her head hit the doorframe of the dormitory as she went down. The breath was punched from her lungs by the shock wave. The corridor in which she was lying was covered in little pieces of confetti-like paper. Larger remnants of paperwork from the office were floating around like little white flying carpets, slowly descending to the floor. Grace briefly glimpsed the still body of her friend Sian lying across the corridor. She lay still on the office floor. Grace noticed that Sian's beautiful auburn red hair was matted with blood and dust, before everything went dark.

CHAPTER 32

John Tankersley – Liverpool

Tank stepped out of the elevator into the top floor office; it looked like a scene from Hill St. Blues. Men were being escorted in handcuffs in all directions, voices were raised, and tempers were frayed. The volume was deafening as his officers processed the suspects who had been arrested during the raids in Warrington. Everyone was aware of the possible human loss to the team. One long serving officer had been killed, four others, including their senior officer Major Timms, had gone down. No one knew how badly injured they were.

Tank crossed the room and headed for the fishbowl shaped office; he stepped into the room, removed his battle vest, and placed it on the chair nearest to the desk. The battle vests had saved his team's lives today, all except one. The body armour battle vests that his taskforce used were made of a material that, ounce for ounce is stronger than steel, yet it maintains the flexibility of a fabric. The chest and back areas are re-enforced with Kevlar plates to further protect the vital organs. Unfortunately, they're not completely indestructible. A high-velocity bullet fired from proximity could penetrate them.

John Tankersley picked up the phone and dialled the hospital that his friends and colleagues had been taken to. Chen was now out of surgery and was making good progress. The bullet had gone through the meat of the shoulder without smashing any bones. The doctor said that he would be up and about in a week or so. The battle vest that he had been wearing had taken four high velocity rounds and stopped them all. The impact of the bullets hitting the vest would have felt like he'd been struck with a sledgehammer. Chen would be pretty banged up and bruised when he woke up, but he would live.

Grace Farrington needed three stitches to a gash in her forehead and she had suffered a concussion, the blast had thrown her into a doorframe knocking her unconscious. The doctor said that once she was stitched up, she would need to rest under observation overnight. Grace had insisted on being released and had gone to see how Sian and Major Timms were.

Major Timms had a small contusion on the back of his head but apart from that, the old Royal Marine was fine. Once Sian had placed the letter bomb onto the desk Timms had thrown her toward the doorway onto the floor. When the bomb exploded, the blast radius was focused mainly upwards away from the desk. The vests that they wore had protected the vital internal organs from the blast. Timms managed to throw Sian and himself to the floor out of the main blast area. Sian had been cut on the head by some flying debris and the shock wave had stunned her motionless for several minutes.

His team was alive and apparently causing the concerned doctors and nurses no end of problems by refusing to stay in hospital for observation. They were three people that you really didn't want to argue with.

Tank leaned against the desk and breathed a sigh of relief. They had been lucky today; they'd been very lucky indeed. Tank signalled through the office window and gestured to the fat controller to come into the office. David Bell was doing his best to coordinate the organised chaos in the office. Most of the suspects had been transferred to holding cells and interview rooms. The process of interrogation and verification had already begun.

This was not the same as a normal investigation when a suspect can only be held for twenty-four hours before being either charged or released. In theory a criminal suspect is presumed innocent until proven guilty. Terror suspects in the UK are guilty until presumed innocent and can be held in custody for twenty-eight days without being charged.

The fat controller entered the room, he was sweating profusely. He pulled out a chair from beneath the desk and collapsed into it, he wiped sweat from his forehead as he sat down.

'How are the others, is there any news?' asked Dave Bell.

'They are all a bit battered and bruised but apart from Chen, they are on their way back. They were bloody lucky though.' Tank nodded toward an older man who was being processed in the main office.

'Is he the Cleric? Bring him in here, let's have a quick chat with him,' said Tank, his face reddened. This holy man may not have had any active part in what was going on in his community around him, but his tolerance of it was unacceptable to Tank. He must have known something about what was going on in his community. David Bell removed his round glasses as he spoke,

'I have spoken to Mustapha Ahmed at some length and I think he would be willing to help us out if we are careful.'

Tank raised his eyebrows in surprise and gestured with his hands for the fat controller to continue.

'We need to know where Yasser Ahmed is. He is the brain behind these fanatics, he is their inspiration. The majority of the Muslim community would want him caught as much as we do. We need to identify if any of the suspects that we detained last night would recognise Yasser Ahmed in the flesh.' Dave Bell raised his hands palms up as if he had revealed something invisible.

'I think I am getting your drift. If we were to bring Mustapha through the office in handcuffs, the family resemblance is so strong, that to a casual acquaintance he would appear to be Yasser.' Tank stood up mulling the idea over in his mind. It could certainly give them a good indication as to who had actually met Yasser Ahmed. In reality, it would prove nothing from a legal standpoint, but it could be a start.

'I think it would give us a starting place. We could have arrested some of Ahmed's followers tonight, but he is still out there. We need to try it. Let's get the cleric in here and then we can walk Mustapha by the window and see what his reaction is,' Tank said.

The fat controller walked out of the office, hoisting his trousers up over his ample belly as he went. He approached the old man; spoke to him briefly and then escorted him back toward the goldfish bowl. They stepped inside the office and he indicated to the cleric to sit down in the chair opposite Tank.

'My name is Tankersley. I am the lead officer for the Terrorist Task Force. You are in serious trouble at the moment. Everything we have to go on is pointing toward your mosque and the people who use it. We've lost an officer tonight and we have four more in hospital so, I suggest you tell us everything you know about Yasser Ahmed.' Tank nodded to the fat controller who was standing behind the seated cleric. He walked out of the room following the plan they had devised earlier.

'I am a man of God, Officer Tankersley, and I have no dealings with men like Yasser Ahmed. I do not teach the radical interpretations of Islam, in fact, I am in a constant struggle for the hearts and minds of my people. It is especially difficult with the young ones. Your government invades Islamic countries and occupies its people at will. You give Yasser Ahmed and men like him all the ammunition they need. My community is made from good people. We are not terrorists and we will give no support to them.' The cleric finished speaking as Mustapha Ahmed was taken past the window of the office in handcuffs. The cleric looked at him as he went by and then looked back at Tank. There was nothing. Not even a flicker of recognition appeared in his eyes.

Tank immediately knew that the holy man was telling the truth. He had no knowledge of who Mustapha Ahmed was, of that he was certain.

'A letter bomb exploded in your office earlier, injuring some of my officers. It was sent from Dublin. We also discovered a receipt for a payment to a private charter company, relating to a small aircraft that was rented to fly to Southern Ireland. We also have a Usef Mamood in custody. He was arrested crossing from Ireland with a car full of Semtex. He used your mosque regularly. Now I am not Sherlock Holmes, but I suspect that someone from your mosque is involved with Yasser Ahmed and that they are in possession of a large number of high explosives. I also suspect that they are planning to blow up lots of innocent people.' Tank didn't think that the old man was involved, but someone at the mosque was.

The Muslim cleric seemed to sag in the middle of his body. His eyes looked red and watery; his face had turned an ashen grey colour.

'I have an administration assistant called Tariq. He came to us shortly after the Invasion of Iraq in 2003. He was a refugee. He lost his entire family to an American bomb. They were all at a family wedding when the Americans launched an air strike. They said that they believed they had attacked an insurgent hideout. He was the only one to survive the attack. The international Red Cross brought him to Britain and placed him with us. I knew that he was very bitter, and I have urged him to seek forgiveness. I realised not long ago, that he had become involved with some of the more radical young men that pray in my mosque.' The old cleric looked tired and saddened as he spoke.

Tank stood up and walked to the window. He looked out at the river which looked black and oily at night.

'Where can I find Tariq? I need to speak to him as soon as possible.'

The old man shook his head slowly.

'I heard rumours among the congregation that something was imminent. I did not suspect that it was the arrival of this man Yasser Ahmed. Tariq started behaving strangely, he became secretive and distant. Then he became frightened. I think that he had become involved in something that scared him greatly. I challenged him one day to look into his heart, and to see if he could become a part of something that would cause others as much pain as he had suffered. Whatever it was, he said that he was sorry, and that he was going to do the right thing. He left and I haven't seen or heard from him since. I'm beside myself with worry about him. I feel that I've driven him away.'

Tank thought about what the man was saying. It made sense that cleric had little to do with the daily administration tasks. The man he had named as Tariq would have had ample opportunity to camouflage his subversive activities. It would also explain why the letter bomb had stayed unopened.

'Let's assume for one minute that I believe what you're telling me is the truth, I will need to know which men Tariq knew that were causing you concern. Who were the two men asleep in the dormitory at the mosque?' Tank summonsed an officer into the room with his hand. He asked for some hot drinks to be brought into the office.

'They are refugees from Darfur. Our Muslim brothers there are being hunted and slaughtered in their thousands by Somalia warlords. They were also brought to us by the International Red Cross. They speak no English at all I am afraid. As for the young men that I was concerned about, they have not been to prayers since Tariq disappeared. They will not be welcome in our mosque any longer.'

An officer appeared in the doorway with two plastic cups of a coffee like substance. It was from the vending machine and could pass as tea or coffee; only the forensic team could identify which it was through chemical analysis.

Suddenly, there was the sound of raised voices and people cheering coming from the far side of the office near to the elevators. Tank looked up and smiled as he saw Major Timms strolling through the office making mock regimental salutes to everyone as he walked. The noise increased and there were wolf whistles made as Faz and Sian followed Timms, sporting head bandages. There were lots of hugs exchanged as they greeted their relieved colleagues.

Tank excused himself from the office and left the old cleric to drink his coffee alone. He was glad to see his friends alive and well. He spoke briefly to a junior officer and told him to arrange for the holy man to be returned to his mosque. He could be of no more help to them and Tank wanted to keep him as much on side, as was possible.

'Hello, ladies, I really do like the bandaged head look. It suits both of you.' Tank hugged them at the same time, one in each of his big arms. He smiled at Timms over Faz's shoulder.

'I believe you probably saved their lives, sir, well done. I really think you two ladies should go home and get some sleep.'

Timms agreed with Tank. None of them had slept much for the last forty-eight hours. The raids had netted several key pieces of information and experts were interrogating all the men arrested.

'I think that we should call it a night and meet bright and early in the morning. Go home and get some rest.'

CHAPTER 33

Yasser – Liverpool

Yasser and Yasmine parked the Honda Blackbird next to a metal railing in front of a four storey Victorian town house in Anfield, Liverpool. They had travelled without incident along the M62 Motorway from Warrington. The town house was part of a terraced row of similar buildings. There were four large stone steps leading up to a huge wooden front door. The ancient gloss paint was cracked and peeling exposing the layers beneath. The steps themselves had ornate iron railings on either side of them. The railings were cracked and rusted. Another set of stone steps went down to a dingy basement apartment whose door was beneath the stairs above. The building was old and covered in green moss. The paintwork on the window frames was cracked and peeling. The wide arched windows were covered from the insides with blankets and dirty net curtains that belonged in a skip. Either side of the tall house the properties were boarded up ready for renovation or more likely demolition.

This part of the city was not a desirable area to live in anymore. Unlike the days when the port of Liverpool was in its heyday, merchant ship men would have owned these once ornate Victorian buildings, but now they belonged to the drug addicts and prostitutes that infested the area, the area was rife with crime. Yasmine fastened a thick safety chain around the motorbike and locked it to the rusty metal railings.

Yasser led the way down the dark slippery stone steps to the small door at the bottom. The steps and the area below were littered with old fast food cartons and empty beer bottles. The whole area smelled of rotting food and garbage. He opened the door and went inside shutting the door behind them. Yasmine was surprised when he switched on the light how deceiving outside appearances could be. The basement apartment had two bedrooms that led off the living area and an open-plan kitchen. Two big black sofas dominated the room. The laminate wooden floors had sheepskin rugs scattered randomly about making the flat feel warm and comfortable. It smelled of saffron and spices.

Yasser took a mobile phone from a worktop in the kitchen and switched it on. It started to vibrate in his hand and beeped noisily. He opened the text messages and read them. They were from one of his affiliates, Nasser. Nasser was the Egyptian pillion rider who had escaped the police in Warrington after shooting one of them dead. Yasser rang him immediately.

Nassir informed Yasser of the evening's events, the distribution centre shooting and the raid on the mosque. They were of little concern to him. The warehouse containing the ice cream vans was undetected, and none of the men who knew of its existence had been taken in for questioning. Not alive anyway. Yasser was amused by the fact that the police had raided a mosque with armed police. Actions of this nature just widened the gap between Christians and Muslims. The old cleric that had been arrested knew nothing of his whereabouts or his plans. The man they'd used from the mosque, Tariq was dead; Yasser had slit his throat himself. His body had been weighted down and dumped into the River Mersey with the hands and head removed to hamper any efforts to identify him should he be found. Nassir had escaped with his life, which was also good, because Nassir was his scuba diver. He was making his way to him now by train, to Lime St. Station in the city centre. It was a short taxi ride from there to Anfield.

Everything was still going to plan, except that was, for his property owner. Members of his group Axe had rented the apartment for two years. Several fugitives from the law had sheltered behind its inconspicuous façade. The problem was that property values in the Anfield area had doubled when Liverpool was awarded City of Culture status. It entitled the city's property owners to apply for a whole raft of grants that were now available. They could be used to demolish and renovate run down parts of the city. Yasser's landlord owned the whole block above him, and he wanted them to vacate the basement, so that he could demolish the ramshackle buildings and build new, more lucrative ones in their place. The rental agreement had now expired, and the landlord had threatened legal action to evict them from the apartment. He had threatened to call the police in if they did not vacate.

Yasser needed this location for his plans to work. He couldn't risk a visit from the police at any costs. In a last-ditch effort to keep the property, Yasser had offered to buy the whole block from the landlord at an inflated price. Yasser did not intend to complete the deal he was just stalling for time. Yasser had arranged to meet his landlord at the apartment tonight, to talk business. There was a knock on the door.

Yasmine opened the door and a little weasel of a man stepped in wearing a crooked grin and a cheap black suit. His suit trousers were too short, so they exposed the soiled white socks that he was wearing with his slip-on loafer shoes. His name was Paul Tomas. Tomas, who was originally from London, had been a crook and a fraudster all his life. Even as a schoolboy he made money from his fellow pupils by wheeling and dealing. He would sell anything that he could get his sticky little hands on, out-of-date potato crisps, second-hand porn magazines, and single cigarettes. As he got older, he progressed to drugs and stolen property, but he crossed some dangerous men along the way and had to leave London in a hurry. He moved north to

126

Kingston upon Tyne and started up a franchise business; he called it Cleani-Kingdom. He invested a great deal of time making sure the advertising was glossy and slick. The advertising made it look like a genuine business venture and it persuaded people to invest huge sums of money into cleaning contracts that were unprofitable and useless. He was responsible for hundreds of financially ruined lives.

With his ill-gotten gains he had started buying properties around the Liverpool area. He was taking the gamble that the prices would boom if the city won the culture awards. It had worked, the city won its valued award and his portfolio of property would eventually make him a millionaire.

He was an odd-looking little man. He had started to go bald at an early age, which made him look much older than his years. In the early 1990s he took out a bank loan to pay for what was then, a pioneering hair transplant. The surgeons had removed plugs of his own hair from the back of his head and transplanted them to the top. It had left him with a wide ugly scar on the back of his scalp were the hair plugs had been removed. He looked as if he had been hit with an axe from the rear view. His new transplanted hair had the appearance of a child's doll, the clumps of transplanted hair looking ridiculous on his bald head. Yasmine disliked the grinning little weasel instantly.

Yasser put on a warm coat and walked toward Tomas, ushering him back out of the door.

'I thought that you could show me the condition of the surrounding properties. I am intending to renovate and restore them rather than demolishing them,' Yasser lied convincingly.

Paul Tomas looked disappointed. The buildings were just empty shells that had been boarded up to keep the junkies out. He did not really feel like playing at estate agents in the dark. The problem he had was that this Arabian man, Yasser someone, had offered twice the asking price for the whole block. He also remembered that when Yasser's affiliates had signed the original two-year rental agreement; they paid the whole amount in cash up front. *Wherever there is oil there is money*, he thought. He sighed and walked back up the dark steps to his car. He opened the boot and took out a flashlight and a large bunch of keys.

Yasser walked toward the far end of the terrace and stood expectantly in front of the building. Tomas fiddled around with a large bunch of shiny silver keys, finally coming up with the correct one. He fumbled with the lock and opened the metal grill that covered the entrance. The original wooden door was long gone. Yasser moved in front of Tomas and headed straight up the rotten staircase, the property owner tried to keep up with him, the flashlight cast dark shadows in the dank building. Yasser could smell damp and vermin; the stench was overpowering, but he turned the corner and climbed up the second flight of stairs, anyway.

127

'Listen, Mr Yasser, we really shouldn't be using these staircases. I'm sure you can get a reasonable idea of the condition of the buildings from what you have seen so far.' The weasel landlord shone the beam around the room at the top of the stairs, but Yasser was gone. He thought that he must have taken the third flight up to the top floor, so he shone the beam up the stairs into the pitch-blackness. No daylight at all could penetrate the boarded windows; the darkness beyond his torch beam seemed almost solid.

Yasser stepped out from an empty bedroom further down the corridor, making the little man jump with fright.

'I am sorry to keep you, Mr Tomas, but I need to be certain in my own mind that the properties are repairable. Am I keeping you from your wife and family?' Yasser enquired; his answer would dictate which direction this encounter would take.

'No, the bitch left me last year and took the kids with her. They moved back to London. I'm living the bachelor life again… I've never been happier. I have a different woman every night.' Paul Tomas didn't realise he had signed his own death warrant.

'I am sure that you have to pay for the women to be with you. They would not do it freely I am certain.' Yasser goaded the weasel. Paul Tomas looked offended and a bit confused; he couldn't understand why this Arabian man had suddenly decided to insult him.

Yasser moved quickly and his hands were imperceptible in the torchlight. He stabbed his middle and index fingers into the landlord's eyes blinding him. Paul Tomas dropped to his knees; his hands instinctively covered his throbbing eyeballs. Yasser stepped behind the little bald man and slit his throat with the box cutter blade that he always kept hidden up his sleeve. The jugular vein was severed completely, and Yasser could smell warm blood as it sprayed from the artery. Tomas opened his eyes in total bewilderment as all the years of defrauding people flashed before him. He clutched at the massive gash in his throat and his blood soaked into his cheap suit and ran down his arms. Paul Tomas fell to the floor and thrashed about for a few minutes as he bled to death. All he could think about as he choked on his own blood was the people he had ruined and the overpowering smell of rat urine.

The blood seemed to disappear into rotten wooden floorboards as Yasser pulled Tomas's body by the legs into the bedroom he'd been in earlier. Someone had pulled up the floorboards to salvage the copper central heating pipes that once warmed the house. Yasser stuffed the body down into the void between floors and hurriedly placed the rotten floorboards over him. He had taken his wallet, mobile phone, and car keys from the body already. By the time the body was discovered the rats would have made him unidentifiable. Yasser doubted that anyone would report the nasty little man missing for weeks. By that time, the building would have served its purpose and Yasser would be gone. Yasser would have the dead man's vehicle hidden for now. The little fraudster had finally been shafted himself, permanently.

CHAPTER 34

At Home

Major Stanley Timms stood in his living room. He had a thick crystal glass in his hand half-full of Jack Daniels. He sipped the amber fluid and relaxed as he felt the warming sensation descending to his stomach. When he had arrived home earlier, he had showered; the hot water soothed his bruised body. His muscles were beginning to stiffen and become sore from the impact of the bomb blast. He had donned his favourite dressing gown and slippers and then joined his long-suffering wife in their living room. They had been married for thirty-years. Ceria, his wife was a French Vietnamese national. Born in Vietnam to Vietnamese parents, she had been orphaned at a young age and was then adopted by French parents. They had met when the Major had completed a tour of duty in war torn Cambodia. He had been on two weeks leave in neighbouring Vietnam and had met Ceria in an art gallery. She was a beautiful oriental woman with stunning dark eyes and a smile that lit up the room. Timms had fallen in love the first time he laid eyes on her and they married shortly after.

Ceria passed her husband the crystal glass with his favourite tipple in it. She could see that he was troubled by the events of that day. They chatted a while about what had taken place, Stanley was always sad when he lost a man.

He looked from his window out over the River Mersey. They had lived in this house for twenty-years; the views of the estuary below persuaded them to buy it. Helsby Hill was six miles from Liverpool city centre. The views from the hill were spectacular. To the left were open fields and river marshes and the rolling peaks of North Wales rose in the distance. In front and to the right, the Mersey estuary twisted its way to the Irish Sea. The river at this point is some three miles wide. The right-hand bank of the river was the home to a huge chemical processing plant. ICI manufactured fertilisers and paint ingredients. The chemical processes involved the use of thousands of gallons of water necessary for cooling huge tanks of chemicals. Hence its site on the bank of the river where there was an endless supply of water. The plant took on the appearance of a small city at night, thousands of lights illuminating the metal structures that stood on the riverbank.

The left-hand bank was the home of another large industrial plant called Stanlow Oil Refinery. Dozens of large white metal tanks stood in geometric rows housing millions of gallons of crude oil, petrol, diesel, and high-octane jet fuel. Tankers from all over the world sailed in and out of the Mersey estuary delivering their precious black cargo. At the centre of the oil refinery was a tall white metal chimney that stood over one hundred feet tall. From the top of the chimney a permanent flame could be seen from miles around. Timms looked from one riverbank to the other slowly and sighed shaking his head. There were Soft Targets everywhere he looked, and he couldn't guard them all.

'What is the matter, Stanley? What are you thinking?' Ceria walked to him and hugged him tightly, hurting his bruised ribs. He winced sharply and laughed.

'You don't want to know what I'm thinking, my love, it really doesn't matter.'

CHAPTER 35

Grace Farrington

Faz put her coat onto the back of a kitchen chair and sat down. She rubbed at the bandage on her head; the stitches that she had received for the wound on her scalp were starting to itch. She stood and walked over to the fridge. She opened the door and took out a cold bottle of Pinot Grigio. Grace always bought this type of wine because it had the twist open top. She hated trying to use a corkscrew. She poured herself a large glass full and headed for the bathroom taking a big sip of the cool wine on the way. She picked up the remote control for the stereo system and pressed play, Oasis started playing through speakers that were wired up all over the house.

She took another sip of wine and looked at her reflection in the mirrored tiles that covered one wall of the bathroom completely. She chuckled to herself when she saw the bulky dressing on her head. *That is just so not cool, Grace*, she thought. She turned her head to the side and peeled the bandage gently from the wound. The blood had started to form a scab already and she had to pull a little harder than was comfortable. Grace dropped the bloody dressing into the small stainless-steel waste bin that lived beneath the sink. She looked at the neat stitches and decided that any scaring would be minimal. Grace turned and reached into the glass shower cubicle and switched on the hot water. She let it run for a while so that it could reach the perfect temperature while she undressed. She stood naked in front of the mirrored wall and looked at her body, turning one way then the next. Grace liked her body, she was lean and muscular, her breasts stood up on their own. Her black skin accentuated her physique; she narrowed at the waist and then curved at the hip. Her stomach was flat and defined with a small diamond piercing through her belly button. She ran her hands down her smooth lean body feeling the firmness of her breasts and the softness of her skin. 'You're looking good for your age, Grace Farrington,' she said as she stepped into the shower. She let the water run onto her skin soothing the troubles of the past few days away.

Grace heard the front door opened with a key and then shut again. She heard heavy footsteps heading toward the bathroom and she froze, holding her breath. The door opened and the man stepped into the room. She smiled and said,

'What took you so long?' She arched her body provocatively.

'I couldn't get away from Timms. Is there room in there for two?' Tank was unfastening his shirt as he spoke.

CHAPTER 36

Sian and Mustapha

'Why didn't the cleric from the mosque recognise you?' one of the agents that had been assigned to protect Mustapha asked.

'He must be relatively new to the mosque; he wasn't there when I lived in Warrington,' Mustapha said.

The agent nodded silently and looked out of the window of the Jeep. They were driving through Toxteth, an area of Liverpool that had suffered huge race riots in the 1970s, on the way to a safe house. Sian squeezed Mustapha's hand in support; he looked tired from the hours of questioning that he had received. Sian had been asked by the fat controller to keep Mustapha positive about helping the taskforce to capture his brother. She would have to use their relationship to manipulate him if needs be; she decided to stay in Liverpool with Mustapha for a few nights. It wouldn't be a very romantic experience staying in a safe house with two goons hovering around all night.

They were heading for an area of the city called Woolton. The area was a wealthy part of leafy suburbia and was heavily populated with Jewish families. There was a synagogue and a Jewish burial ground in proximity to each other. On top of a small hill, which was surrounded by open parkland, there stood an old sandstone building. The building was tall and Gothic in design; it had a sandstone perimeter wall and big iron gates to the front. The gates were locked with a heavy rusted chain and an old padlock, there was a large coat of arms welded to the gates. 'Newborough Preparatory School' the crest read, but it had been many years since the building had heard the voices of young children in its grounds. The old building looked more like an asylum than a school.

One of the agents opened the gates and the other drove the vehicle into what was once the old playground. The concrete school yard still had wooden benches dotted around its edges, but they were now green with moss. There would have been many games played here in the playground once upon a time, little girls running around giggling while the little boys battled it out with conkers tied to a piece of string. Now large hinged wooden shutters covered the windows of the old school making it look deserted and foreboding.

'What is this place?' asked Mustapha, he was curious about this unusual building and also a little concerned.

Sian laughed as she opened the door and stepped from the Jeep. Mustapha followed closely behind her. Sian climbed the three mossy steps to the front door and swiped her identity card through a reader that was hidden behind a thick wooden mailbox. The front door clicked and then opened, and Sian entered first.

Mustapha stepped out of the darkness of the playground into a brightly lit reception area. The interior of the building was bright and new, the floors were oak wood block shined and polished.

'This is a safe house that the taskforce uses. From the outside it just looks like an old school, which it is. Inside we have accommodation, control rooms, and a great big kitchen. I'm starving let's get something to eat,' Sian said.

She headed toward the rear of the building where a wide sweeping staircase that led to the first floor. They went by a large room full of banks of computers. Three men sat staring at the screens undisturbed by their presence. They walked down a small flight of stairs into a large kitchen area. Sian put water into a silver kettle and switched it on to make coffee. She took four cups from a mug tree and put powdered coffee into each one. Mustapha put his hand gently to the bandage on the side of her head.

'Does it hurt?' he asked.

'A little but it could have been much worse. The Major saved my bacon today.' She reached behind his head and pulled him forward into a gentle kiss.

'I am going to do whatever I can to help you to catch my brother,' he whispered quietly and kissed her again.

Sian kissed him harder and pushed her body gently against him. The tension of the previous days had dulled her senses but now they were stirring again.

'I'm not tired anymore,' she said. 'Let's go to bed.'

CHAPTER 37

Newborough Preparatory School

Sian was woken from her sleep by the ringing phone on the bedside table. She was in the bedroom of the accommodation suite located on the upper floors of the old school. Mustapha stirred next to her. She picked up the handset and listened to the excited voice on the other end of the telephone. The old preparatory school that they were staying in was used as a listening post for the government's security services. The basement and the ground floor areas were packed with receivers that picked up information from all over the northern part of the country. Telephone taps, bugging devices, surveillance cameras, and a thousand hidden microphones all relayed their information to the equipment fitted into the old school. MI5, MI6, and the Terrorist Task Force all had their operatives using the information from this facility.

When Chen and his surveillance team bugged the house in Warrington, they'd placed motion trackers inside as many items as they could, in the time given. They then entered the corresponding code of the bugging devices into a computer, which identified the item into which the bugs were planted.

One of the bugs that Chen had planted was now moving at speed. Alarm bells were ringing all the over the country as the TTF was alerted to the situation.

The agent on the telephone informed Sian and she got out of the bed and quickly dressed. Mustapha snored quietly in the warm bed. She left the accommodation suite situated on the fourth floor of the old school. It had once been a science laboratory for young children, but the gas taps and Bunsen burners had long since been removed. The accommodation suite was the temporary home for tired agents from a myriad of security services. It was also used as a safe house for high profile informants, whose lives could be threatened.

She headed down the wide wooden staircase, her footsteps echoed through the open stairwell. She entered the ground floor control room that she had seen earlier with Mustapha; the room was busy with excited security agents.

'What have we got?' asked Sian as she scanned the bank of screens that filled the wall in front of her. On the centre screen was the image of a motorbike which was being ridden at speed on a motorway that she didn't recognise.

'We have a motion sensor that has been tagged to a Scuba diving wet suit. It was picked up from a marked address in Warrington ten minutes ago, by the rider of this

136

motorbike, which we know is a Honda Blackbird with false registration plates fitted to it.' The surveillance agent never took his eyes from the screen as he spoke. He was concentrating on a small joystick in front of him. This was the control for the pilotless helicopter drone that was silently following the Honda.

'The wet suit is in the rucksack that the rider is carrying, and the bike is heading west on the M62 motorway toward Liverpool. We are using the drone to follow it and we have the bike on visual. The Terrorist Task Force has been informed, and there is an armed response team on the roundabout eight miles ahead of the target. They are on the Tarbock Motorway Island at the junction with the M57. The section of the motorway that they are positioned on is elevated. The motorbike will pass underneath their position in approximately four minutes,' another agent said talking into a telephone on a desk to the right of the screens.

'I've got Inspector Tankersley on the line for you,' he said passing the handset to Sian. Sian took the handset from the agent and spoke to Tank.

'Who do you think the motorbike rider is, Sian?' Tank asked. He couldn't see the visual information that was in front of Sian.

'We don't know who it is yet. Whoever it is, they knew where to find that wet suit. All the occupants of that house are in our interrogation rooms in the city, except for one man. He is an Egyptian national called Nassir al-Masri. He is registered on the electoral roll as having lived at that address for six months, but he wasn't arrested at the distribution centre raid. He is the most likely suspect for the shooting of our officer at the raid in Warrington. We have to assume that he's armed and dangerous.' Sian summarised for Tank.

'Well, if it's him he has escaped from us once already, we can't risk losing him again. If he's heading toward Liverpool, he could be going straight to the river with that Scuba gear. Can you get the x-ray from the drone on to that rucksack to tell us if he is carrying explosives?' Tanks voice had come through the room's speakers.

'I am switching to X-ray now,' a surveillance agent said. He was controlling the remote drone. The camera that was sending images to the centre screen on the wall zoomed in on the rider's rucksack. The picture changed to a black-and-white image. The X-ray penetrated the material and photographed the contents that were inside the rucksack.

'We have a mobile phone in the side pocket which could be used as a detonator. There is some non-metallic bulky material, which is probably the wet suit. There is also a cylindrical container in the bag. It could be explosives, but it could just as easily be a bottle of liquid, even water.'

'Where is the bike now?' Tank asked.

'Just passing the old Burtonwood Air Base, he's now six miles from the Armed Response Unit. If he passes the Response Teams' position, he'll be three miles away from the River Mersey Tunnels. If he takes the bike into one of those tunnels, we'll lose him completely,' said the drone's pilot.

There were three traffic tunnels beneath the River Mersey, each crossed from the city centre to the town of Birkenhead, which was three miles away, on the opposite bank. The tunnel entrances were in the city centre. Inside the tunnels there was a labyrinth of ventilation shafts and small access tunnels that a fugitive could hide in.

'Is it possible that we could put a roadblock across the M62 to stop him before he reaches the city?' Sian asked; being from Holyhead she was unfamiliar with the local motorway networks.

'There are too many exit roads between the target and the city centre. He could use any one of a number of them to escape. We need to take him out before he gets there.' The drone's pilot turned briefly to look at Sian emphasising his point.

A digital printer on the desk lit up as a profile of the target was sent electronically from the CIA headquarters in Langley USA. The target's name had tripped a software programme that allowed security services worldwide to share information.

'Nassir al-Masri is the CIA's top suspect for the bombing of the USS Cole in 2000. She was an American destroyer that was anchored in the Yemen when extremists sailed a small boat alongside her and blew a huge hole in the side. CIA pointed the finger at al-Qaeda, but it looks like Axe was involved now.' Sian read the information out for everyone to hear.

The room remained silent for what seemed like an eternity as they waited for orders to be given.

'Put the drone in front of him and see if he is willing to stop. If he doesn't stop, then order the Armed Response Team to drop him before he reaches the city.'

Tank gave the order. The choice to live or die was now the motorbike rider's decision.

The drone's remote pilot flew the helicopter directly over the speeding motorbike. He turned the engines from silent mode to normal. The sudden booming noise from the helicopters' rotor blades as it flew above startled the motorbike's rider. The bike veered across two lanes of motorway before the rider regained complete control. A powerful spotlight mounted beneath the drone illuminated the Honda with its dazzling beam. The drone hovered only metres above the road surface in an attempt to stop the bike.

The remote pilot activated a loudspeaker on the helicopter and demanded that the rider stop the Honda. The motorbike veered around the hovering drone and accelerated by it

138

heading toward the city. The bike was now just two miles from the Armed Response Teams position, in just over a minute's time the motorbike would pass beneath some of the country's best sharpshooters.

'He has not responded. I will place the drone in front of the motorbike again to obscure the riders view as he approaches the armed unit.' The agent remotely flew the drone overhead the speeding Honda Blackbird and shone the dazzling beam onto the target. The motorbike increased its speed again trying to escape the blinding light.

'Have we stopped normal traffic from entering the motorway?' Tank asked through the room's speakers.

'Yes, sir, the area is clear. We have thirty seconds before he is in range, Sir.' The surveillance agent focused a second camera from the drone to the Armed Response Teams position. They were positioned ready to take out a moving target. Four men wearing full body armour were lying prone on the elevated section of motorway above the targets route. They were aiming 0.5 calibre Barrett sniper rifles. Each sniper had a section of road to aim for. They would fire at one second intervals to counteract the oncoming speed of the Honda until the target dropped.

'Tell the Armed Unit that they have my authority to fire.' Tank had to think long and hard about the decision to shoot at an unidentified target. The risks of allowing a potential bomber to escape gave him no option but to take the shot.

'Armed Response Unit, you have a green light to engage the target. Inspector John Tankersley has given full authorisation. Lethal force is required.' Sian relayed the order to the firearms unit. Lethal force was ordered in case the target was carrying explosives; a wounded man could still press a detonator button, and so they had to make sure he was dead.

The four snipers from the Armed Response Unit simultaneously chambered a 0.5 calibre bullets into the firing chambers and deactivated the safety catches. The Honda Blackbird came into sight, spotlighted by the helicopter drone.

The rider of the Honda saw only two of the four muzzle flashes that lit up above the motorway, before they died. The huge high velocity shells tore baseball size holes in the rider's chest, smashing and tearing vital organs. The fourth bullet had shattered the face guard of the crash helmet before splintering the teeth and jawbone of the Honda's rider. The Honda Blackbird scraped along the motorway for a hundred yards before it stopped, leaving a shower of sparks behind as it travelled.

Mustapha had been standing in the corridor outside of the control room for about five minutes he was mesmerised by the action on the big screen, and also a little shocked at what he had just witnessed. The man who appeared to be controlling the pictures was zooming in on the dead motorbike rider. The face guard had gone, as had the face behind it, and it had been replaced a bloody mess of bone and tissue. He watched as heavily armoured men approached the dead rider. They were still aiming their guns at the body as if it may suddenly come to life and attack them. The men removed the rucksack using sharp combat knives on the straps and they made it safe by placing it into a thick lead blast proof bin that two of them carried.

They searched the pockets of the rider and removed a small leather wallet. The jeans that the rider had been wearing were in tatters due to hitting the road surface at high speed. Another agent unzipped the leather motorcycle jacket that the rider was wearing, and he looked up at the on-looking officers an expression of shock and horror was on his face. He stood up and snatched the small leather wallet from the hands of the agent who had removed it and opened it quickly.

'Who gave the order to shoot? This is a woman. We've just shot a fucking woman.' The Armed Response Team men started to remonstrate with each other on the screen.

'Are you sure the target's female, the face looks pretty messed up from here?' Asked the drone's remote pilot.

'The last time I looked women had breasts, right? This body has got breasts.'

Mustapha looked at the small photo identity card that the agent on the screen was holding. The picture was of his older sister Yasmine. He had just watched Sian giving the orders that resulted in the death of his sister, and he couldn't cope. Mustapha turned and walked toward the big wooden front door of the old school in total shock, opening it he stepped out into the cold night air unseen by anyone inside. Yasser had caused this terrible thing to happen, and Mustapha had no doubt that his brother and his followers had been responsible for Yasmine's shooting. He walked through the big rusting metal gates into the night.

CHAPTER 38

Yasmine Ahmed

The dead woman's identity card confirmed that she was Yasmine Ahmed. As far as mistakes go this one was a classic. A preliminary search of the woman's rucksack confirmed that it contained no explosive materials, but there was a scuba diving wet suit and a mask that had been tagged by surveillance agents in the bag, and there was also a two-litre bottle of mineral water and a mobile telephone. To all intents and purposes, she was an innocent young woman, riding her motorcycle.

To top it all Mustapha Ahmed had escaped protective custody during all the commotion and was nowhere to be found. All the agents from the Terrorist Task Force had been summoned to the top floor of the station in Liverpool city centre.

Tank was stood by the window looking at the River Mersey. The weather was wet, and the sky was still gloomy despite it being nearly midday, and the river looked dark green and murky. Major Timms was in the goldfish bowl office. He was pacing up and down with a telephone placed to his ear, and from the look on his face the conversation was not a pleasant one. The Press had already picked up the story and they were having a field day with it. A young Iraqi woman had been shot four times while riding her motorbike. 'Islamophobia hits Liverpool' the tabloids would read later that day, speculation that the young woman was related to the wanted terrorist leader, Yasser Ahmed was rife. Records from Iraq stated unequivocally that Yasmine Ahmed had died in an allied bombing raid near Baghdad, there was no concrete evidence that this woman was Yasser Ahmed's sister and there was no solid evidence that she had left Iraq alive, or that she had ever entered the United Kingdom.

Major Timms put the phone back in its cradle and banged on the glass partition. Tank looked toward the noise and Timms gestured him into the office. David Bell was already seated at the desk opposite Major Timms and he looked very uncomfortable. He was the man that collated information, but the information that had been gathered from the raids in Warrington was useless. The man they knew as Tariq had handled all the money transactions between Dublin and the mosque, but he had been missing since the customs officers made the first arrests in Holyhead. The rest of the information gathered was rumour and speculation, Bell knew that Timms needed solid facts to work on but there were none. Major Timms nodded toward the fat controller indicating that he wanted an immediate update. Tank stood to the side of the desk leaning against the glass wall.

'All the information that we've gathered from our interviews is pointing toward this man called Tariq. He seems to have been the logistical organiser of the arms deals in Dublin. He is also associated with Nassir al-Masri but we don't know the whereabouts of him either. We have concrete proof that Yasser Ahmed, Nassir al-Masri, and Tariq are working together, but nothing beyond that,' David Bell wiped his sweaty brow with a handkerchief.

'What is our theory on Yasmine Ahmed's involvement in all this? The Press is going to have a field day on this one. It won't be long before they link the shootings in Holyhead with the raids in Warrington,' Tank said.

'The forensic evidence recovered from the men that attacked you in Holyhead only confirms what we already know. They were all living in Warrington and working for several employment agencies carrying out temporary work. Sometimes they worked at the distribution centre but not always. They were known to worship occasionally at the mosque there and were friends of Tariq. We've been looking for Yasmine Ahmed ever since Yasser used her identity to enter the country. We can only assume that she went to the marked address in Warrington and picked up the Scuba gear on her brother's instructions. The majority of people that we've interviewed are asylum seekers. They won't jeopardise their residency applications by associating themselves with the incidents that we are investigating,' the fat controller paused for a sip of water.

'I am assuming that Yasmine Ahmed was heading toward Liverpool when she was shot therefore, I am also assuming that Ahmed and his affiliates are in the city somewhere.'

'We need to make a press release that indicates that Yasmine Ahmed was shot whilst being involved in terrorist activity. Tell them nothing more specific than that. As far as the press are concerned you will tell them that the incidents in Holyhead and Warrington are unrelated. I do not want London on our backs while we are looking for this bastard.' The Major stood and pointed at the digital photograph of Yasser Ahmed.

This wouldn't be the first time that the truth was massaged by the security services. After the shooting dead of a Brazilian immigrant following the July 7 bombings in London, the Press was initially reporting that he had run away from and resisted being arrested by, armed security service officers. Eventually the Metropolitan Police issued a full apology stating that the innocent Brazilian had not run away or resisted arrest. He was the victim of mistaken identity. Some members of the public sympathised with the police who had to make a split-second decision. Other sections of the public condemned the killing as police brutality. The door opened suddenly, and Grace Farrington popped her head round it.

'I am sorry to interrupt but the coastguard has just recovered a body from the river.' Grace stepped into the room.

'There would be nothing so unusual about this except that the man they recovered was of Middle Eastern appearance. He has also had his hands and his head removed. The body is with the coroner now. It could be an isolated boating accident; he could have been injured by a propeller blade, but initial reports say that it looks like the injuries were caused deliberately. I've sent some DNA samples that we recovered at the mosque and the house in Warrington to the coroner's office. They can cross reference the tissue from the body found in the river to see it could be our missing man Tariq.'

'The cleric that we interviewed said that Tariq might have been having a change of heart. He had indicated that 'he was going to do the right thing'. It looks like someone disagreed with his good intentions,' Tank said recalling his conversation with the Muslim cleric.

'That could explain the tip-off that the customs office received. It could be that Tariq knew about the explosives coming into the country and decided that enough is enough,' the fat controller said as he headed toward the door. He nodded to Timms as he left indicating that he was going to prepare the press release.

'What are we going to do about Mustapha Ahmed going missing?' Timms asked.

'We've sent his picture to uniformed police officers both here, and in North Wales just in case he heads back to Holyhead. The problem is that he looks so much like his brother. The armed units are on the lookout for Yasser Ahmed. It would be easy to confuse the two of them. We don't need another dead sibling of Yasser Ahmed on our hands.'

Tank and the Major talked about the information that David Bell had summarised earlier. They decided that Sian should return to her undercover position at the customs office in Holyhead. They agreed that Mustapha would more than likely head back there, eventually. It would kill two birds with one stone; Timms was under pressure to discipline Sian for allowing Mustapha to escape from protective custody. He had not informed his superiors in London that Mustapha had probably witnessed the shooting dead of his sister.

Although the investigation had been a roller coaster of events, it seemed that little progress had been made. They still had one of the most dangerous terrorists on the planet at large. They knew for definite that he was in possession of Semtex explosives. The scuba diving gear made them assume that the potential target could be on or near to the River Mersey. The possibilities were endless. Along the length of just ten miles, the River Mersey had an international airport; an oil refinery; a huge chemical processing plant; one of the biggest coal fired power stations in the country; local ferry ports; international ferry ports plus three miles of busy cargo docks. These crucial economic sites were all situated on the riverbanks.

Tank and the Major both agreed that while security on the river could be increased, it would be impossible to stop a determined attack from underwater. The coastguards were already increasing their patrols following Chen's discovery of the scuba equipment in Warrington. The fact that Yasmine Ahmed had tried to retrieve the equipment meant that the focus must be on the River Mersey.

The airport and the oil refinery worried them the most because of their proximity to the water's edge. The oil refinery at Stanlow covers 1900 acres of riverbank, and at any one time can store two million tonnes of crude oil. It had the capacity to produce three million tonnes of petrol and two million tonnes of jet engine fuel every year. An explosion at the refinery would cause an ecological disaster on top of the human cost. Financially an attack on a facility like Stanlow could bring the country to its knees. In recent years the site had been the target of protest against the British government's high taxation on fuel. The protesters had used farm machinery to blockade the refinery stopping fuel tankers from leaving the site. Within twenty-four-hours the effect of strangling fuel supplies brought the north of England to a standstill. Supermarket shelves were empty, and the public couldn't travel to work. Human reliance on the internal combustion engine was highlighted during the protest; without petrol or diesel fuel, nothing moved.

The Terrorist Task Force knew that an attack on this facility or one like it would be devastating. They decided that the site must be a priority red. This was the code given to a potential target if it was felt that an attack was imminent. The international airport at Speke, which was seven and a half miles south-east of Liverpool city centre, was also given a code red status.

The John Lennon Airport was a concern as the main runway, which ran parallel to the riverbank, was less than one hundred yards from the water. A large passenger jet laden with jet engine fuel would make an easy target for a determined terrorist, and the accessibility of airport perimeters was a major headache for security services worldwide. Liverpool was no different to any other passenger airport. It was a 'Soft Target'.

CHAPTER 39

Tariq Al-Masri

Tariq was born in 1986 in the small village of Mukaradeeb in Iraq, near the border with Syria. His father had been a musician, and his mother cared for and educated Tariq and his six siblings. They were raised in the Shia Muslim faith and lived far away from the religious sectarian fighting that the more densely populated areas of Iraq experienced. While the more unfortunate teenagers of Baghdad were learning to make war on the allied forces, Tariq was learning to play the guitar. Tariq and his family were often invited to village weddings to provide the musical entertainment. As most of their neighbours were poor people they were generally paid for their services with food and hospitality.

On May 19, 2004, a wedding was being celebrated in the village which formed a union between two of the largest families from the area. Traditional weddings in this part of the world involved the wedding party and their guests setting up large marquee type tents in the desert outside of the town itself. There the guests would eat and dance to the musicians' music for days. At 3 a.m. on May 19, American forces bombed the wedding using helicopter gunships. Local accounts reported forty-two men woman and children were killed in the attack. Amongst the town's dead were Tariq's entire family.

A military representative for the coalition forces claimed that there was no evidence of a wedding taking place and this was a suspected foreign fighters' camp. A video made during a visit to the site of the massacre, by members of the Associated Press, showed the remains of brightly coloured decorations and musical instruments. The remains of pots and pans and large quantities of food contradicted the military's claims. The reports from local hospitals showed that the bodies of thirteen dead children had been recovered from the bombed-out tent.

The American Major General who was put in charge of the incident was challenged with the video evidence. He replied, 'There may have been some kind of celebration going on, but bad people have celebrations too.'

Tariq had been left an orphan. Once he had recovered from the extensive burns that he had received, the International Red Cross brought him to England. Tariq had been given an administration job at the mosque in Warrington, mainly thanks to the schooling that his dead mother had given him. His grief had turned to hatred during his rehabilitation and soon his hatred was harnessed by the extremists in the community. He had plotted and planned with the conspirators and he used his position in the mosque to mask their activities. Too late he had realised that what was being planned would cause misery and death to more innocent people. He decided that he could no longer be a part of that process. His decision cost him his life. Now the end of his tragic journey had brought his headless mutilated body to the coroner's table.

The coroner Graham Libby switched on his tape recorder and proceeded with his autopsy report.

'The subject is a young male, between the ages of twenty and thirty-five years old. He is of Asian or Middle Eastern origin. The body weighs approximately ten stones, the approximations are because the body is missing the head and both hands. Cause of death was shock and massive haemorrhaging caused by a wound to the throat. The wounds to the arms were inflicted post-mortem. The removal of the head was carried out with a saw of some description, again post-mortem.'

Grace Farrington was attending the autopsy on the Major's instruction. He was desperate to know if the body belonged to Tariq.

'Can you estimate when he died?' Faz asked.

'It's difficult to say because the body has been in the water. The body has gone through different stages of putrefaction, but the limbs are less putrefied than the trunk. Bodies pass through certain stages of disintegration, but the water could have accelerated the process. Hypostasis, or lividity, starts about four hours after death. It is caused by the sinking of red corpuscles in the blood to the lowest part of the body. If the body were found standing for instance, hypostasis would be in the legs and feet. The general discolouration of the skin and the fact that the body has no rigor mortis leads me to believe that the subject was dead at least eighteen hours before it was put into the river. Putrefaction has begun and the body is stained and is starting to distend. Several of the internal organs have started to burst so we are looking at least a week or more, definitely not more than two weeks.'

'That would fit into our missing person profile. How can you be so sure that he has not been dead longer than two weeks?' Faz asked. She wanted to be sure that this was Tariq. There had been enough mistakes made already.

'There are maggots here around the neck wound. They are the third-stage larvae of the common bluebottle fly. The bluebottle fly only lays eggs on fresh meat so we can safely deduce that the eggs were laid within twenty-four hours of death. The larvae become new flies within twelve days. These little fellows are still wriggling about in here so I can assume they are not twelve days old yet.'

'What about identification can you match the tissue to the DNA samples from Warrington?' Faz asked trying to avoid looking at the wriggling maggots.

146

'The test results are not back yet but we know that he is the same blood group. I will call you as soon as they are returned.'

Faz turned and left the laboratory. She took off the gloves and sterile gown and placed them into an industrial laundry bin. She checked her hair in a mirror fixed to the wall above a small hand sink. She was pleased with the image that she saw, and she smiled. Faz was almost certain that the body in the mortuary was Tariq al-Masri. They knew that he had his throat slashed and that the removal of the limbs and head were post-mortem.

Faz considered the removal of the head was to hamper the identification of the body. There was another reason that needed to be considered though. The removal of the head was commonplace among the Islamic extremists in Iraq. It seemed that these groups deemed it to be the ultimate affront to a human being to be beheaded, and Grace had looked at the possibility that Yasser Ahmed and his affiliates were sending some kind of message.

In 2004, a Korean translator, an Italian photographer, and two Bulgarian truck drivers were all beheaded by extremists in Iraq. The message was clear that foreign workers risked their lives if they chose to work in Iraq. If it was considered that they were in any way aiding or working for the coalition forces, then they were legitimate targets. In 2005, more beheading occurred including the decapitation of two Algerian and one Egyptian diplomat, all three were Muslim. The fact that it was seen that they were cooperating with the occupying armies was enough to condemn them to a terrible death. Perhaps poor Tariq had been beheaded for similar reasons. Grace couldn't be certain of the motives behind his death, but she was certain that Yasser Ahmed was responsible. She headed back to the office.

CHAPTER 40

South Stack Lighthouse

Sian left the old Newborough preparatory school and turned right onto Quarry St. She pulled the Jeep into a petrol station and filled the greedy vehicle with fuel. She had over one hundred miles to drive back home to Holyhead, it would take around two hours to make the journey if she stopped for breakfast on route. Sian had been ordered back to the customs unit where she was to oversee the tightened security at the port. Officers were searching for any explosives or munitions that the Irish Republicans may have traded, to stop them reaching the mainland. She was also to look for Mustapha. The general consensus of opinion was that he would head to wherever he felt was home, in this case that would probably be Holyhead.

Sian didn't like to leave the case, but she understood that recovering Mustapha was a priority, after all she had been in charge of his protective custody; it was her responsibility to find him. She put a compilation CD into the disk player as she joined the A55 expressway, which would take her along the North Wales coast to Anglesey. She reached a small Welsh coastal town called Penmaenmawr and decided to stop there and eat breakfast.

She sat by the window in the Little Chef and enjoyed the view across the Straits to Puffin Island. She smiled as she remembered the story that her father had told her about Puffin Island. The island had once been the breeding colony of thousands of puffins however in the early 1900s an old wooden sailing ship had run aground on the treacherous rocks that surrounded it. The rat-infested ship sank quickly, leaving the drowning rats no option but to swim to the safety of Puffin Island. Being an island, it was ecologically isolated and there was little for the rats to eat except Puffin eggs. Puffins nest on the ground where their eggs were an easy meal for the hungry vermin invaders; therefore, Puffin Island no longer had any puffins on it.

She ate breakfast and washed it down with three cups of strong coffee. Sian used the washroom on her way out to the Jeep and brushed her auburn red hair. Feeling refreshed she started the Jeep and pulled back onto the A55 toward the island of Anglesey.

The Britannia Bridge was the crossing point from the Welsh mainland to Anglesey. It would take her twenty minutes to cross the island from the bridge to Holyhead.

Sian drove the Jeep across the island feeling anxious about Mustapha's disappearance. She drove through a small village called Valley, and she could see Holyhead Mountain towering in the distance. The mountain lies about a mile west of the town, which is built at its foot; it slopes steeply down to the Irish Sea on two sides. Sian decided to take the coast road through Treaddur Bay and Porthdafarc beach. She was hoping that Mustapha might have made his way back to his caravan there.

She slowed the Jeep down as she approached 'cow shit corner' looking for evidence of their shoot-out with the Axe men. She shuddered as she looked at the deep holes in the stone wall where bullets had struck. Sand had been sprinkled over the tarmac to cover any bloodstains. There was a solitary bunch of flowers tied to the farm gate. Flowers were generally left at the scene of a death by someone who cared about the deceased. Sian thought this was a bit odd but didn't read too much into it.

The Jeep climbed the crest of the hill away from the scene. As the vehicle came over the crest, Mustapha's caravan came into view on the cliff tops across the bay. The caravan was in darkness, Sian's heart sank. She drove the Jeep up the hill towards her house on the mountain. An idea occurred to her. Mustapha loved the lighthouse that was at the bottom of the mountain; he might have walked there. The South Stack Lighthouse had stood on its little island warning passing ships of the treacherous rocks since 1809. It could be seen from up to twenty-eight miles away. An iron suspension bridge was added in 1828, which crossed the deep-water channel between the island and the mountainside. Before the suspension bridge was built, the only means of crossing to the island was by means of a basket suspended from a hemp cable. Sian drove up the steep mountain road passing her own house on the way. About a mile past her house she reached the car park which serviced the lighthouse and its visitors. The car park was empty apart from an estate car parked in the far corner of the lot. Sian got out of the Jeep and reached inside her jacket for her gun. She opened a lock box positioned between the front seats and placed the Glock inside. She put on a warm coat that was in the back seat over her jacket; the wind on the mountainside was bitterly cold.

She walked toward a gap in the low stone wall that lead to a path which made its way down the mountainside to the lighthouse. She could see the white building perched on its island in the sea below her. Local legend suggests that there are 365 steps descending to the suspension bridge, which leads to the island. It's believed there was one step for each day of the year. In fact, that's just another urban legend. There are actually over 400 steps, which zigzag down the cliff face to the lighthouse bridge. In the summer, the steps are crowded with tourists and birdwatchers. The cliffs at South Stack are home to thousands of sea birds and puffins.

Sian started down the path toward the steps. She descended the first flight of smooth stone steps and reached the first tight turn. The path turned back on itself and descended sharply. Sian looked over the edge of the low wall toward the flights of stairs below her looking for any signs of Mustapha.

She saw him three flights below her, he was walking up the steps toward her. There was another man with him that Sian did not recognise. He was definitely not from Holyhead but then hundreds of people used the area for bird watching, he could just be a tourist. The two men looked up at her simultaneously and stopped their ascent. Sian knew immediately that something was wrong. She reached inside her jacket instinctively and touched the empty holster. The stranger reached toward Mustapha pressing a small revolver into his ribs. Sian was confused by the situation; the man didn't look Asian. She watched as the men started to ascend slowly up the steps the gun was still pointed at Mustapha. Sian quickly stepped back away from the wall and out of sight of the two men. She turned and started to run toward the Jeep. It was at least 200-yards across the heather to the car park.

Rasim Janet was a Bosnian Muslim. He looked like any other white European male. He had been allowed to leave the raid at the cold room in Warrington because the taskforce had focused only on Asian or Middle Eastern men. He was pointing a Colt revolver at the younger brother of his Caliph, Yasser Ahmed. Rasim was born in Sarajevo in 1970. He had still lived in the city when the breakup of Yugoslavia began, and the country descended into civil war. He was trapped in the city with hundreds of thousands of its inhabitants for four years. The siege of Sarajevo is the longest in modern history. The Serbian army surrounded the city in 1992 and laid siege to it for nearly fifty months. Rasim and his fellow Muslim countrymen made up less than a tenth of the city's population. Rasim fought bravely alongside his fellow Muslims, some had travelled from other countries to help their religious kin. Many of the Muslim fighters from the Afghanistan conflict, the Mujahideen, travelled to fight alongside their Muslim brothers in Bosnia.

The Christian Serbian forces carried out a campaign of genocide, seeking the annihilation of the Bosnian Muslims. There were mass killings, mass gang rapes, and torture conducted by different Serbian forces. Rasim escaped the city in 1995 and fled to Poland. As the immigration barriers in Europe began to fall, he travelled to England using a Polish passport; along with hundreds of thousands of other Eastern Europeans looking for work. He headed for the north where rental accommodation was cheap and settled in Warrington. Rasim worked for employment agencies moving from one casual job to the next. It was while working for one of these agencies that he had met Nasser al-Masri. They found that they had a lot in common. Both men had fought as Mujahideen in Muslim struggles against Christian invaders the colour of their skin was irrelevant. It wasn't long before Rasim joined 'Ishmael's Axe'.

Nasser had told Rasim to drive to Holyhead and to look for Mustapha Ahmed. He had waited on the cliff tops opposite Mustapha's caravan with a pair of binoculars. He looked like all the other bird watchers and tourists who visited the island.

When Mustapha arrived at his caravan, he had gone inside only briefly. He came back out shortly after and started walking along the headlands toward South Stack Lighthouse. Rasim had followed at a safe distance until he had Mustapha alone on the steep stone steps that led down to the suspension bridge. He had approached Mustapha in a friendly manner at first but when he mentioned that his brother Yasser had sent him Mustapha had become frightened. That was when he had pulled the gun out. Now he had been spotted by a woman with red hair who seemed to know Mustapha, he could tell by the look on her face when she had leaned over the small wall, this changed the dynamic of the whole situation.

'You had better run because she is a policewoman and she has a gun. Go now while you still can. I don't want to go to my brother. Just leave and say you couldn't find me,' Mustapha hissed at the man.

'Of course, she's a policewoman. Do you think that I'm stupid? There are hundreds of women cops around here carrying guns. Now shut up and keep walking,' Rasim pushed the muzzle of the gun hard into Mustapha's ribs.

'Look, my brother is a lunatic and I don't want anything to do with him. My sister has just been shot because of that bastard. He is not worth the trouble that he'll cause you. Whatever he is paying I'll double it, please just let me go.' Mustapha finished what he was saying when Rasim punched him hard in the solar plexus. The breath in his lungs was forcefully expelled and he dropped to his knees gasping for breath.

'If you were not his brother, I would cut your tongue out and feed it to you, you whining dog. You are not fit to speak about a Muslim warrior of Yasser Ahmed's calibre. How dare you speak of him that way? Do you think that I follow him for money you little pig?' Rasim kicked Mustapha hard in the side of the head jerking it backwards violently.

A high calibre bullet smashed into the low wall a yard to Rasim's left-hand side. Splinters of stone and hot metal spat into face making him lose his balance. Mustapha saw his opportunity as Rasim staggered to maintain his footing on the smooth steps. He lunged at Rasim grabbing him around the knees making him fall backwards down the hard-stone steps.

Rasim tumbled head over heels backwards for what seemed like an age until he hit the low wall which stopped his momentum. He cracked his head on the hard rock and cried out. Warm blood started to trickle down the side of his face. Rasim looked for the gun but he had lost it in the fall. He spotted it lying close to Mustapha who was lying stationary just a few yards away. Mustapha stirred and looked at the gun. Both men launched themselves for the weapon at the same time.

Sian rounded the sharp corner of the second flight of steps and pointed the Glock at the two men as they tumbled down the third tier. She couldn't shoot at the stranger without endangering Mustapha. She ran down the steps keeping her weapon trained on Rasim. *He must have laid the flowers at the scene of the shoot-out*, she thought. He wasn't Asian or Middle Eastern in appearance, which didn't make sense.

The two men collided as they leapt for the weapon. Rasim managed to grab the revolver first. Mustapha punched Rasim hard in the mouth. His lip split as they were forced back against his front teeth, and the coppery taste of blood filled his senses. Rasim grabbed Mustapha by the hair and pulled his face down toward his bleeding lips. He bit down hard on Mustapha's face and twisted his head sharply at the same time. A large flap of cheek flesh tore away from Mustapha's face and he screamed in agony. Rasim was on him in a flash and he pinned his arms together tightly. He smashed the hard bone of his forehead into the fleshy bulb of Mustapha's nose crushing the cartilage and making it bleed profusely. Rasim had fought hand to hand for his life many times during the Bosnian war; he had killed many men with his bare hands. He stood over Mustapha and kicked him violently in the groin. The blood vessels in one of Mustapha's testicles burst under the power of the impact. Mustapha kicked out in desperation knocking the Bosnian over, and he fell on top of Mustapha. Rasim raised his right elbow and smashed it into Mustapha's windpipe, and the blow closed the already winded Mustapha's throat momentarily and he blanked out.

Rasim stood up quickly and turned to face the approaching woman with the gun. A bullet slammed into his shoulder knocking him over the low wall onto the thick heather that clung to the steep cliffs. Rasim lifted himself to his knees and fired twice at Sian. The first bullet hit her in the chest and smashed her sternum into splinters of bone. The shards of bullet and bone ripped tissue and punctured her lungs as they travelled through her body. She had felt nothing as the second bullet hit her in the middle of her forehead, she was already dead. Sian's body tumbled down the steps and landed crumpled next to Mustapha. His eyes were watered by the impact of the head-butt that he had received, and he had to blink to focus them on Sian's ruined face. The woman that he loved was dead beside him. It was only half a day since his sister met a similar fate. The rage inside him surpassed the pain that he felt in his body. He looked like a man possessed as he rose, covered in his own blood from the cold stone steps to face his lover's killer.

Rasim raised the gun toward Mustapha but he was seconds too slow. Mustapha cleared the low wall and struck Rasim in the chest with both feet. The impact catapulted the Bosnian down the steep slope toward the cliff face. Rasim grasped at the thick heather and managed to stop himself from falling over the precipice. Mustapha ran headlong at Rasim hitting him in the midriff with his shoulder. The momentum took the two men over the edge. They fell, locked together in a violent embrace toward the foaming surf far below.

CHAPTER 41

Glasgow Airport

Chen walked into the top floor office and was greeted by cheers and applause; his right arm was slung in a loose hospital fastening across his chest.

'Some people will do anything for a few days off!' He heard someone say as he made his way across the office toward the goldfish bowl. There was a buzz around the far side of the room as new information was coming in. Tank waved at Chen and summoned him over to them. The digital screen was descending into its operating position and the image of a burning vehicle came into focus.

'Good to have you back, Chen,' Tank said slapping him on the back a little harder than was necessary. Chen grimaced in exaggerated pain and then smiled.

The image on the screen showed a green Cherokee Jeep wedged in the doorway of the main terminal building at Glasgow Airport. The Jeep was ablaze, as were the two Asian men that had jumped from the burning vehicle. Four members of the Strathclyde Police Force pounced on one of the burning Asian men and handcuffed him. Flames were jetting out from the rear of the Jeep and gas canisters could be seen clearly in the boot.

The Major stepped out of the goldfish bowl office to address the assembled agents of the Terrorist Task Force.

'We have an incident at Glasgow Airport as you can see. The Prime Minister Gordon Brown has called a meeting of COBRA, the emergency committee. The home secretary has raised the national terrorism threat to its highest level 'critical', meaning that we are expecting attacks imminently. Tank, there is a helicopter on the way for you. You need to be at this COBRA meeting with the PM.'

'I'll take Chen with me, if that's okay with you.' Tank grabbed his suit jacket and started to fasten his tie properly. Tank and Chen headed to the elevator that would take them to the landing pad on the roof.

'It would seem that we are finally getting some response from London. Faz, you had better get yourself up to Glasgow, and report back to me when you know what the bloody hell is going on there.' Grace Farrington nodded and headed toward the lift.

The Major and Tank had been frustrated by the lack of urgency that the government had displayed since the arrival of Yasser Ahmed. The home office didn't want to spark off widespread panic across the country. Incidents of terrorism both at home and abroad led to mistrust in the communities where Muslims lived and worked. During the 1970s when the troubles with the Irish Paramilitaries were in the news every day, anyone with an Irish accent became a potential bomber. The public would become suspicious of anyone with olive skin if the government were not very careful.

The Major had asked the home office for troops to be deployed around the Stanlow Oil Refinery and heightened security at the country's airports. The strain of British forces stationed in Iraq, and at war in Afghanistan left domestic issues short of men. There was no definite target, and too much supposition for the home office to agree to deploy troops. The situation had been compounded by incidents the previous day in London. Two abandoned vehicles had been found packed with petrol, gas canisters, and nails. One was parked outside of a busy nightclub in the theatre district of the capital; the other was left abandoned on a major traffic route. Neither home-made explosive device had detonated, but the intention shocked the nation. The green Jeep that the Major was watching on the screen was packed with gas canisters. This was the work of the same group that had attacked London the previous day.

Tank had already given the Scottish airport police orders on what to do until Grace Farrington arrived to control the situation. The two Asian men who had been in the burning vehicle had suffered severe burns. It was only because of the quick thinking of a taxi driver that they were still alive. The taxi driver was an ex-marine who had seen action in Northern Ireland. He had located a fire extinguisher and doused the flames that were consuming the two suicide bombers. Eyewitnesses reported that the two Asian men were not at all grateful for being rescued. They were now in the accident and emergency department of the Royal Alexandra Hospital in Paisley. Tank ordered the rest of the department to be evacuated until it was clear that the two men had no further devices hidden on their person. All the aeroplanes that were on the runway were to be parked, and all passengers were to be left on-board. Any air traffic that was due to land at Glasgow was redirected to other airports in the north of England.

Airports all over the country were closed to traffic. Nothing was allowed to approach the terminal buildings at any airport in the country. Tank's mobile buzzed in his pocket. He answered it and spoke to Grace.

'I'm in touch with the Strathclyde police; they've given me a rundown of the situation. The set-up is the same as the two cars in London yesterday. The vehicle is packed with gas canisters but there doesn't appear to be any sophisticated explosive devices involved.' Grace had already deduced that this was an independent extremist terror cell. The type of attack that they'd attempted in London and now in Glasgow was amateurish.

'This is not Yasser Ahmed's work then. This is another cell. Have we got any indication of who they are?' Tank asked.

Often bombers and the bomb makers could be identified by the type of device that they use. The 7/7 London bombers had used home-made explosives to devastating effect. A few weeks later, on 21 July, copycat terrorists tried to imitate the bombs. They used a mixture of Hydrogen Peroxide and a type of baking flour. They had incompetently weighed out the incorrect amounts of ingredients and the bombs failed to explode.

On August 11, 2006, the Terrorist Task Force and British police foiled the worst airline terrorist plot since 9/11. Tank believed that had they not uncovered the plot it would have caused death and destruction on a massive scale. It was believed that the suspects were just days away from carrying out their plan. They planned to take down multiple aircraft using liquid or gel explosives. The plan was to hide the explosives in a sports drink bottle. The bottom half of the bottle was to contain dyed explosives; while the top of the bottle would still be sealed containing innocent sports drink. Water-gel explosives are now the most commonly used commercial blasting agent and have almost completely displaced the use of dynamite and plastic explosives in industry. The liquid explosives were to be detonated using a camera flash. Since this plot was discovered the carrying of liquid through security at airports has now been banned.

'We have ID on one suspect; it appears he is a doctor. He is badly burned and keeps shouting that the attack is in revenge for the people of Haditha,' Faz said. She was around an hour drive from the Glasgow airport.

'I will call you after your meeting with the PM.'

Tank asked Chen what the connection was with Haditha and Muslim extremists. Chen had researched Iraq and Afghanistan as the conflicts developed. All wars have casualties but many of the dead in Iraq were non-combatants. The allied forces there were fighting a faceless enemy. They did not wear the uniform of an enemy army. The fight was impossible to win without creating innocent casualties.

'Haditha is a nightmare situation. It is a city in the western Iraq province of Al Anbar. There are so many conflicting reports about the incident that it's hard to get to the truth. The incident took place on 19 November, 2005. The Iraqis will tell you that the American Marines shot and killed twenty-four men woman and children, in cold blood. They claim that the killings were in retribution for an attack on a convoy, with an Improvised Explosive Device that killed an American lance corporal. The Americans will tell you that they were chasing known insurgents through the area when they took small arms fire from two houses. Standard procedure is to clear the building with fragmentation grenades then pepper spray each room with machine gun fire.'

156

'What happened then? Were there non-combatants in the houses that they attacked?' Tank asked. 'You can't really attack peoples' homes like that and not expect civilian casualties.'

'Well that's not the only problem. When the deaths were first discovered a Marine Corps communiqué initially reported that fifteen civilians were killed by a bomb blast and that eight insurgents were subsequently killed when Marines returned fire. An investigation found that five men, four teenagers, and a taxi driver were shot dead in a taxi. Nineteen dead bodies were found in the three houses that were attacked; apparently all of them were killed by well-aimed shots to the head and chest.' Chen shrugged his shoulders as he told Tank the tragic story of the Haditha killings. The horror of war changes peoples' lives; normally good men do strange things.

'Eight American Marines were charged in connection with the deaths. Not all of them were convicted, but the incident doesn't exactly make the Iraqi people think that the coalition is there to help them.' Chen finished with a one-arm shrug.

'It's not just the Iraqi people we need to be worried about. That's the type of incident that so-called preachers of hate used to motivate potential extremists. Just like this incident in Glasgow where we have a doctor, who has decided to set fire to himself and his Jeep,' Tank said. He wished that the Americans could be a little more diplomatic sometimes; but then diplomacy wasn't Tank's best attribute either.

Tank's mobile phone buzzed again, He looked at the screen and saw that it was the Major calling.

'Tank, put the phone onto conference mode. I need to speak to you all immediately.' Tank switched the mobile over which allowed multiple agents to be involved in the call simultaneously. Tank could see the names of fourteen other agents who were attached to the call including Grace.

'The North Wales Police Force has just found a body at South Stack Lighthouse. I'm sorry to have to inform you all that it's Sian. She has been shot twice. There is evidence of a fight at the scene and forensic teams are there now. Her gun and her Jeep are missing. As soon as we get the results back from forensics, I'll update you all.' Major Stanley Timms cut the conference call connection. There was no point in saying anything more. Sian was one of the team and now she was dead.

Tank and Chen made the rest of the helicopter flight in silence.

CHAPTER 42

Mustapha

When Mustapha had fallen from the cliff, he managed to hold on tight to the Bosnian. The journey to the crashing waves below felt like it had taken forever to complete. The two men hit the waves and were separated immediately. Mustapha could barely breathe; he was winded badly by the fall into the freezing sea. The water around the Anglesey coastline rarely rises above twelve degrees; without the aid of a wet suit, hypothermia is never far away. He plunged beneath the surface of the waves; the impetus of his fall dragged him deeper and deeper. He felt like his lungs would explode any second and he kicked desperately to reach the surface.

As he finally broke the surface, he sucked in fresh air deep into his lungs. He was coughing and spluttering as he tried to get his bearings. He was 200 yards from land on either side of him. The steep black cliffs at the bottom of the mountain looked impossible to climb. The waves crashed against them rising twenty feet up the sheer rock before falling back into the ocean. He would be broken like a piece of driftwood if he attempted to reach the mountain. He turned gasping for his breath all the while and looked toward South Stack Island. The tall white building of the lighthouse itself, which looked so small from above, now towered above him, the rocks looked sharp and treacherous and the waves pounded against them, he would be ripped to pieces in minutes if he tried to exit there. His muscles started to cramp in the freezing water, his wounds already felt numb. He lay on his back and tried to float; he had no more energy to swim. Consciousness started to fade, and darkness crept into his vision. The huge black cliffs seemed to reach up to the sky. He thought he could see a young girl dressed in a white dress up on the headland far away. She was waving to him and he thought he could see her smiling. *It looks like Yasmine*, he thought, as he passed out.

Rasim Janet crashed into the water at high speed. The young Ahmed was above him and seemed to be driving him deeper down. His lungs screamed at him to breathe. The bullet hole in his shoulder stung as saltwater entered his flesh. He kicked wildly trying to reach the air above. Desperation gave him strength and he drove himself upward to the surface. The enormous swell of the Irish Sea lifted him up and down. He could see no sign of Mustapha. He looked toward the lighthouse and quickly decided that to try to leave the ocean there would be suicidal. He turned toward the mountain and started to swim. The swell was helping his progress by pushing him toward the cliffs. He was now directly below the suspension bridge that crossed 150-feet above him from the mountain to the island. He was losing his strength rapidly as he tried to swim to the cliffs. Rasim looked up at the steep rock face that loomed above him and he wondered how he was going to climb it even he did make it to the rocks. He pushed himself harder; he wouldn't give in now. Rasim had weathered horrific times in his fight against Christianity; he couldn't be defeated now, he kicked harder toward the rocks. A glint of metal caught his eye. It was dull not shiny, but it was metal nonetheless, and as the waves receded, he saw it again. It was a rusted metal ring that would be used to tie up a boat, fixed to the rock face. He swam toward it, the swell aiding him, and as he approached the cliffs, he saw the smooth rounded shape of ancient steps cut into the rock face. The steps climbed the cliff zigzagging toward the bridge. The steps had been cut when the lighthouse was built. They serviced small boats that were used to ferry the builders and architects with their materials to the island. God had saved Rasim from the nightmares of Bosnia, now here he was helping again.

CHAPTER 43

Liverpool Anglican Cathedral

Yasser Ahmed stepped out of the black Hackney taxi and pulled his baseball hat firmly onto his head. His long black hair was tied in a ponytail which hung between his shoulder blades. Yasser fastened the zip on his leather jacket, he placed on his dark sunglasses and paid the driver with a five-pound note, and then he tucked his black wallet into his faded blue jeans. It had been a short journey from his apartment in Anfield to Liverpool city centre, and now he looked around at the busy city and contemplated his plans. The infidel had killed his sister. He found out from his informers that the taskforce that hounded him were based in the city, so this would be the target of his revenge. They had made it personal. He adjusted a small camera that he was wearing beneath his jacket; he intended to film his reconnaissance trip. The building in front of him was the Adelphi Hotel, once one of the country's finest hotels. The square shaped building was built from grey marble and it had large columns either side of the wide entrance. The doorway consisted of a large wooden revolving door with etched glass panels and brass handrails. It stood at the bottom of Mount Pleasant just five hundred yards from the Catholic cathedral which was built on Brownlow Hill.

Opposite him was an enormous department store which sported a twenty-foot high statue of a naked man above the main entrance. Liverpudlians called the statue Dickie Lewis. To his right was The Vines, a massive Victorian pub that looked more like a stately home than a public house. Yasser looked up the hill toward the Catholic place of worship.

The cathedral was an unusual circular building. The base was a circular shape beneath enormous metal girders that comprised the roof. The girders met two hundred feet above in a cone shape. Local people affectionately called it 'Paddy's Wigwam' because of its shape. From a distance it looked like an enormous Red Indian Tepee made from glass and stone. Paddy is a reference to the city's large Irish Catholic community that worshipped there. Yasser walked up Mount Pleasant toward the holy building. The construction of the cathedral was started in 1933 when the foundation stone was laid. The original plans would have made it the second biggest church in the world. It would have had the largest dome in the world on top. The outbreak of the Second World War interrupted the building work and by 1958, the plans were scrapped. The newly designed 'Paddy's Wigwam' was opened and consecrated in 1967 and was the spiritual centre for the Catholic faith in the north of England.

Yasser reached the wide slate steps that led to the main entrance and started to climb them. As he climbed Liverpool's historic skyline unfolded. Just a half-mile away was the sandstone monolith of the Anglican Cathedral, the biggest cathedral in the United Kingdom. Its wide Gothic arches and gigantic bell tower made it an iconic landmark that could be seen from forty miles away. Between the two huge places of worship, he could see the St John's Tower. The tower resembled a gigantic concrete pole seventy feet wide and one hundred and fifty feet high, with a flying saucer stuck on the top. The flying saucer had once contained a revolving restaurant that boasted panoramic views of the city; it was now home to a local radio station. The two cathedrals with the St John's Tower between them, and the gigantic bronze Liverbirds in the distance made a truly awesome skyline. Each of the famous landmarks was also a potential target.

Yasser looked toward the Catholic cathedral now in front of him. The circular building incorporates a nine-acre site at its base. The vast space inside the cathedral can seat two thousand people, who can participate closely in the services. Yasser stepped into the huge cathedral and looked up. The top of the building was an enormous cylindrical shape made entirely from coloured glass. The effect of the light as it filtered through this huge prism was breathtaking. Yasser walked around the perimeter of the cathedral secretly filming everything that he saw. The hushed voices and footsteps of eager tourists echoed around the enormous holy chasm. He stopped for a moment when he spotted a metal cleaning gantry high up in the glass conical ceiling. He followed the perimeter wall searching for the access door that would lead to the maintenance walkways. From above, the cathedral's base would look like a huge cogwheel. The main body of the church was surrounded by smaller chapels, which would be the cog teeth. At the back of one of these smaller chapels was a velvet curtain. The curtain was billowing gently as if it was being blown by a draft. Yasser lifted it away from the wall slightly. There was a door marked 'maintenance' that had been left slightly ajar. The perimeter of the building has great concrete buttresses that bear the weight of the glass and steel structure. Inside this particular buttress was a labyrinth of service tunnels and access stairwells. Yasser noted its position and moved on.

This holy building definitely had potential. He marked a mental tick next to it as a possible future target. He completed walking the full circumference of the building and walked outside into the drizzling rain. He stood at the top of the wide slate steps and scanned the city's skyline again.

The skyline of a city and the buildings that compose it give its inhabitants a feeling of ownership. A feeling of belonging can grow even in the short time a tourist spends in its presence. The loss of the Twin Towers was felt worldwide. Sales of pictures of the New York skyline that still contained the towers in them, still outsell those pictures that don't contain them.

In February 2006 Yasser's affiliates blew up the Al-Askari mosque in Samarra, Iraq, destroying one of the holiest sites in Shia Islam. The domes of the mosque however remained standing, as if in defiance of the bombers. The skyline was still intact despite the destruction of the revered place of worship. 165 Sunni Muslims were slaughtered in revenge attacks over the days following the attacks and guards were placed to stop the bombers returning to destroy the holy domes. The Sunni insurgents eventually returned and murdered the guards. They destroyed the magnificent domes with explosives bringing them to the ground in pieces. Despite the fact that the mosque was ruined and unusable, the Sunnis needed to remove the domes from view. The skyline itself can be symbolic of a people and their religion. Mosques and cathedrals alike are visible beacons of hope to the people that live and work beneath them.

Yasser descended the steps of the Catholic cathedral and saw the Everyman Theatre. He made his way down Rodney Street toward the biggest cathedral in the country.

Rodney Street was once home to many famous private medical practices. The doorframes of the street were once adorned with shiny brass plaques proudly displaying the doctors' names and their speciality. As private medicine became more lucrative, the doctors moved to new private hospitals and the area became the haunt of Liverpool's street girls. This was the red-light district. Yasser crossed Hardman Street and looked in awe at the gigantic Gothic cathedral. Its dark sandstone colour emphasised the sheer scale of the building. The cathedral has three towers, one at the head of the transept above the main alter; the two centre towers are at the middle of the transept forming the shape of a cross, if the building was viewed from above. Yasser looked at 260-foot high towers and ruled out sniper rifles. They were simply too high. The cathedral bells started to boom. At 219 feet above floor level, the bells of Liverpool Cathedral are the highest and heaviest ringing peal in the world. They consist of thirteen bells grouped in a circle around the great fourteen and a half tonne Bourbon bell. The whole peal weighed thirty-one tonnes. Yasser listened to the bells ringing the hour and could feel the noise vibrating in his chest. He stepped into the cathedral; the enormous vaulted ceilings and stained-glass windows gave the transept a feeling of immense space surrounding you. He walked through the cavernous naves surveying the building, looking for its weak spots. He arrived beneath the bell tower and gazed at its size. The plaque on the wall informed him that this was the highest and heaviest peal of bells in the world. What a blow to Christianity it would be to bring them crashing down. He smiled as a plan began to form in his evil brain. There was little thought given to the human cost of his attacks. All faiths had their martyrs, Muslim, Christian, Jews, it mattered little to Yasser. His faith was under attack and had been

162

since its conception; there would be no respite in his Jihad until the one true faith had triumphed over the infidels of other religions. Yasser checked that his camera was still filming his reconnaissance and he headed toward the exit. It was still raining outside.

Yasser walked down the hill of Duke Street toward the city centre. He counted thirteen giant construction cranes dotted about the skyline as he walked toward the river. The city was enjoying a massive period of regeneration and rebuilding due to receiving City of Culture status. The tall T-shaped cranes worked non-stop like giant robots lifting girders up to build new structures. Museums, art galleries, and bright new shopping precincts were springing up all over the city. He turned toward the dock road and looked right toward the Albert Docks. Just by the old dock building was the looming fortress shape of Merseyside Police Headquarters. The Terrorist Task Force was stationed on the top floor. Yasser smiled as he toyed with the idea that the country's top agents could be stood at the window of their offices looking right at him. He walked toward the ferry terminal at the Pier Head, directly in front of the police buildings.

There had been a ferry service from Liverpool across the River Mersey since the year 1150. Yasser bought a return tourist ticket and walked up to the top viewing deck of the Royal Iris. The old ferry had seen action at Zeebrugge in World War 1 and was granted the prefix 'Royal' shortly after returning to her home on the Mersey. The seats on the ferry quickly filled with eager tourists who wanted to see the city and its buildings from the river. The view from across the wide river estuary allowed one to put the city in perspective.

Yasser wasn't interested in the history of the city that the tour guide was explaining over the loudspeaker system. He was more interested in the river view of the oil refinery at Stanlow and the airport that occupied the opposite bank. The tourist ferry gave him an ideal opportunity to scout these potential targets without arousing suspicion. Yasser took a small digital camera from his pocket and snapped the coastline on both riverbanks. He was disturbed only once when a small Japanese girl tapped him on the shoulder and asked him to take a photograph of her with her grinning parents. The three of them never stopped nodding their heads in appreciation of the favour. The cold wind from the Irish Sea made him shiver, but it did not dampen his enthusiasm. He wished he had more explosives; there were just so many potential opportunities to cause utter destruction.

CHAPTER 44

The Corpse That Cried

It was early morning on Porthdafarc beach when two council workmen driving their sand lorry spotted the body of a man drifting in the shallow waters close to the shore. The workmen called the police who in turn called a local doctor. The local doctor attended the scene and reported that the man was not breathing and there was no sign of a pulse. The body was bruised and had facial lacerations, which indicated that he could be a jumper. Many people with suicidal tendencies chose the cliffs at South Stack as the place to end it all. He certified the body as dead, and the dead man was covered with loose tarpaulins to hide him from curious onlookers while a home office pathologist was called. A local policeman who attended the scene lifted the tarpaulin and recognised the body as that of Mustapha Ahmed. He had dated a local female customs officer Sian Hughes. The name Ahmed, once reported, triggered alarm bells in the security services system. Agents from the TTF were alerted and Graham Libby, the coroner, was flown from Liverpool by RAF helicopter to the morgue at Holyhead Hospital, where the corpse was to be taken.

Taskforce officers were still combing the headlands above South Stack Lighthouse where Sian's dead body still lay. Forensic teams were searching her house and the area around where her death occurred for clues. There was a blood trail all the way from the ocean to Sian's Jeep. Now that Mustapha's body had turned up the crime scene investigation would spread to incorporate the beach at Porthdafarc.

Dr Graham Libby stepped from the Sea King helicopter and ducked low as he ran across the landing pad. He entered the morgue and was handed the attending doctors report as he dressed in his sterile scrubs. The doctor had certified the man's body as dead, cause of death unknown. Libby lifted the cover from the corpse. He sensed something different about the body immediately. He often thought that he had a sixth sense with his subjects. He felt that the more he could find out about the way they met their end, the closer he became to them.

'The body is a male in his early twenties, he is neatly dressed. He is of Asian or Middle Eastern origin. The body is displaying signs of trauma. There is a chunk of the right cheek missing and definitive teeth marks. From the size and shape of the teeth marks, I would say that they are human. I am not swabbing the cheek wound for DNA because of the time the body has spent in the Irish Sea. There is bruising to the nose and below both the eyes, indicating that he had been in some sort of fight before he died.' The doctor cut open the T-shirt that the body wore and looked for signs of lividity or discolouration.

'There is no dew on the corpse which I would expect to see. There is also no rigor mortis or post-mortem lividity. The body temperature is 27.2 degrees centigrade, which is completely inconsistent with the on-call physicians report. This is all wrong. I am taking the body temperature a second time using the mouth as the reading point. The thermometer is reading 27.2 degrees.'

Graham Libby looked at the thermometer and noticed fresh spittle on the glass bulb. Dead bodies don't produce saliva. He was now seriously concerned about the attending doctor's report. Of the three cardinal signs of death, algor (cooling), rigor (stiffening) and livor (staining), there was only algor present. A body pulled from the waters of the Irish Sea either alive or dead would be considerably cooler than normal. He was not convinced that the doctor's report was correct. He held the broken nose bone of the dead body and squeezed it hard between his finger and thumb. He stared at the corpse as a tiny tear trickled from the eye down the cheek.

'This man is still alive for God's sake, unless dead people have suddenly started to feel pain,' Dr Libby cried.

There was a flurry of activity around the hospital as emergency teams ran to the morgue. Hot water bottles were placed around the body and oxygen was administered. They wired him up to an ECG machine but still the vital signs were negative.

'The body has been in the water so long that the blood circulation has slowed down. He has effectively been frozen alive and is in a hypothermic stupor. We must raise his body temperature immediately,' Dr Libby had never experienced a patient in a hypothermic stupor, but its effects were well chronicled.

Silver thermal blankets were applied to the corpse and the hot water bottles were changed quickly as they cooled. A faint pulse appeared in the neck of the corpse and the ECG monitor registered a heartbeat.

Mustapha had no idea where he was as he awoke seventy-two hours later. He knew that he was awake and that he wasn't alone. As his eyes started to focus, he could see a pretty young nurse leaning over him. Beyond her was a bright light fixed to a white ceiling. The light hurt his eyes and he squeezed them closed again. The smell of antiseptic hung heavily in the air. He felt very weak and tired. His nose and face caused him pain. He wanted to drift back to sleep away from it all.

Mustapha slept fitfully for hours. He drifted in and out of consciousness. He dreamt of Sian and the terrible way she had looked when she died. He dreamt of his sister Yasmine and

165

how they used to play outside in the sunshine when they were children. Yasmine was always laughing when he dreamt of her. Mustapha was pulled back toward reality by the sound of voices around him; the image of Yasmine laughing was replaced by one of her lying shattered and broken on the cold tarmac of a motorway.

He opened his eyes and saw the smiling face of a nurse; she placed a glass of water to his lips and he sipped it. His mouth and throat were sore from the tubes that had been inserted into him to help him to breathe and eat. Behind the nurses he saw a policeman standing near the doorway. He was wearing padded body armour and held a vicious looking black machine gun of some description. Reality was creeping back to him slowly. A big man, that he recognised vaguely, greeted the armed guard and approached the bed. He had a shaved head and his muscular frame stretched the material of his black suit to the limits. Mustapha remembered that he was Sian's superior officer. His name was Tank. He knew why he was here; he would want to know why Sian was dead. Mustapha wasn't really sure that he knew the answer except that it would involve his brother Yasser. The killing would never stop until Yasser was dead.

CHAPTER 45

Majeed

Majeed stepped out of his hotel into the historic centre of Istanbul; the only city in the world that's built on two continents, where the waters of the Black Sea meet the Sea of Marmara. Istanbul was once the home of the Sultans of the Great Ottoman Empire. During the years of Ottoman rule the Islamic Empire was the mightiest force on the planet. Majeed looked at the beautiful Blue Mosque in the distance. It was illuminated by a hundred spotlights after dark making its six tall minarets and giant arched domes a breathtaking sight. The seventeenth century Ottoman mosque was spectacular against the skyline of this vibrant city. Majeed headed toward the Bosphorus Bridge where he would meet his contact.

Majeed had driven the truck that had contained the IRA's surplus Semtex explosives from Ireland to Warrington. It wasn't long after that the British security services descended on the town looking for the conspirators. He was told that his friend Tariq had betrayed the Caliph, and that he had been murdered for his actions. After the Warrington raids police attention on the mosque and its community had been too severe for Majeed to remain in the country safely. Majeed was given false papers by Yasser Ahmed's affiliates and he was flown to Islamabad in Pakistan. He had been here many times since the end of the war in Afghanistan in 2001. Majeed was one of the thousands of disaffected young Arab extremists who flocked to Pakistan. These Mujahideen veterans now turned their attention to different enemies. Pakistani President Bhutto was under massive international pressure at the time of the Afghan Arabian influx. Western and Middle Eastern governments were demanding a crackdown on the foreign militants in Peshawar. In the aftermath of the World Trade Centre attack, Egypt, the USA and Saudi Arabia had all given Islamabad lists of the radicals and suspected terrorists that were hiding in Pakistan. The Egyptians were especially incensed because the men they suspected of reducing their Islamabad embassy to smoking rubble in 1995 were still at large in the city. Al-Qaeda and other extremist organisations used the country as a safe haven for their members. It was here on his last visit that Majeed decided to break away from the mainstream activists to join 'Ishmael's Axe'. He spent only a few days in Islamabad before travelling to Istanbul. His journey of Jihad was nearly over, and he was proud that he had contributed so much to his cause. From the mountains of Kabul where he fought and killed the invading Soviet soldiers with much enthusiasm, to the streets of Britain, he had been a loyal servant of Islam. His reward would be in heaven.

167

Majeed continued toward the Bosphorus Strait to meet his contact there, unaware of the two British agents who had followed him. When Majeed left the house that he shared in Warrington, following the raids there, he was immediately tracked. The bugs that Chen and his agents had planted in the house transmitted their signals to the surveillance centre in the old school. The listening post tracked Majeed as he travelled to Pakistan and then to Istanbul. He had checked in his luggage at Manchester Airport's terminal three, which was immediately searched without his knowledge. TTF affiliates made sure that extra electronic tags were attached to his belongings. There was no sign of anything illegal in his luggage so the TTF allowed his journey to proceed in the hope that he would lead them to Axe's leaders abroad. So far, the operation had highlighted two new safe houses in Islamabad, and several previously unknown activists were now under observation. The international war on terror needed as much information as it could gain to be effective against the faceless enemy. Surveillance and espionage were key weapons in the struggle against terrorism of any description. The two TTF agents walked faster to close the gap between themselves and Majeed.

Majeed approached the Bosphorus Bridge and saw a silver taxicab parked at the side of the road. He knew that was his contact waiting for him. The taxi was a Skoda Octavia, whose driver was a fat man with a large head. The fat taxi driver was eating a greasy kebab when Majeed approached the vehicle. He had large dark patches beneath his arms where his deodorant had failed to stop him sweating. He chewed noisily on the spicy meat.

'My friend Morris had a taxi that was just like this one. How much would it be to take me to the Grand Bazaar?' Majeed said to the driver. Many of the Turkish nationals that worked in the busy tourist industry used English names to impress their customers, hoping for a bigger tip no doubt.

The fat taxi driver opened the door and wrestled his huge frame out of the vehicle. Without saying a word, he walked toward the bridge still eating his kebab. Majeed looked around nervously. He sat in the driver's seat and closed the door. He had to adjust the seat forward so that he could drive the vehicle. The fat man had pushed the seat back as far as it would go. The car smelled of sweat, cigarettes, and chilli sauce.

Majeed was given five minutes to drive the car bomb to the American embassy and detonate the huge device in the boot. He took a deep breath and engaged first gear. The embassy was only a mile away over the bridge.

The TTF agents had to intercept their target. Majeed had been tailed since leaving Britain but presented no imminent threat until now. Once he made the switch with the taxi driver, the agents no longer knew what the threat level was. The possibility of the taxi containing explosive was high. To try to identify a potential target at this stage would be impossible. Istanbul contained many cultural and political centres, any of which could be attacked without too much trouble, 'soft targets'. In recent years the TTF had agents stationed in Istanbul permanently. The city had been targeted frequently. British interests in the city had been attacked resulting in the British consulate being destroyed and a British owned bank being reduced to smoking ruins. The same day two synagogues were destroyed. The attacks resulted in fifty-seven dead and over seven hundred injured.

John Tankersley had visited the city in August 2006 when terrorist bombers launched a twenty-four-hour campaign of destruction across the country. The bombing campaign was aimed at the tourist industry in an attempt to destabilise the government by damaging the economy. British tourists were attacked, not for any specific nationalist reasons but for Islamic ones. Extremists saw them as allies of the invaders from America. Tank helped to investigate twenty separate bomb attacks, eight of which occurred in August. The investigation discovered that the bombs were not the work of an international extremist group. It had been the work of Kurdish extremists who were trying to spotlight their struggle for an independent state. The worst of the attacks occurred in the resort of Antalya, on the Mediterranean coast. A busy tourist marketplace was attacked causing the deaths of three people. Tank identified that these attacks were the result of an internal political struggle and deployed TTF agents to monitor the situation. They would also be activated to respond to any future international threat. Majeed now constituted an international threat and hence came under TTF jurisdiction; terminal force could be used if necessary.

Agent Anthony John removed his Smith and Wesson MP15 9mm pistol from its holster. The black tungsten weapon was the modern-day pistol of choice carried by undercover agents the world over. It was extremely lightweight and had a short three-inch barrel that made it difficult to detect visually. Despite its smaller design the MP15 would stop a rhino at one hundred yards. Agent John fired twice as the vehicle started to move forward. The fat bullets destroyed the driver's side front tyre, shredding the rubber before continuing into the engine block. The Skoda seemed to tilt to one side as the tyre burst and a jet of smoke and steam hissed from the engine block; the car spluttered one last time and stopped completely.

'If you move your hands from the steering wheel, I will blow your head off. Remain very still and keep your hands on the wheel.' Agent John moved slowly. He kept himself parallel with the vehicle but maintained his distance from it. His partner stepped in front of the crippled silver taxi and levelled his weapon at Majeed's head. The agents had no idea what type of detonator the car bomb was wired to, but the chances were that the suicide bomber would try to reach for it. Majeed was starting to sweat profusely and his hands were trembling on the wheel. He had been told that there was a five-minute timer applied to the car bomb in the boot

169

that would be activated when the driver's door was closed. He couldn't stop the device from exploding, nor could he drive the vehicle to its intended target. He had no weapon to attack the infidel with. Agent Anthony John looked to his colleague to confirm what he was thinking. He thought the bomber would have detonated the explosives by now if he could. His colleague nodded his head almost imperceptibly. The two agents started to move backward away from the taxi slowly, keeping their weapons pointed at Majeed. This device was attached to a timer or a remote detonator which could be activated from a distance. Bombers sometimes used both systems so that their bombs could still be detonated even if the driver was killed or incapacitated.

The seconds ticked by, seeming like hours. Majeed began to think that the device had failed and that he would be spared the humiliation of dying in a failed car bomb attack. After all, he had been through his final glorious act of Jihad failed. The sound of police sirens were approaching from across the Bosphorus Bridge, the blue flashing lights now visible. The Turkish police were notoriously uncooperative and corrupt. The presence of armed foreign agents would agitate the local police force and make this delicate situation very complicated. The TTF men didn't need any complications. Agent Anthony John fired three bullets into the boot of the taxi and the device exploded. The taxi disintegrated into shards of jagged metal as the vehicle was blown three feet into the air. Ball bearings and nails formed a lethal metal spray that radiated out from the blast area. Majeed's blackened right hand was still attached to the charred steering wheel when the shattered vehicle returned to the tarmac; nothing else of him remained.

CHAPTER 46

TTF Liverpool

Tank and Grace stepped from the elevator onto the top floor of the police station. The office was buzzing with activity; agents were at every desk talking hurriedly into telephones. Major Timms and Chen were standing next to the large white digital wipe board the team used to illustrate ideas. Chen was pointing his finger and then pulling whole words across the board as if his finger were magnetic. As Chen rearranged words on the board, he was talking quickly to the Major. He always talked quickly when he was excited. The Major and Chen had both rolled their shirtsleeves up to their elbows; their shirt collars were tie-less and unfastened. They spotted Tank and Faz as they approached.

'That's very funny, Chen. What's going on here then?' Tank said as he pulled up a chair. He patted Chen on the back hard, nearly knocking him over.

Major Timms picked up the remote handset that controlled the digital board and pressed play. The screen changed immediately to an image of a man stood in front of the Iraqi flag. It was Yasser Ahmed. He was holding a 9mm Uzi machine gun for effect. His long black hair was tied tightly behind his head and he wore a dark headband.

'Our message to the people of the West is a simple one. If you choose to vote for your crusading governments, then you are legitimate targets for the soldiers of Islam. Your leaders have led an illegal invasion into the lands of Islam, and we, the Mujahideen will defend ourselves. The people of the West must denounce this unholy invasion, and demand that the United Nations acts to stop this military action with its own troops. All Muslim prisoners illegally held in Guantanamo, and across the world must be freed. I have spelled it out to your governments before. Now I spell it out to you again. You will read the message and weep. We will not stop until every last Muslim brother is free from Christian and Zionist oppression.' Yasser Ahmed fired the machine gun into the air and the image disappeared.

The digital board lit up again and the words that Chen had been moving around reappeared on the screen.

'Chen's onto something I think,' Timms said pointing to the screen.

'Ahmed specifically used the phrase 'spell' in the message several times. He likes to play games and tries to prove that he is more intelligent than we are. Look at this.' Major Timms gave Tank a typed list of recent attacks. Tank studied the list with Faz but there appeared to be no pattern at first glance.

'Watch this please,' Chen said as he added the chronological order of the bombings to the screen.

'We haven't noticed this before because not all the attacks are successful. We generally only put actual successful contacts onto the index rather than all the attempted attacks. The foiled plots and plans we disregard. We give ourselves a gold star for solving them and forget about them. The attacks that took place overnight make no sense at all if you apply my theory to them, because Istanbul and Hamburg were stopped. So, we couldn't see the pattern until we applied my theory to them, then it was obvious,' Chen was very animated and trying his best to get his theory across but without success.

'Chen, I haven't got a bloody clue what you're talking about so please just 'spell' it out for us. Excuse the pun, Major,' Tank said shaking his head. He hated it when Chen spotted something before he had, but he often did.

'Okay then, pay attention please. We registered successful car bomb attacks overnight in Johannesburg, Amsterdam, and Dubai. We also recorded foiled attacks in Hamburg and Istanbul. Now then if we forget what the outcome of each attack was, and just put them all on the same list. Then we need to apply the chronological order in which they should have happened.' Chen moved the digital names around on the screen, placing them in an imaginary order.

'Now, we have Johannesburg, Istanbul, Hamburg, Amsterdam, and Dubai.' Chen pointed to each city as he read it out trying to emphasise his point.

'Well, they aren't in alphabetical order. They aren't even on the same continents. They are not all British colonies or American interests either. I still don't see your point, Chen,' Tank stared at the list but the more he stared, the less sense it made.

'I'll add the attacks from last week to the board in the same chronological order, Glasgow, London, Oslo, Boston, Athens, and Las Vegas. We discovered the London plot before the Glasgow attack took place. Forensics has told us that the car bomb in London was actually timed to explode after Glasgow airport had been attacked.' Chen was straining at the bit now. His theory was so obvious to him that he couldn't understand why no one else could see it.

'Yasser Ahmed said he would 'spell' it out to us. If we put the attacks in the correct sequence and use the first letter of each city, we can spell the words, GLOBAL JIHAD.' Chen shrugged and held his hands palms up like a magician finishing a trick.

'You can't be serious. Have you checked this theory with his other attacks?' Tank stood up and stared at the list in disbelief. Now the theory had been explained it made perfect sense.

172

'Run some of the others past me. I'm not convinced that this isn't just a coincidence,' Grace said shaking her head incredulously.

'In 2002 when Ahmed first splintered from al-Qaeda he was involved a series of incidents. If we take all the successful and attempted events in systematic order, we have the word ISHMAEL. There were attacks in Istanbul, St. Petersburg, Helsinki, Manchester, Antwerp, Edinburgh and London. Now bearing in mind that he was just starting to branch out, he was already sending us messages. He has been playing games with us from the beginning,' Chen shrugged again to emphasise his point.

'What about the attacks in America before he landed here?' Tank asked with a confused look on his face. He couldn't make any sense or word from the attacks there.

'Well this one is a little more difficult. If we apply the same logic to it, then we have a series of attacks that would give us the letters, SLGF: San Francisco, Las Vegas, Grand Canyon, and Florida were all Ahmed targets. There is an Islamic extremist group in the Philippines that were formed in 1991 that use the same initials. The Sayyaf Liberty Group Freedom Fighters, they are responsible for over a thousand deaths, and they are highly revered by Ahmed and his affiliates. At the time of the American attacks, SLGF had just bombed a passenger ferry killing 323 people. Spelling their initials from his own attacks was a gesture of salute from Ahmed.' Chen smiled at the look of amazement on Tank's face.

Tank knew that Chen's theory was correct. Yasser Ahmed's message to *The Times* had just highlighted the obvious.

'If we can identify an Ahmed plot, then we may be able to second guess the next target. It's not much to go on. It would be pure speculation and guess work but it's better than nothing,' Tank said thinking out loud.

'What do we have from the tape apart from that, any suggestion of where it was made?' Grace asked. Identifying a potential target wouldn't help them to catch Yasser Ahmed. He was unlikely to be near to the attacks when they happened. Grace Farrington made an incorrect assumption.

'Forensics has it at the moment but there isn't much to go on at the present time. The fact that he emptied a machine gun clip into the ceiling during the tape would indicate that they're using an empty building somewhere, an industrial unit perhaps. There are no neighbours. That is certain.' Major Timms looked across the room as he was speaking, the fat controller David Bell was hurrying toward them.

'We've located Sian's Jeep at a railway station in North Wales. There is a lot of blood in it, which indicates that she wounded her attacker. The DNA matches the samples of blood that we took from the steps where she was shot. Whoever drove that Jeep also killed Sian. Our initial DNA searches have thrown up the name of a Bosnian Muslim called Rasim Janet. He is a veteran of the siege of Sarajevo, but our records have him listed as missing presumed dead after the war.' David Bell stared at the list of cities that was on the digital screen.

'Has anyone checked the local hospitals in the area? He can't have boarded a train unnoticed with a bullet wound in him,' Faz said.

'There are no reported gunshot victims at all but there is a Polish immigrant in a recovery room at Bangor hospital. He has had emergency surgery to a shoulder wound that was apparently caused by a metal spike. It went right through him in some kind of farming accident. He could be lying, and it's possible that he is our Bosnian friend with a through-and-through bullet hole in his shoulder. The local uniform men are checking it out now,' the fat controller said.

'The chances are that if he is Rasim Janet, then he is armed. I want you to send an Armed Response Unit, to back them up immediately,' ordered Major Timms.

'Do they have him on CCTV entering the hospital? If they do, then we need to get his picture to the hospital in Holyhead and see if Mustapha Ahmed recognises him. Look, I know that this Rasim character shot Sian, but we really don't need another terrorist in prison that's refusing to say anything to us. We have an opportunity here and we shouldn't waste it.' Tank stood and walked toward the window. Everyone in the taskforce would want this man imprisoned or dead for killing Sian.

'What are you saying, Tank?' Chen asked.

'I'm saying that if it's him, then we need to let him go and keep him under surveillance. He could lead us straight to Yasser Ahmed.' Tank knew that it would be an unpopular suggestion, but it was the correct thing to do. Yasser Ahmed was the number one priority.

'Tank's right. We need to know that it's Rasim Janet first. Get the Response Team to keep him under observation. Tell them to send that CCTV footage to us immediately. Bell, you need to get that information to Mustapha Ahmed for confirmation that this man is our target,' Major Stanley Timms patted Tank on the back. It was a hard decision to allow a man that has killed one of your officers to remain at liberty. The job of taking him to task would be delayed. He could lead them to the most wanted terrorist on the planet; justice would have to wait.

CHAPTER 47

Trooper Bob Duncan

Trooper Duncan was standing in the middle of the one thousand nine hundred-acre Stanlow Oil Refinery. Next to him was his spotter. They were both using binoculars to survey the refinery, trying to assess its weak points. Following the governments meeting of the COBRA committee that Tank attended earlier that week, armed troops were deployed to defend Britain's refineries. Stanlow had been identified as the number one priority because of its size and proximity to the recent extremist activities. There were twelve million tonnes of extremely flammable fuels being stored in huge metal tanks. Terrorists or no terrorists, the use of high velocity bullets in the vicinity was out of the question. Just one stray round could cause an ecological catastrophe. The army were instructed to issue their soldiers with tactical combat shotguns only. Each refinery would also be defended by sharpshooters where it was thought to be appropriate. The tactical shotguns had only a limited effective range. They were devastating at close quarters, but the army had to prevent terrorists from getting close enough to the storage vessels to attack them. Snipers would be deployed to protect the weak points in the refinery's perimeter.

Trooper Bob Duncan was revered by Special Forces the world over as the best of the best. The American SERT sharpshooter had been seconded to advise British forces on the best positions, and the best weapons and munitions to use.

The wrong calibre or incorrect bore of bullet used in this sensitive arena could end in disaster. A ricochet bullet could pierce a storage vessel; the resulting explosions would be felt sixty miles away. In December 2005 maintenance workers at a similar refinery situated at Buncefield, Luton, not far from London, caused a spark that ignited a fuel line. The following series of massive explosions were heard in the country's capital city eighty miles away. Surrounding areas were evacuated and road networks in the vicinity were closed. It took fire crews days to bring the flames under control. They used 1.4 million litres of water and 20,000 litres of foam. That was an accident, but harsh lessons were learned about the vulnerability of this type of storage depot. The SERT team leader pointed to one of the white storage containers close to the bank of the River Mersey.

'If you think that the threat is most prevalent from the river, then that's the position we need to take. We need a CheyTac M-200 .408 calibre sniper rifle. What is the distance to the water's edge?' Trooper Duncan asked his spotter. The spotter looked again through his binoculars and gauged the distance.

'It is approximately 2200-yards from that row of storage tanks to the river. It's well within the striking range of an RPG or even a home-made EFP,' the trooper advised.

Chen was confused. He knew that a Rocket-Propelled Grenade launcher could be carried by a determined diver to the refinery. All it would take would be a waterproof covering of some description to keep the ordinance dry. A terrorist could deliver his RPG attack from well beyond the effective range of most expert shooters, if he made it to the riverbank.

'What is an EFP? I am not familiar with that abbreviation?' Chen asked. He hated not knowing and felt a little ill equipped in front of the two military men.

'An EFP is a new phenomenon that our forces in Iraq are encountering frequently. It's a form of Improvised Explosive Device that the insurgents have developed with Iranian know how and training. Our vehicle armour in Iraq will withstand most explosive attacks but the EFP is a whole different ballgame. It's very simply an Explosively Formed Penetrator. The Iranians have shown the Iraqi insurgents how to place a cylindrical shaped explosive charge behind a concave copper disc. The force of the explosive launches the metal disk at 6,000 feet per second, which will penetrate our armour. Once the metal projectile is inside the armoured vehicle, it ricochets around ripping any of our Marines in there to pieces. It could do the same here with your storage tanks. It would be like a big pinball bouncing from one tank to the next, Boom, Boom, Boom,' Trooper Duncan explained. He had witnessed first-hand the devastation that had been caused by the EFP devices in Iraq. By the time the penetrators had stopped bouncing around inside the armoured troop carriers it was difficult to identify the casualties.

'I want some target disks set onto wooden posts along that riverbank. Let's make sure that if we get the chance to make a shot, we are ready to make it count,' the spotter saluted Trooper Duncan and jogged away to make his preparations.

'The river is over 2000 yards away. Can you seriously take a man down from that distance?' Chen asked incredulously.

'Well now, let's go and see shall we.' Trooper Duncan slapped Chen on the back, and they headed toward the storage tanks close to the river. The white metal tanks were sixty feet high and one hundred feet in diameter. They had black metal access ladders that hugged the circumference of the containers, leading to the top of them. Chen and the trooper climbed the stairs to the top of the container. From the top of the fuel storage tank they could see Liverpool city centre across the River Mersey on the opposite bank. They could also see passenger jets landing and taking off from the John Lennon Airport. It was two miles away across the water. Between themselves and the water's edge was a flat marshy area of waist high grasses. Two soldiers were hammering wooden stakes into the mud and attaching white disks to them. Chen had to look through his binoculars to see them clearly; they were just over a mile away.

'We have another problem here that you may not be aware of,' Chen said to the SERT officer. 'There are forty-two refineries similar to this one across the country with over a thousand miles of underground pipelines. The airport on the far bank of the river is supplied with high-octane jet fuel via an underground pipe. There is no feasible way we can protect every pipeline.'

Trooper Duncan's spotter returned with the M-200 sniper rifle and a small handheld computer. The rifle was nearly five feet long and was fitted with a large black scope. The end of the barrel was thickened by a built-in suppressor, which was designed to quieten the supersonic bullets as they were fired. The computer was called an ABC, Advanced Ballistics Computer. When relevant information such as wind speed and bullet velocity is fed into the ABC, it delivers super accurate adjustments for the rifles scope. It is essential that a two-man team be deployed on a weapon such as the M-200. The sniper and the spotter are equally important. The SERT team set up their weapon and programmed all the variable information that was required into the computer.

'We are trying to eliminate some very important factors that come into play when we are shooting over long distances. The spindrift of the bullet and even the curvature of the earth affect shots fired over this distance. We have a ten to fifteen mile per hour wind up here at the rifle; that will be twenty to twenty-five at the target,' Trooper Duncan adjusted the scope in line with the information that was appearing on the ABC.

Chen watched fascinated by the preparation and technical skill that the two sharpshooters were demonstrating. Trooper Duncan squeezed the trigger and a loud crack sounded as the supersonic bullet headed toward the river. Chen raised his binoculars and looked at the circular targets. He thought that the bullet had missed at first, but it takes a full four seconds for the bullet to travel 2200-yards. Suddenly a white disk just twelve inches in diameter shattered into pieces as the big bore .408 mm bullet struck it.

'Well, I think we have the river covered,' Trooper Bob Duncan said as he fired another dead eyed shot.

CHAPTER 48

York

Yasser Ahmed pulled the van to a halt. He turned to the passenger who occupied the front seat and smiled. Omar Squire smiled back at him nervously. Omar had entered Britain just two days earlier on a flight from Pakistan. He was born a Muslim in the African country of Gambia and was just twenty-three years old. His childhood had been typical for that part of the world. Education was for the wealthy and war and poverty were the only certainties. The Gambia was a satellite country completely surrounded by the country of Senegal. Civil wars in the region had raged on and off for centuries creating famine and strife. The capital of Gambia, Banjul situated on the west coast of Africa had a healthy tourist industry. The influx of western European tourists coming into Gambia was a constant reminder of the inequalities of life. Tourists would spend more on an evening meal than the average Gambian could earn in a month. Bitterness and anger had festered in Omar Squire until he had reached the point where he felt that he had to act.

Omar travelled across West Africa to the Sudan where he found solace in a religious training camp sponsored by Yasser Ahmed. The camp Mullahs had taught Omar that there would be no peace for the oppressed Muslim people of the world until the Jewish and Christian enemies were crushed. Omar Squire spent two years in the Sudan until he had answered the call to arms from Yasser Ahmed himself. Now he was sitting next to his Caliph wearing a suicide bomb vest.

Explosive vests had first been used by the Tamil Tiger group from Sri Lanka in 1991. A female Tamil Tiger suicide bomber blew herself up and killed Rajiv Gandhi. Omar had made his explosive belt the previous day using some of the IRA Semtex that Yasser and his affiliates had purchased. He filled six metal cylinders with the plastic explosive and strapped them around his abdomen. He put on a waistcoat packed with steel ball bearings and screws. The explosive force would turn his jacket into an omnidirectional fragmentation grenade. A deadly spray of metal shrapnel would be unleashed upon detonation of the device.

'Thank you, Caliph, for this great task that you have given to me. I will not let you down.' Omar Squire opened the door of the ice cream van and walked toward the vast bulking towers of York Minster.

York Minster is the largest Gothic cathedral in northern Europe and is situated in the City of York, England. There has been a Christian house of worship on the site since the 300s

AD. The Minster is one hundred and forty metres long, and its three towers stand sixty metres high. Built from limestone the cathedral is a creamy white colour. Omar looked at the massive Great East Window as he approached the stone edifice. The seventy-six-foot-tall Great East Window is the largest expanse of medieval stained glass in the world. It towered above him as he entered the building, heading for the main altar. The huge vaulted ceiling loomed overhead as he walked through the cathedral, Christian images were all around him and he suddenly became very frightened of dying. Every window depicted a story of Christ, everywhere Jesus seemed to be staring at him. The two million pieces of glass that make up the Minster's one hundred and twenty-eight stained-glass windows glowed as the sunlight filtered through them. The building felt so serene and holy that real doubt started to weaken his desire to commit this horrible evil act of aggression. Yasser had prayed with him that morning and he told him that fear and doubt would be sent to him by the devil, he must ignore them both and complete his task. Omar Squire heard a small girl crying close to him. He looked at the little girl and his heart softened even more; she had black African skin just like his own, her eyes were wide and bright, full of life. Omar reached out and touched the wiry black hair that she wore plaited against her head and she stopped crying immediately. She looked up at him, her eyes still full of tears and she tried to smile. The little girl looked similar to the three sisters that Omar had left at home in the Gambia. It seemed like such a long time since he had seen them. He didn't even know if they were still alive and he felt very guilty for leaving them.

'What is wrong with you, little one?' Omar asked the little girl. He wiped a tear from the corner of her eye, and she tried to smile again. Her nose was running, and Omar wiped the fluid away with the edge of his sleeve.

'That statue makes me really sad. I don't want Jesus to be hurting like that.' The little girl pointed to a plaster statue of Christ on the cross. It was a realistic image of a white European Jesus nailed to a wooden crucifix. The bloodstained nails and thorns were clearly visible. The statue depicted how horrific crucifixion would be and left little to the imagination. It was a terrifying image for a five-year-old girl to face.

The little girl's father approached and looked at Omar suspiciously as he led her away; he scolded the child for becoming separated from her family. Omar was left alone with the memories of his young sisters in Africa and the image of a crucified Christ suffering on the cross to console him.

Yasser looked at his watch and he knew that something had gone wrong. There had been no explosion, yet he had watched Omar enter the cathedral fifteen minutes before. Suddenly people started running from the Minsters entrance doors in a panic. Tourists piled through the opening becoming squashed between the huge wooden doorframes and falling over each other. Hundreds of people were escaping the building. What was happening in there? Yasser couldn't investigate now; instead he started the engine in case he needed to leave in a hurry. Police sirens started to sound from a distance away, obviously alerted to the incident at the Minster.

Omar Squire watched as the tourists left the holy building in a panicked crush. He waited until the very last one had gone. He had removed his ski jacket and shouted to the tourists to leave as he had a bomb. People ran away from the dark-skinned man in all directions to exit the building as fast as they could. Omar had decided that he wouldn't take any life but his own. His god would understand the reasoning behind his decision. He would still be awarded his place in heaven and hopefully he would be reunited with his long-lost family there someday. He pressed the detonator button on his explosive vest. The statue of the crucified Christ seemed to smile at him as his body liquefied beneath the power of the bomb blast.

Yasser felt the deafening thump of the explosion as the stained-glass windows around the Minster disintegrated into a million pieces. Glass was blown three hundred yards from the building showering panicked tourists with coloured debris. The first part of the message had been delivered.

CHAPTER 49

Mustapha – Rasim Janet – Wales

The yellow Sea King helicopter landed on the car park at Holyhead Hospital, where Press photographers and TV camera crews laid siege to the building. Tank and David Bell ducked as they exited the helicopter and ran toward the rear entrance of the hospital, reporters raced toward them shouting questions trying desperately to be heard over the rotor blades. The Press had become interested in the growing news story about Islamic extremism, and they were feeding the public enough disinformation to cause a media frenzy countrywide. Random racist attacks had become commonplace in response to the growing suspicion being generated by media coverage. The shooting dead of Yasmine Ahmed and Sian had just added fuel to the flames. Stories that the dead body of Mustapha Ahmed had been misdiagnosed were leaked from sources within the hospital. The press had not taken long to connect Mustapha with the death of a female customs officer hence the massive media presence in the small Welsh port.

Two armed policemen stood aside as Tank walked toward Mustapha's room. There was no way Mustapha could remain in the small hospital any longer. Yasser Ahmad and his cronies would be aware by now of where he was and why he was there. He would be a target for Yasser one way or the other. Sian lost her life trying to protect Mustapha, and Tank had to shoot three men that were sent to collect the Iraqi, so he needed to be moved immediately away from the eyes of the press and out of harm's way.

Mustapha sat up when Tank walked in followed by the fat controller. The bite mark on his cheek looked nasty, and a large blackened scab covered the stitches that closed the wound. Tank nodded at David Bell.

'Is this the man that tried to abduct you from South Stack?' The fat controller asked.

'Yes, that's him. Who is he?' Mustapha seemed to pale as he looked at the grainy CCTV still.

'Are you positive that this is the man that shot Sian?' David Bell needed to be certain that the man who claimed he was a Polish immigrant was actually a Bosnian mercenary. He was recovering from a shoulder operation in a hospital that was just thirty miles away.

'Well I did get pretty close to him, so yes I am certain,' Mustapha pointed to the bite mark on his face sarcastically.

'We need to be sure, Mustapha. We are keeping this man under observation until he leads us to his accomplices,' Tank said trying to calm him down.

181

'You mean my brother, don't you? Why don't you just say that then?' Mustapha was becoming upset. He had lost his sister and his lover in the space of two days and nearly died himself along the way. Now he was lying in a hospital bed surrounded by armed policemen and besieged by hundreds of paparazzi, he could see no end to it at all.

'Okay, Mustapha, we are hoping that he will lead us to your brother. We need to remove him from society and then you are a free man,' Tank said. He could see that Mustapha was breaking under the strain.

'I will never be free of him unless he is dead. You need to kill him, or his people will haunt me as long as he lives. I cannot see any future while he is still alive.' Mustapha touched the thick scab on his face thoughtfully.

'Why don't you use me to lure him out? If he knows where I am, he will send his people to find me. You could follow them back to Yasser. You could follow me back to my brother,' Mustapha said exactly what David Bell wanted to hear. He couldn't suggest this as a valid option himself without compromising the taskforce's position. Mustapha had volunteered which was completely different.

'You would be putting yourself in a position of intense danger. You are fully aware of what your brother is capable of. You need to think about this very carefully,' Tank said pacing the room as he spoke. It was a valid option. Yasser had twice tried to contact his younger brother by sending armed men to retrieve him and Tank had little doubt that he would try again if knew where he was.

'I would rather die trying to help, than to live in my brother's shadow any longer. I have spent my life running and hiding from him and his enemies. They would kill me to get at him if they could. I will hide no more, I want to do this,' Mustapha sounded certain.

Thirty miles away, Rasim Janet pulled a jumper over his head and his shoulder wound raged at him. He gritted his teeth and pulled a coat on over the jumper. He squeezed into a pair of Adidas trainers that were two sizes too small and fastened the laces. Rasim was stealing the clothes from a staff changing room that was located just down the hallway from his recovery ward; he thought that it was odd that there was only one set of clothes hanging up in the room. It didn't matter though; he had to move before his cover story was exposed as a lie, and so he had stolen extra painkillers from the pharmacy trolley earlier that morning. Once the morning doctor's rounds were completed, he used the opportunity to escape without arousing suspicion. He pulled on a baseball cap and headed for the fire exit sign posted at the end of the corridor. Rasim opened the door and instinctively pushed it with his shoulder. The fresh wound hurt terribly he felt the stitches straining and a trickle of blood run down his back. The cold fresh air revived him he stood on the fire escape and leaned against the wall to recover a little before moving on.

Rasim could see across the hospital car park to the train station, it was only a few hundred yards away. He climbed down the metal staircase and then reached into a small grid that was situated underneath it. He retrieved Sian's Glock 9mm from where he had hidden it when he arrived at the hospital. Rasim had kept it dry by wrapping it in a plastic shopping bag. He crossed the parking lot and entered the small station without incident; he bought a single ticket to Warrington and sat on a bench seat to wait for the next train to arrive. His shoulder was causing him pain and he swallowed two of the stolen painkillers that he had in his pocket. He scanned the railway platform nervously. There were three other people waiting for the train, an elderly couple and a young woman. The young woman stood nearby reading a celebrity magazine. The people of the West seemed to be obsessed with celebrity, and he couldn't understand it. It seemed that football stars and pop singers were more revered than God to most people.

The young woman wore tight faded denim jeans and a loose knitted jumper that clung to her curvy body. Rasim flushed as he felt sexual desire pulse through his body. She was sexy; there was no doubt about it he tried not to stare at the woman, but he found it very difficult not to. She looked up and caught him staring he flushed again, this time with embarrassment. She smiled at him and he looked away quickly. He should not have such thoughts on his mind, but he couldn't help it. She tossed her long black hair over her shoulder and he stared at her again.

The Holyhead to London express train appeared, heading toward the platform that Rasim was waiting on, he stood and walked toward an empty carriage as the train came to a halt. The train wouldn't stop again until it reached the fortress city of Chester, built on the border of Wales and England as a garrison town for the invading legions of Rome. Rasim would need to change trains at Chester to continue his journey to Warrington. He sat at an empty table next to the window of the express train, the dark-haired woman had chosen to sit in the same carriage as him, but she was further down the train. He couldn't see her from where he was sitting. She could see him though. Detective Constable Ruth Walsh was an experienced Armed Response Officer. She was approaching thirty but looked much younger. Surveillance, detection, and undercover operations were her specialities. She placed her celebrity magazine on the unoccupied seat next to her and checked that she could see her target. His reflection was mirrored in the carriage glass; she could watch every move that he made without compromising her cover. She typed a message into her MMS communicator and pressed send. The communicator looked like a mobile phone and was just as simple to operate. The Bosnian man

183

looked uncomfortable when he moved; Ruth knew that the hole in his shoulder would negate the use of his right arm. If he still had a weapon, he would have to use his left hand to shoot. He would also not be able to support his shooting arm, which made accurate shots almost impossible to achieve. DC Walsh had assessed most of this information in the short space of time that she had been watching him. The taskforce had correctly guessed that he would use a train when he left the hospital, and they'd placed DC Walsh at the station in case they were correct.

CHAPTER 50

Anfield – Liverpool Football Club

Chris Lampie was a Liverpool Football Club fan, he had been a fanatical supporter all his life to the point where his long-suffering wife, Denise, had allowed her three sons to be named after previous players and managers. Chris Lampie hadn't missed a game home or away for six years, neither had his friends. Les White, mad Adie, and dodgy Si as they were known, they'd travelled the world with Chris watching Liverpool play football. The only time they missed any of the season was years ago. All four die-hard fans had missed three months of the season six years earlier after being sentenced to twelve weeks detention at Her Majesty's pleasure. They were allegedly attacked by a much larger group of Chelsea fans at an away game in London, and in the process of defending themselves, they managed to hospitalise all bar two of the Londoners. Their combined yearly spending budget for season tickets and paying for hotels and airfares would be grounds for divorce if their respective wives ever found out.

When Liverpool played their matches at home, Chris Lampie and his crowd of friends always met in a pub in proximity to Anfield Stadium. From the public house, which was called The Sandon, to the Anfield Stadium, was three hundred yards. Lampie and his group of fellow supporters sat in the same seats in the Sandon every time Liverpool played at home, and it had affectionately become known as 'Compost Corner'. Anfield Stadium had been built in 1884 and had been the home of the most successful British football club in history ever since. Liverpool had won the European Champions League Trophy a record number of times.

Chris Lampie and his friends always sat in a section of the ground known as the famous 'Kop', to watch their beloved Liverpool play. The Spion Kop, after which the stand is named, is a hill in Natal, and it was the site of a battle in the second Boer War. During the battle over three hundred men of the Lancashire Regiment were killed, many of them were Liverpool fans.

Kick off for the game today was scheduled for 3 p.m. Chris Lampie stood at The Sandon door waiting for it to open, he looked at his watch and it was 10.55 a.m. He would have to wait just five minutes until the pub opened its doors. Chris leaned his back against the wall of the pub and looked down Breck Road toward the city centre. He could see the Liverbirds perched on top of the Liver buildings next to the river. They were the emblem of LFC and he thought it would bring him luck to see them towering in the hazy distance before the game started. As he looked back toward the stadium, he noticed a slim Asian-looking man climbing

185

some basement steps up to the street. The rest of the old Victorian terrace looked derelict which wasn't unusual for this area. A strange shiver ran down his spine as he watched the little Asian man climb into an ice cream van and drive away.

CHAPTER 51

Carpenray Scuba Dive Centre

Nassir al-Masri had been a trained diver from a very young age, so diving in the River Mersey wouldn't be a problem for a diver of his experience. He had to swim across the Mersey underwater, which meant that he would need a dry suit to combat the cold conditions, and he would need propulsion. He couldn't swim the required distance underwater with only one aqualung. Yasser was aware that the security services would be tracking every equipment sale that was made country wide because Yasmine had been killed retrieving the bugged wetsuit, so they needed to acquire the equipment some other way.

Nassir worked for many years in the Egyptian holiday resort of Sharm el Sheik as a diving instructor. He loved his job at first, but as political and religious tensions grew in the region so did Nassir's resentment. The predominantly European tourists that he dived with paid more for a forty-minute dive than he earned in a month, and he relied on the generosity of his allocated group of divers to increase his wages by paying him a tip. Unfortunately, Nassir was not very good at disguising his true feelings toward his customers and he rarely got tipped at all.

On one particular day he had to instruct an English diver who was taking an advanced diving qualification. The course involved diving to the legal recreational limit, which is forty metres deep. Nassir hadn't taken the proper time to ensure that diver's equipment fitted properly. He hadn't completed a safety check dive with the Englishman either, which would have highlighted any potential problems. As they descended deeper, the Englishman's ill-fitting suit began to tighten as the water pressure increased the deeper they dove, the worse the restricting effect became. Eventually starved of oxygen the diver had panicked at around ninety feet below the surface and dumped his weight belt heading for the surface like a rocket. By the time he broke the surface the expanding oxygen and nitrogen trapped in his blood stream had burst his lungs like an over inflated balloon. Nassir was arrested and charged with the equivalent of manslaughter and thrown into an Egyptian jail in Cairo. Luckily, for him the prison guards were corrupt, and he managed to escape in exchange for his life savings. With his occupation taken away from him, he became all the more resentful toward the West, and it wasn't long after that he joined a group of Egyptian extremists whose goal was to cripple the government by driving tourists away in fear.

Nassir had driven sixty miles north from Liverpool on the M6 Motorway to the Lake District of Cumbria; he arrived at the Carpenray dive site just after 6 a.m. that morning. The former quarry was a popular destination for divers from all over the British Isles. Nassir had dived here often, trying to build his resistance to the cold-water temperatures that he would have to encounter in Britain's coastal waters. When Nassir had dived at home in Egypt, the waters of the Red Sea rarely dropped below twenty-four degrees. The River Mersey was rarely above twelve degrees and the quarry was even colder still.

Nasser parked the car that belonged to Yasser's dead landlord in the gravel car park which serviced the dive site. He exited the vehicle and walked up a steep slope that led to the reception area. He showed his diving credentials to the attendant and then paid the young girl for the hire of a dry suit and gear. Dry scuba suits are completely sealed from the surrounding water by a series of wide rubber cuffs that prevent the liquid from entering the sleeves, legs, or neck. The mask and tank apparatus are generic to other types of scuba diving. The dry suit would extend his time under water dramatically without him suffering from aqua hypothermia. Nasser walked further up the slope to the equipment shed where he handed the equipment steward his ticket.

The steward sized Nassir up correctly and dispensed him all the equipment that he required to complete three, forty-five-minute dives in the ice-cold waters of the murky quarry. The equipment shed was a redundant articulated lorry container that had been converted into the dive site equipment storage facility. Nassir collected his equipment and then noticed some unusual machines stored to one side of the container. Nasser recognised them immediately as DPVs. He had only seen prototypes at home in Egypt, but he recognised them anyway. The Diver Propulsion Vehicle consisted of a battery-powered electric motor fitted into a circular plastic body that was fitted with two handles. The battery powered a propeller which pulled a diver along underwater greatly increasing the distance that he could cover with the limited air supply that he had. Nasser paid the extra twenty pounds to hire the DPV for the day.

Once issued with all your equipment it's traditional to change into your scuba gear next to your motor vehicle in the car park, so that you can leave your belongings safely. The freezing Cumbrian wind almost made the icy waters of the quarry seem attractive as the divers kitted up and headed for the water. The car park started to empty of people as divers waddled to the quarry and non-participants headed for the warmth of the café inside the main building. No one noticed Nassir al-Masri loading his newly acquired scuba gear and DPV into the boot of his car. No one would notice until the next day when all the hire equipment had been dried out and inventoried that Nassir had stolen everything that he needed to cross the River Mersey underwater.

188

CHAPTER 52

Yasser – The FA Cup

Yasser drove the ice cream van to the end of the derelict terrace in which he lived. He stopped and opened the driver door and an Iranian man, called Ali waited for him to exit the van before climbing into the driver's seat himself. Ali nodded to Yasser and grasped his hand tightly. He didn't speak as he drove the vehicle away.

Ali had been at home in Bandar Abbas, Iran on Sunday 3 July 1988. His father had taken Iranian Air flight 655 to Dubai, which was shot down by a missile launched from the US Navy, Ticonderoga class guided missile cruiser, USS Vincennes. All two hundred and ninety passengers and crew were killed including sixty-six children. According to the American government they'd mistakenly identified the Iranian Airbus as an attacking F14 fighter plane. The Reagan administration at the time, represented by the then Vice-President George H Bush, defended his country's actions at a news conference held on August 2, 1988 said,

'I will never apologise for the United States of America, I don't care what the facts are.'

Ali promised his mother that one day he would avenge his father's murder, today he would fulfil that promise. Four more ice cream vans pulled in line behind him. The strange procession turned right and headed for Anfield Stadium. Two more were already in the city centre.

The city of Liverpool had a double celebration going on. Liverpool Football Club would be playing their old local rivals from across the city, Everton FC. The game was to be played at Anfield and the winners would be rewarded with a place in the semi-finals of the FA Cup. The FA Cup is the oldest football competition in the world, beginning in 1871. It involves clubs from every division of British football right down to the grass roots amateurs. Because it involves clubs of all standards playing against each other, there is always the possibility for 'giant killers' from the unpaid lower divisions defeating one of the top clubs. The romance of an underdog victory enhanced the importance and credibility attached to winning the trophy.

Football fans from all over Liverpool and the surrounding Merseyside area were packing the streets from early in the morning. Some were looking for the opportunity to purchase a late seat from a ticket tout outside the ground; others were just soaking up the carnival atmosphere. The pubs and bars across the city were packed with armchair supporters who weren't lucky enough to purchase a ticket at the ground itself. The red shirts of Liverpool and the blue shirts of Everton mingled in the busy streets of the city.

190

Ali slowed down and waved into the rear-view mirror to the driver of the ice cream van behind him, and the driver pulled his van onto the kerb as instructed. The process was repeated until all four vans were positioned strategically around the Anfield Stadium. It was eleven thirty in the morning and the kickoff was scheduled for three o'clock that afternoon. By twelve noon, the streets would be packed with excited fans enjoying a few beers before the much-anticipated game began.

A man dressed in a red Liverpool shirt banged on Ali's window making him jump. The fan's friend banged on the other side of the ice cream van frightening Ali even more. It was mad Adie and dodgy Si fooling around on their way to compost corner in The Sandon.

Yasser stood at the north end of Hope Street and looked up at the giant towers of the Anglican Cathedral. He had already been into the sandstone monolith that morning and planted four kilos of Semtex explosives around the massive Bartlett Bells. The cathedral bells, the highest and heaviest in the world, would peel out at 3 p.m. that day for the last time. The huge central bell was called Great George, the Bourbon Bell, and it weighed over fourteen tons on its own.

As Yasser watched, two ice cream vans entered the cathedral grounds they parked either side of the monstrous cathedral. They would stay there until Yasser's bomb exploded in the bell tower. Panicked tourists that survived the bomb would try to exit the huge front doors and then the secondary charges in the ice cream vans would be detonated.

Yasser wished that he could be close by when Great George, the Bourbon Bell came crashing down, but he had to be somewhere else. The logistics of his plan were already in motion. Yasser felt that the net was closing in. Today he had a plane to catch. It was time to move on.

CHAPTER 53

Terrorist Task Force

Chen and David Bell were staring at the digital operations board on the wall in front of them. York Minster had been bombed the day before and it was almost certain that Yasser Ahmed was responsible. Forensics had identified the explosive used in the Minster bomb as Semtex, from a batch that was identical to some that was seized en route to Ireland, from Libya in 1998. The suicide bomber had left no clues as to his identity, but strangely he had forced the visitors in the cathedral to leave before he blew himself to pieces.

'It looks like he may have had a change of heart at the last minute,' Chen said thoughtfully flicking through photographic evidence from the scene. The suicide vest had been packed with steel ball bearings, which had only one purpose; that purpose was to maim and kill as many human beings as possible. The bomb was not designed to destroy buildings, although the damage it had caused was extensive.

'If we are certain that this is an Ahmed sponsored attack, then we have a message of some kind beginning with the letter Y,' said the fat controller trying to get one step ahead.

'Well, I don't believe that he is sending us anything Islamic, or in Arabic. His name starts with the letter Y, and so does his sister's name, Yasmine,' David Bell continued.

'If your theory is right, then the next attack should be on a site beginning with the letter, A and the one after that should be the letter, S.'

Chen typed the letter A into the digital computer screen and pressed search. The screen came back with two hundred and fifty thousand places that began with the letter, A. He narrowed the search to the UK only and reduced the number to sixty-two thousand. It was still like looking for a needle in a haystack. Chen tried several different searches. Cathedrals beginning with, A, produced just twelve possible targets countrywide. Churches or synagogues beginning with, A, increased the possible number to twelve thousand. It was all supposition and speculation; they needed more information to narrow the search.

'We must have something else that we can use to cross reference this information with. What else did we really discover from the raids in Warrington?' Chen said thoughtfully, scratching his head.

'There was nothing that we can use here. The only information that we haven't received yet is a report from uniform division. They were going door to door on the industrial parks checking out businesses to see if any of them were not legitimate. They were supposed to cross reference all the vehicles that entered the park against their registered business addresses. I'll give them a call now and see if anything jumps out as being useful to us,' David Bell said reaching for the telephone.

Chen radioed the Armed Response Unit tailing the Bosnian suspect Rasim Janet. He had shot Sian, and everyone was keen to bring him down, but they were also hoping that he would lead them to Yasser Ahmed. Chen was informed that the Bosnian was on a train heading for Chester. That made sense because he would have to change trains there to continue his journey north to Warrington. Alternatively, he could transfer to a train travelling east to Liverpool. He was being tailed by a very competent undercover agent named DC Ruth Walsh whom Chen was familiar with. There was a full surveillance team already assembled at Chester waiting for Rasim Janet to make a move.

David Bell tapped Chen on the shoulder making him jump with pain. His bullet wound was still fragile despite him no longer using the sling. He signed off with the Armed Response Unit and turned back to the intelligence gathering.

'This is very interesting. I can't believe uniform haven't spotted this and sent it on to us the bloody idiots,' Bell said taking off his round spectacles and wiping spittle from around his mouth. He always spat a bit involuntarily when he became annoyed, and even more so if he was drunk.

'Calm down and tell me what you think it is that is so important,' Chen said hiding a smirk.

'We gave uniformed division the job of cross checking every vehicle that moved on and off that industrial park against the Companies House records in London. One company on the list did not exist as a legitimate business. They apparently buy and sell reconditioned vehicles from a unit not far from the cold room operation that we raided,' Bell stopped to take a drink.

'Have uniform been to the business in question to investigate?' Chen asked, not quite keeping up with conversation.

'Yes, they have, and the unit was empty. They cleared out a week ago according to their trading neighbours. It was completely scrubbed down and gutted, apparently. Now here is the best bit, guess what type of vehicles they repaired?' Bell said dribbling a little again and waving his round spectacles about in frustration.

'I have no idea, please get to the point,' Chen encouraged.

'They repaired ice cream vans and hot dog wagons. The neighbours saw several rundown machines being taken there and just assumed that's what business they were in,' Bell stood up and kicked the desk.

193

'We need to get sniffer dogs into that building to see if there was ever any explosive in there. I mean right now, today.' Chen walked to the digital screen and typed in the word 'events' beginning with, A. Nothing of any significance appeared.

'What are you looking for now?' Bell asked. He had just ordered the dog teams to the industrial unit to search for trace evidence.

'We must be able to use this ice-cream van information to narrow down the search. Ahmed will look for an event where there are large crowds of people if he is going to utilise this van theory,' Chen looked out of the window toward the River Mersey and watched six men cross the road all wearing red Liverpool football shirts.

'Oh my God, it's the FA Cup-tie today. Liverpool are playing Everton in the quarter finals. There will be thousands of people there today. The game is being played at Anfield,' Chen spoke as if he was in a dream as the realisation of the horrific scenario hit home. It was twelve thirty and kick off was scheduled for three.

CHAPTER 54

Rasim Janet – DC Ruth Walsh, Chester

The train approached the station at Chester and Rasim stood up and walked to the carriage door. DC Ruth Walsh waited by the carriage door at the opposite end from Rasim, the wheels of the train squealed as it came to a standstill and Rasim left the carriage. He walked over to a refreshment stand and bought a bottle of mineral water. Rasim gulped down another two stolen painkillers to try to give him some relief from his shoulder wound while he checked the station timetable to see what time his connecting train would arrive. He had an hour to wait, so he decided to telephone Yasser.

DC Ruth Walsh headed to a news stand and flicked through the magazines that were laid out there while she watched her quarry. She noticed that Sian's Glock was in Rasim's waistband next to his right pocket. The gun was useless apart from the frightening effect it could have on the public if it was brandished in a crowded place. The Armed Response Unit had searched the hospital grounds and Sian's stolen Jeep as soon as they were alerted to Rasim's possible whereabouts. The gun had been recovered from its hiding place and made safe by having the firing pin removed before being replaced. They didn't want to alert Rasim to the fact that he was being followed, but he had already shot one officer, so the gun was rendered useless. Rasim was also unaware that the clothes and shoes that he had stolen had been left there purposely for him to steal. Everything he was wearing had microchip trackers in it. DC Ruth Walsh couldn't lose Rasim if she tried.

Rasim Janet seemed agitated as he made a telephone call from a bank of pay phones. It was obvious that there had been no reply. Rasim scuffed his foot hard, repeatedly against the wall beneath the phone as he waited for his call to be answered. The call had been tracked by a team of surveillance experts sitting in a replica furniture van in the station car park. The information from the number dialled was processed at the old Newborough Preparatory School thirty miles away in Woolton. The number that Rasim had dialled was listed as a British Telecom landline at an address in Anfield, Liverpool. Tank and his team would already be on their way to the address by the time Rasim hung up the receiver.

Rasim knew that something had gone wrong. The number that he had dialled at Yasser's basement flat always had a messaging service attached to it. The caller would leave a coded message and a contact number and Yasser would call back on an untraceable mobile phone. This time there was no answer machine. The number just rang and rang. It was as if someone was trying to make the caller stay on the line long enough for a trace to be made on it. Rasim knew that he had made a huge mistake by waiting on the telephone for so long. The pain in his shoulder and the effect of the painkilling drugs had dulled his usually sharp instincts. The only way anybody would be able to trace a call from a public telephone would be if they knew where you were going to be and had bugged it prior to you arriving. He realised that he was being followed. This was a set up.

There were six undercover Armed Response agents on the platform including DC Ruth Walsh. She was the lead officer, and so none of them would make a move until she gave the signal. The suspect's demeanour had changed dramatically since he tried to make a phone call. He was nervous and he was behaving furtively. Rasim looked around the station platform and studied the passengers that he could see. Every one of them could be a police officer for all he knew. Rasim started to panic. The pain in his shoulder was returning as his stress levels increased. He could feel the warmth of blood soaking into the bandage. Sweat trickled down his back as he tried to fathom a way out of the trap that he was in. He felt like a rat in a cage. Rasim spotted a public lavatory block about ten yards from where he was standing, and he decided to buy some time by heading into it quickly.

The white tiled walls were covered in graffiti and the stale smell of urine was overpowering as Rasim entered the toilets. There was a small narrow window at the far end of the block above a stainless-steel sink. He ran to the sink, jumped up onto it, and then tried to open the window. It opened enough for him to able to squeeze through, but he swore loudly when he saw the metal bars that were fixed to the outside wall preventing him an escape route. Rasim noticed that the pretty woman from the Bangor station was talking hurriedly to two men. The men had small earpieces and were looking directly at him. Realisation that they'd been spotted made the six agents spring into action. DC Ruth Walsh pulled her Glock 9mm and pointed it toward the toilet block at Rasim's head.

Rasim dropped quickly from the toilet window and banged his shoulder on the door of a stinking cubicle. The cubicle door flung was open revealing a startled punter who was enjoying a blow job from a local station prostitute who called herself Jo. Rasim hit the man in the face hard knocking him to the floor. He grabbed Jo up from her knees and put his arm around her throat tightly. He pulled out Sian's gun and put it to the prostitute's head. Rasim could hear the frantic voices coming from the platform outside, it sounded as if at least half a dozen agents were clearing the public away to safety.

Rasim edged slowly out of the stinking lavatory using Jo as a human shield. DC Ruth Walsh couldn't understand where Rasim had found this tarty looking woman from at first but then it dawned on her. Rasim edged along the toilet wall toward the tracks, sweat was soaking his shirt and stinging his eyes. His shoulder wound was openly bleeding he could feel the blood running under his armpit and down the side of his body.

'Rasim Janet. Let the woman go and lie down on the floor, or I will instruct my officers to kill you. Your gun has been rendered useless so just let the girl go and you live. You have got two seconds to comply,' DC Walsh shouted. Rasim couldn't understand how this pretty policewoman knew his name. He also couldn't believe that his gun was useless. The pain in his shoulder was making him feel physically sick. Rasim felt a warm sensation running down his thigh and he realised that the prostitute Jo had wet herself in fright. The warm liquid soaked down his jeans and into his stolen trainers. The shock of being peed on made him loosen his grip on the woman and she stamped her foot hard into Rasim's shin. He lost his grip and she bolted toward the police officers.

A startled looking man staggered out of the toilet block that Rasim had just left. He was bleeding from the nose and his limp penis was hanging out of his trousers.

In all the confusion, Rasim squeezed the trigger of his gun. It made a loud click in his hand. He was devastated. Rasim was sick that his journey had ended here on this station platform far away from his home. Armed police surrounded him because he had killed a policewoman and now he had a decommissioned weapon in his hand, and he was covered in urine. Rasim heard the roar of an approaching express train and he bolted.

As he ran toward the edge of the platform DC Ruth Walsh fired her Glock 9mm three times. The first bullet hit Rasim in the lower back splintering his spine into dozens of tiny pieces; the second hit his wounded shoulder shattering the ball joint and nearly separated the damaged limb from his body. He stumbled over the edge of the platform and fell onto the dull metal rails. Rasim tried to lift himself up but his ruined spine wouldn't allow him to move. It took just eight seconds between Rasim Janet landing on the rails, and the 12.45 from Liverpool squashing his head against the dull metal. He had remained conscious as he watched the speeding express come toward him.

CHAPTER 55

Terrorist Task Force – Liverpool

Chen replaced the handset of the telephone and he slammed his fist against the desk in frustration.

'What's wrong now?' David Bell asked. Information was pouring into the taskforce office all afternoon. Uniformed police were deployed to identify the location of every ice cream van and hot dog stall they could find. No one could approach the suspect vehicles in case the suicide bombers became suspicious and detonated their device. The streets of Liverpool were swarming with people wearing replica football shirts enjoying the carnival atmosphere. Chen had sent a uniformed officer to a local sportswear warehouse to purchase two-dozen replica shirts. They were distributed to uniformed officers so that they could reconnaissance any potential vehicles without raising suspicion.

Grace Farrington called Chen with some urgent developments. Faz and Tank had raided an address in Anfield. It was a basement apartment close to the football stadium and it was completely sterile. Everything had been wiped down and cleaned. In the middle of the living room of the apartment was a wooden coffee table; in the centre of the coffee table was the severed head of the old Mullah whom Yasser had entrusted with caring for Mustapha and Yasmine. The old man's tongue had been pulled between his teeth and was left lolling out of the dead mouth, stapled to it was a photograph of Yasmine Ahmed.

Grace also received a call from the diving centre at Carpenray. She had spoken to them previously when air tanks marked with their brand, were found at the mosque in Warrington. The owner there had kept her number in case anything untoward happened. The owner informed Grace that a dry suit had been stolen along with all the relative equipment and a DPV. The name of the man that hired the equipment couldn't be identified, but the staff remembered that he was of Middle Eastern appearance. The theft of the Diver Propulsion Vehicle was significant in the fact that the distance being patrolled along the River Mersey would now increase tenfold. This would dilute any attempts to search for a submerged diver.

'Uniform has found a car abandoned near the Mersey promenade. They say that it has a man's clothing and shoes on the back seat. It could be a suicide drowning, or we could have a diver in the river. This has to be related to the other incidents that we have.' Chen feared an attack from the river the most. The Coastguard was on heightened alert, but they couldn't prevent a determined diver from reaching the water. Now that they had the information from Carpenray, they could only assume that an attack from the river was imminent.

'We need to launch every available unmanned spy drone and have them patrolling the River Mersey immediately. Order them to concentrate their searches around the John Lennon Airport and the Stanlow Oil Refinery. If we are correct in assuming that Ahmed is spelling Yasmine with his attacks, then Stanlow is the more likely target. The drones have infra-red thermal imaging but it's still nearly impossible to trace a diver in a dry suit…' before Chen had finished giving the order four black helicopter drones lifted off from the roof of the taskforce building. They headed off to their programmed search areas like a swarm of huge black metal wasps.

'Coastguard control has three motor patrol boats fitted with specialized diver-detector sonar. They are widening the search area to include the approach water between Otters Pool and the potential targets. If the terrorists are using a DPV, then they should be able to pinpoint the sound of the electric motor using high power passive sonar,' the fat controller had been tasked to borrow the sonar equipment from an American Warship. It was prototype equipment that was still in the development stage, but it was far more advanced than anything the Royal Navy possessed. The Americans also had a trained sea lion and four dolphins that were used to locate scuba divers on behalf of a specialised Navy Seal Team. Unfortunately, they were in the Philippines seconded to the government there looking for al-Qaeda trained terrorists. It would take the navy two weeks to fly the animals into Britain, so the idea had been shelved.

'We've deployed sharpshooters at Stanlow, and we have a team of Special Boat Service divers in the water near the refinery and the airport.' David Bell had struggled to get the British Navy to deploy the Special Boat Service initially but once the terrorist threat seemed imminent, they'd responded with two teams of divers. They were experts at maritime counterterrorism. The Special Boat Service was responsible for the Liberation of the British embassy in Kuwait in the first Gulf War in 1991. On May 12, 2007 the British Special Boat Service killed Taliban leader Mullah Dadullah in Helmand province during a raid on his compound.

The SBS divers were armed with APS Underwater Assault Rifles. APS stands for Avtomat Podvodnyy Spetsialnyy, which translates, to Special Underwater Automatic Rifle. The underwater weapon was derived from the Russian made AK47. Because ordinary bullets are inaccurate and have a very short range if fired underwater, the APS Assault Rifle is fitted with a magazine that holds twenty-six, five-inch long steel bolts that can penetrate even reinforced dry suits. If Nasser al-Masri was attempting to cross the River Mersey, he would have to avoid the Special Boat Service.

'What is the situation with Tank and Grace?' Major Timms approached the two intelligence agents.

'The address in Anfield that they searched is sterile, Major, apart from this.' Chen handed the Major a digital crime scene photograph of the old Mullah's severed head.

'That looks like Yasser Ahmed's handy work. What is the situation regarding the location of the suspect vehicles?' The Major asked. The problem was there would be approximately four hundred ice cream vans in the city that day. They couldn't risk panicking the public or attracting further press interest by ram raiding every ice cream and hot dog vendor in the vicinity.

'We have plain clothes officers all around the Anfield stadium. They are marking the position of every vendor of Middle Eastern or Asian appearance first. Once we have all the information back Tank is going to eliminate each suspect site one by one,' Chen explained. It would be a painfully slow process, but they had very few options without alerting any potential suicide bombers.

'What about cancelling the game itself, is that an option?' The Major mused.

'At the moment the imminent threats are from the river, and outside the stadium. The fans will probably be safer inside the ground. From the intelligence that we have we could make matters worse. We are concerned that if the bombers get wind of the fact that we are onto them then they may just detonate their devices at random,' Chen was using a lot of supposition to support his theories but his gut feeling was that the bombers would be aiming to detonate their bombs shortly before the stadium filled up. He was guessing that three pm would be the time when the streets around the ground would be the busiest. It would be the optimum moment to explode a series of bombs. If they called off the game and alerted the bombers, there was no telling what might happen. They still had two hours to locate and neutralise the bombers. The River Mersey was well protected from a maritime attack; the focus now was on finding Yasser Ahmed's affiliates.

'We could use Mustapha to weed out the bombers,' Chen said. Everyone looked shocked at the suggestion, but he continued anyway.

'If we assume that any potential suspect bombers must know what Yasser Ahmed looks like, then we could disguise Mustapha and get him to signal the bombers away from their vans from a distance. If he wears dark sunglasses for instance, then the likeness is uncanny. From a distance of say fifty yards they would not know that it was not Yasser until it was too late,' Chen was talking quickly and using hand gestures to enforce his idea. He shrugged as he finished his suggestion and a bolt of pain shot through his shoulder making him wince.

'I think that the idea might just work. We haven't got much time left to try anything else. This could be our only realistic chance of identifying the bombers before they act. Get Mustapha in here quickly and let's prep him with what we want him to do.' Major Stanley Timms knew that it was a risky plan, but he couldn't think of any other way to lure the bombers from their vehicles.

Mustapha was escorted into the taskforce office and briefed by Chen and David Bell. A pair of donated dark glasses was placed on him and a female officer applied some foundation to the nasty scab on his cheek. From a distance he could pass as Yasser Ahmed. Mustapha was frightened silly. He was still suffering from the effects of his adventure at South Stack Lighthouse and his ordeal in the waters of the Irish Sea. The thought of being bait for a group of potential suicide bombers was not a pleasant one. He laughed with Chen and the fat controller about getting a ticket to watch the game if all went well with Chen's plan, but on the inside, he felt very scared indeed.

'We also have a mobile phone that was posted to your address in Holyhead. We are assuming that your brother sent it to you in order to make contact with you at a later date. Take it with you just in case. Please don't worry about anything. Tank and Grace are already there, and they'll be with you every step of the way.' The fat controller placed a small micro-camera to Mustapha's jacket lapel. It would record and transmit images and sound back to the taskforce. A tiny plastic flesh coloured device was placed into Mustapha's right ear. Chen tested it and now Mustapha could receive orders via the tiny speaker. Mustapha was stripped to the waist and he was dressed in a battle vest before getting dressed again.

'The vest is just for safety sake as a precaution. I don't think for one minute that you will need it but it's best to be on the safe side,' Chen said lying.

Mustapha felt a bit safer with the vest on but was still very anxious. He placed the mobile phone into his pocket and followed the Major into the lift that would take them down to the car park. It was only three miles to the Anfield area of Liverpool, but the streets were packed to bursting point with football fans dressed in red and blue. Mustapha felt his throat drying out and he suddenly felt very thirsty. It was the longest three-mile journey that he had ever had to make. It was one fifteen pm when he stepped out of the unmarked police car in Anfield and shook hands with Tank.

CHAPTER 56

Stanlow Oil Refinery

Nasser al-Masri checked the dive computer on his wrist; it was like a big digital watch that told the length of time that the diver had spent underwater, and the depth that the diver had reached. There was also a compass incorporated into the programme. Underwater navigation is very difficult especially in strange waters where there are no recognisable landmarks beneath the surface to guide you. Nasser had been submerged for twenty-minutes and had been using the Diver Propulsion Vehicle to speed him across the River Mersey toward the Stanlow Oil Refinery. The waters of the Mersey were dark green, and his visibility was just three feet in front of him. It would make him harder for enemy divers to locate, but it made his passage slow, and he had just twenty-minutes of oxygen left before he would need to start surfacing in stages to avoid decompression sickness. Nasser could hear the propellers of small craft passing above him and then fading into the distance. He knew that they were the motor patrol boats that he had seen trawling the river before he entered the water.

Nasser knew that he had just one chance to destroy his target and he would be under intense fire from the moment that he was located. His journey had been hampered by the weapons that he had to carry with him on his underwater journey. Strapped to his thigh he had a British made Scorpion machine pistol, and it was fitted with a suppressor permanently, and was capable of firing short distances underwater. The magazine was waterproof, bulky, and held sixty-two 9mm rounds. He couldn't carry any extra ammunition; once the sixty-two high velocity bullets were gone, he would be at the mercy of the British security services.

His main weapon of destruction was an RPG-29. The plan was to reach the riverbank submerged and then try to get close enough to fire his Rocket-Propelled Grenade at one of the huge petrol storage tanks.

The RPG-29 that Nasser had was far more accurate and deadly than its predecessor. It also had a self-destruct timing device, which meant it could be fired from long distances and timed to explode. It was sealed inside a watertight carrycase protected from the murky waters of the River Mersey. The weapon had one grenade fitted, ready to fire, and in the case was a spare grenade to reload the weapon with. Nasser would need around forty seconds from leaving the water to being set to launch his first Rocket-Propelled Grenade. Under the intense fire that would be waiting for him, he knew that his chances were slim to say the least.

Nasser heard the sound of a propeller belonging to a motor patrol boat closing in on his position. This time instead of fading into the distance it maintained its location directly above him. He realised that the ship's sonar must have located the battery-powered engine of his DPV. Nasser checked his computer again and he estimated that he was five hundred yards from the shore. He checked his compass to make sure he was heading west. Once he had plotted west, he released the DPV. He launched the small machine into the opposite direction sending it buzzing off alone beneath the waves heading east.

Nasser swam away from the DPV in the direction of the riverbank. His weapons suddenly felt incredibly heavy without the use of the DPV. The engine noise from above drifted slowly away in the other direction. They were following the underwater machine which was barely out of Nasser's vision. Suddenly the water around the small machine seemed to explode into a seething mass of foam and bubbles. The motor patrol boat had relayed the position of the DPV engine to the control centre at the old school in Woolton. The location was then passed to an armed remote helicopter drone already positioned above. The drone immediately opened fire on the position with an American made rotating air cannon. The air cannon looked similar to an old Gatling gun used in cowboy films from the '70s. The cannon's sixteen-barrels rotate at high speed powered by compressed air, unleashing a lethal barrage of high velocity bullets at the rate of one hundred bullets per second. The effect was devastating and the DPV was shattered into a thousand pieces in just seconds.

Nasser reeled away from the wreckage and dragged his heavy load along the riverbed toward the shore. He caught a glimpse of two small silver objects glinting in the gloom. They seemed to be descending slowly from the surface toward the area where the DPV had been destroyed. The two anti-personnel concussion grenades exploded in a blinding flash. The blast wave ripped Nasser's face mask from his head and somersaulted him through the murky water. He reached for his mask and pulled it back over his face. He tipped his head backward toward the surface and exhaled through his nostrils to remove the water from the mask. He settled himself by breathing slowly and deeply. He regained his composure and thought that he could only be two hundred yards from the riverbank now. He checked his oxygen capacity gauge and assessed that he had approximately ten minutes of breathable air remaining.

In the gloom ahead Nasser saw air bubbles rising toward the surface, sunlight reflecting from them as they headed toward it. He knew that there was an enemy diver close by. Nasser stopped swimming and looked around scanning a full circle. He saw the glimpse of a scuba tank in the dark water and he laid the RPG down to rest on the riverbed. He removed the Scorpion machine pistol from its leg holster and remained still, trying to reserve as much precious oxygen as he could.

The noise of another propeller closed in above his position. The shadowy silhouette of a Special Boat Service diver appeared and then disappeared just as quickly in the murky green water. Nasser unleashed a spray of bullets in a deadly arc from his Scorpion machine pistol. A five-inch stainless-steel bolt whizzed past Nasser's face fired from an APS underwater assault rifle. A second steel bolt was on target and penetrated his dry suit. The hot metal stuck into his right calf. Water rushed into his suit and mixed with the gushing blood; his body temperature dropped dramatically as the ice-cold water covered his exposed flesh. The suit had been breached and his body couldn't last any length of time underwater at that temperature. Nasser knew he had just minutes to survive at this depth. He swam as hard as his injured leg would allow him. He recovered the RPG from the riverbed and pressed on. There could only be a hundred yards to cover now and the river was becoming shallower making it easier for him to make progress.

The dead body of an SBS diver floated into view. His face mask had been shattered by Nasser's bullets and red liquid filled the mask. Nasser ripped the respirator from the dead diver's air tank and a huge plume of bubbles escaped rushing to the surface. He moved away from the lifeless body as quickly as he could. The rush of bubbles hit the surface and the location was transmitted immediately to the old school. The coordinates were electronically sent to the unmanned drone, and it unleashed a sustained attack on the position of the bubbles with its lethal air cannons. The body of the dead SBS man was shredded into mincemeat in seconds.

Nasser was now just five feet below the surface of the river where the motor patrol boats couldn't sail this close to the riverbank because of the dangerous shallows and mudflats. Nasser could see the silhouette of a remote drone in the air above him. He aimed his Scorpion machine pistol and fired a volley of shots at the wasp-like machine from underwater; the high calibre bullets shattered two of the rotor blades and the drone started to spiral out of control. Smoke poured from the rear of the stricken craft as it plunged toward the river. The drone crashed onto the bridge of one of the motor patrol boats scattering debris in all directions. The patrol boat suddenly exploded in a fireball that climbed sixty feet up into the air.

Nasser was waist deep now and running for his life across the salt marshes. The thick mudflats were covered in indigenous river grasses that offered Nasser little cover. He ran in a zigzag pattern trying to avoid enemy fire. Nasser crouched low in the now ankle-deep water and opened the carrycase for his RPG-29. A Special Boat Service diver had followed Nasser out of the water and opened fire at him with his underwater assault rifle. The stainless-steel bolts had no range or accuracy out of the water and the bolts whistled past Nasser's position. He placed the RPG-29 onto his shoulder and aimed at the row of huge white storage tanks.

Nasser saw a muzzle flash coming from the top of one of the white metal structures. He squeezed the trigger and released his Rocket-Propelled Grenade with a loud whooshing sound it sped off toward the petrol tanks. As the grenade sped away, it passed the high-velocity bullet from trooper Bob Duncan's sniper rifle coming the other way.

Nasser never knew if he had hit his target or not. Trooper Duncan had sent his bullet expertly through Nasser's forehead leaving an ugly round hole the size of a walnut. The exit wound was more the size of a coconut and Nasser's brains sprayed the salt marshes around him for more than ten yards.

CHAPTER 57

Anfield – Anglican Cathedral

Tank had gathered his team around him before Mustapha arrived in an unmarked police car. They had identified a total of twelve ice cream vendors working around the stadium. Four of them had men of Middle Eastern appearance working in them. In addition, they'd located eighteen hot dog stands dotted around the streets outside the stadium. Tank and his men commandeered clothing from the Liverpool FC souvenir shop so that they would blend into the crowds of football fans that packed the streets. They wore padded club jackets to conceal the weapons that they carried. If the crowds saw a gun panic would ensue, and the bombers would be alerted. The plan was risky but simple. Mustapha Ahmed was to approach the vans from a reasonable distance and then signal the occupants to come to him. Once the suspects had left the vehicle they would be neutralised, and the vehicle could be made safe by the bomb squad. It would be too risky to remove the vans in case they'd been booby trapped with motion sensors or mercury switches. Mercury is a liquid metal which can conduct an electric charge to trigger a bomb. It moves like a liquid does. If a device was moved, the mercury moves too, making a circuit contact complete.

Grace had been in contact with the Anfield Stadium management and had informed them that there was a large security operation in motion outside the stadium. Their cooperation was required to make the operation run smoothly. Terrorist Task Force Agents were located in the stadium control room monitoring the CCTV. Grace had also asked the ground staff to pipe music through the external sound system to nullify the nose of any gunfire. They couldn't risk the arrest of one terrorist alerting another. The club cooperated and music was blaring on the streets outside the ground. The volume was so high that it was making it very uncomfortable for sightseers to just wander aimlessly. The crowds started to drift slowly away from the ground. People chose to use the bars and shops located a safer distance from the stadium.

The crowds had thinned significantly when Mustapha arrived. The music was deafening. Tank briefed Mustapha on the plan and they approached the first target near to the Shankly Gates. The gates were a memorial to one of the clubs greatest ever managers, Bill Shankly. Mustapha stood across the street from the idle ice cream van and leaned against the wall behind him. He looked through his darkened sunglasses at the man who was in the vehicle. Mustapha pretended to be making a call on his mobile phone. The ice cream vendor appeared to recognise Mustapha. He looked intently at Mustapha and half raised his hand in a gesture of acknowledgement. Mustapha waved to him and beckoned him over. The Asian man hesitated briefly and then opened the passenger door and climbed out of the vehicle. He crossed the road heading toward Mustapha through the crowd.

Tank grabbed the man from behind crushing the breath from his lungs as he lifted him off his feet. He pinned both the man's arms to his sides in the vice like grip that he held him in. Agents rushed in and fastened the terrorist's wrists and ankles together. Startled members of the public quickly moved on when ID cards were displayed. The bomb squad cordoned the van off by parking a huge truck alongside it to protect innocent passers-by from any potential blast. The bomb squad confirmed their worst suspicions. The freezer storage space was packed with Semtex and ball bearings.

'That's one suspect down with no weapons drawn, ladies and gentlemen. Target two is two hundred yards away on Breck Road,' Tank instructed his agents and Mustapha through their coms earpieces.

'We've just received information that an attack on Stanlow Oil Refinery has been foiled. The suspect was neutralised. He managed to release an RPG, but it exploded short of his intended target. We need to get the same result here,' he continued.

Mustapha crossed the busy street and made himself visible to the occupant of the second vehicle. Ali stooped low to make sure that it was Yasser that he could see beckoning him out of the van. He was sure it was him, but something made him suspicious. Ali took the safety catch off his Magnum .357 and pushed it into the waistband of his jeans. He opened the driver's door and stepped down from the ice cream van. Mustapha was sweating as Ali approached him, he did not look comfortable as he neared him. Football fans were hampering the taskforce agents as they tried to approach Ali. They couldn't be sure if the terrorists would have the facility to remote-detonate the devices until the bomb squad had analysed the first device. Tank couldn't grab Ali and ensure that his hands had been neutralised because of the crowds in his proximity. Mustapha wiped sweat from his forehead and his sleeve removed the make-up that was covering the bite mark on his cheek.

Ali realised in an instant that this was not Yasser Ahmed although the likeness was uncanny; he pulled his gun from his waistband and aimed at Mustapha. Mustapha froze in fear as Ali fired three rounds at him through the crowd. The deafening music muffled the booming gunshots and only those closest to Ali realised that shots had been fired. Mustapha felt pieces of house brick scratch his face and neck as the bullets from the .357 Magnum shattered the wall behind him. Tank reached Ali and placed his Glock 9mm against the top of the shorter man's head. The gun was pointed vertically down at the floor. Tank fired twice. The 9mm bullets ripped downwards through Ali's brain and into his torso. The devastating effect of the bullets liquidised most of the Iranian's brain before he had even realised that he had been shot. His legs buckled and he crumpled to the floor. Tank had to shoot down through the terrorist's head to minimise the risk of a through and through bullet continuing on its journey into an innocent football fan.

'A second target is down. Was there any response to the gunfire from the other vehicles, Grace?' Tank asked as he made his way to Mustapha through the crowd.

'Nothing, I don't think they heard it. The bomb squad have just informed us that the devices are manually activated. There is no remote detonation facility on the first device,' Grace replied.

Tank reached Mustapha and he noticed how pale he looked. He was going into a nervous shock. The exertion of his ordeal at South Stack Lighthouse combined with losing his sister and his lover had just about finished him off and being shot at by an Iranian with a Magnum .357 was just the icing on the cake.

'Are you feeling all right, there are only two more ice-cream vans that fit the profile, can you carry on, Mustapha?' Tank shook him a little trying to get a response, but Mustapha was staring at the ice cream van.

'Look its Pinky and Perky,' Mustapha said pointing to the driver's door of the van.

'Mustapha, I need you to hold it together for just a bit longer. Don't you worry about the two little pigs right now.' Tank was getting annoyed. They needed to move on quickly.

'You don't understand what I'm saying to you. Both vans had Pinky and Perky decals on the driver's door. It might help to narrow down the search,' Mustapha shouted over the booming music from the external sound system.

'Grace, get every vendor checked for decals. Tell them to check on the driver's door for Pinky and Perky. If the same person re-sprayed all these vans, then he may have left a pattern without even realising it. Chen, you pass the information onto uniform as soon as possible please,' Tank knew that Chen and the fat controller had been coordinating events and information. They had deployed the relevant assets to the relevant situations, and so far, they were on top.

Tank guided Mustapha toward the third target and pointed to the position that he wanted him to maintain. Mustapha looked at the ice cream vendor and the man caught his eye. The Asian man took a double take at Mustapha and then bolted toward the back of the vehicle. Tank watched in horror as the man reached for the detonator in an attempt to blow the van, and the surrounding public to smithereens. For some reason, the man knew that Mustapha was not Yasser straight away.

Tank closed the distance between himself and the van in a few strides. He drew the 9mm Glock simultaneously and emptied the clip of sixteen high velocity bullets through the glass, into the terrorist. The bullets smashed through the man's chest spraying blood and cartilage up the windows of the van. As he collapsed three rounds to the neck area ripped his head from his body completely. The terrorist wouldn't get the chance to detonate his bomb.

The dead terrorist had realised that Mustapha was not Yasser Ahmed, because Yasser had left the van just seconds before. Yasser Ahmed watched the action unfold from the safety of the crowds as his affiliate was gunned down inside his mobile bomb. He was fascinated as he saw his younger brother Mustapha being led away by a big man with a shaved head, Yasser backed slowly into an alleyway transfixed by his younger brother. Yasser hadn't seen his brother since he was a small boy, and so he was stunned by their resemblance.

The shooting of the ice cream vendor had been witnessed by hundreds of people and word had spread around the pubs and bars that the police had shot someone. Speculation was rife that it was a potential terrorist. Why else would the police shoot an ice cream man? Chris Lampie and the supporters from compost corner had left The Sandon as soon as they'd heard what was going on. They stood holding pint glasses on the pavement outside the pub watching the bomb squad going in and out of an ice cream van parked just a few hundred yards away. They were just ten feet from a hot dog stand on the corner of Breck Road and Anfield Road. Speculation was rife that a terrorist had been shot. There was a nervous buzz around the stadium, and no one was really sure if they themselves were in any danger.

Chris Lampie and mad Adie approached the hot dog stand still holding their precious beers in their hands. There didn't appear to be anyone staffing it, and so mad Adie lifted the lid from a stainless-steel pan and looked at the hot dog sausages inside the steaming container.

'Here we are, Lampie, free hot dogs. The bloke must have fucked off somewhere. Tell the rest of the lads and I'll get some more bread rolls out of the bottom here?' Adie said. Chris Lampie called the rest of compost corner's regulars over and they pushed and shoved each other mischievously around the hot dog stand. Mad Adie opened the stainless-steel door beneath the stand and thought that it was odd that there were wires everywhere inside. He never thought of anything ever again, as the stand exploded, and the members of compost corner took the full blast of the shrapnel bomb.

Tank instinctively pushed Mustapha to the ground and covered him with his own body. The crowds around the stadium scattered in all directions as the realisation of what had happened struck home. The remnants of the compost corner members were strewn across the street like bloody confetti, and within seconds the immediate area was almost empty.

'Take the last target down immediately,' Tank shouted across the airwaves. Three agents dressed in red Liverpool FC shirts drew weapons around the remaining van and pumped it full of bullets. The occupant was left dangling from the serving hatch where a pool of his blood spread on the road beneath him.

The remaining hot dog stand bomb was cordoned off and a controlled explosion was carried out. It too had been left unattended and unnoticed by the huge crowds that passed unaware.

'Tank, uniform has reported two unattended ice cream vans next to the Anglican Cathedral. They both have the Pinky and Perky decals on the driver's door. We are evacuating the tourists now and beginning a search of the building. Everyone leaving the cathedral has been searched,' Chen informed Tank of the breaking news.

'What time is it? Get everyone away from the building immediately. Chen, if you are right about the optimum time for exploding the devices being 3 p.m., then we only have five minutes left.' Tank realised that Chen was probably correct in his assumption. He lifted Mustapha off the road onto his feet. The Iraqi man was badly shaken by the blast. Tank walked him toward a police transit van that was parked on the pavement nearby.

Yasser watched from the safety of the alleyway as the big skinhead walked toward the van, carrying his younger brother. The police transit van had a white background with the distinctive orange stripes carried by police vehicles around the middle of it. Tank noticed that the police markings didn't look quite right. He realised that the markings were upside down. There were two parallel orange stripes on a genuine police vehicle. The thicker of the two stripes was fixed above the thinner band. This one was upside down. The disguised police van exploded at exactly 3 pm, as did the Semtex in the bell tower of the Anglican Cathedral. The cathedral bell tower, weakened by the blast, had disintegrated beneath the massive weight of the bells. Huge sandstone blocks weighing tons, had tumbled into the cavernous building crushing six-members of the Terrorist Bomb Squad that had not had time to escape. The skyline of Liverpool had changed forever.

Tank was blown across the street with Mustapha when the police van exploded. The two men were stunned into unconsciousness by the power of the shockwave.

CHAPTER 58

Tank – Mustapha

Tank had woken up in intensive care at the Royal Liverpool Hospital forty-eight hours later. He had woken just long enough to ask Grace, who was waiting by his bedside what had happened. Then he passed out again and didn't come around for another three days. The swelling to Tank's brain caused by the concussion wave had nearly killed him. The surgeons had drilled a hole into his skull to relieve the pressure from the bleeding, and that saved his life.

Seven Terrorist Task Force members lost their lives at the cathedral blast along with the nine members of compost corner, near the stadium.

Mustapha had never arrived at the hospital at all. Witnesses said that he was seen being helped away from the scene by an Asian man who looked like he was related to him.

Tank, Chen, Faz, and the Major, returned to duty as normal once all the scars had healed. The Terrorist Task Force tracked the alleged movements of the ghost like Yasser Ahmed across the planet. Several reports of him were received from the Philippines and Afghanistan over the following six months, but nothing concrete ever surfaced.

Eventually a report came in from an American black operations team that specialised in rendition. These people don't officially exist of course, but they specialise in counter terrorism and interrogation under torture. This process is usually carried out on foreign soil. The American people are not made aware of such procedures being utilised by their government. Countries with a broader moral outlook are used to extract information. Western populations cannot prove the use of torture if there are no Western witnesses to tell the tale.

The black operations team reportedly captured Yasser Ahmed in Iraq. They interrogated him for two months in a prison in Chechnya. His heart had finally given in after eight weeks of intense torture and malnutrition. Tank cried when he saw the autopsy pictures and recognised the bite mark on the cheek of the corpse. Mustapha denied being Yasser Ahmed right up to the point where his heart stopped beating.

A NOTE FROM THE AUTHOR

Thank you for reading my books. This is the first book in the Soft Target series and if you enjoyed it, I would be grateful if you could leave a review on Amazon.

For another free thriller, go to;

www.conradjonesauthor.com

Printed in Great Britain
by Amazon